In the Spirit of Murder

Laura Belgrave

This book is a work of fiction. All names, characters, places, and events are the product of the author's imagination. Any resemblance to actual events or persons, living or dead, is entirely coincidental and beyond the intent of either the author or the publisher.

Hardcover ISBN: 1-57072-108-4
Trade Paper ISBN: 1-57072-124-6
Copyright © 2000 by Laura Belgrave
Printed in the United States of America
All Rights Reserved

1 2 3 4 5 6 7 8 9 0

With love and gratitude, this novel is for my primary and most enduring cheerleader, Mary L. Belgrave, the good, kind, sweet, wonderful, loving mother. (How could I resist that, Ma?)

It's most certainly also for my husband, John C. Caramanica, Jr., a certified charming prince whose spirited optimism and support kept me going when logic screamed at me to stop. I'm glad you won this one, John.

A huge thanks also goes to my sisters, Linda Liska Belgrave, whose thoughtful critiques chapter by chapter improved the story with each round, and to Leslie Curtis, a one-woman fan club whose loyalties were established the day she hugged the rug for me.

Finally, my gratitude extends big-time to Marlene Passell, who was there with me in the beginning and is there for me now.

All of you? You believed when I didn't. You insisted when I couldn't. If you weren't in my orbit, this novel would never have happened. I cherish you all.

CHAPTER 1

DETECTIVE LIEUTENANT CLAUDIA HERSHEY stood with her hands in her jacket pockets and looked at the woman on the kitchen floor. Sometimes dead people looked like they were only napping. An eyelid would appear to move. Lips might twitch. You'd know they were dead, but still they'd play some trick or another, just enough to make you suck in your breath.

Not this woman. Her face had been obliterated along with her last breath. Blood was her pillow.

Claudia's eyes moved restlessly around the kitchen. It was just a little square room with the standard appliances and a small round table. The table had been upended like a gladiator's shield, but it was the only evidence of a struggle. She guessed the woman hadn't gotten the first lick in.

"God have mercy," said a hushed voice behind Claudia.

She turned and took in the chief's spongy face. It still bore traces of pillow creases. "Worst I ever saw, before this, was some fella got pulled out of Little Arrow Lake three days after he went in. Gators'd gotten to him, that and fish and water and whatnot." Chief Mac Suggs pulled his eyes from the body and cleared his throat. "But this? A dog with rabies wouldn't have gone this far. No one deserves to die like this."

The woman lay on her back, her right arm and wrist bent in a question mark. One leg was drawn up at the knee, the victim's skirt hitched past her thigh. Claudia resisted an impulse to straighten the skirt for the woman, to do just that much.

The characteristic rumble returned to Suggs's voice. "Well, looks like you're finally gonna earn your pay, Hershey. Hope you still know your way around a stiff body."

The comment didn't call for a response. In the ten months since she had arrived in Indian Run, Suggs had treated her like a mistake. In a sense, it was true. The burly chief had hired her in error, mistaking her name as *Claude* on the application. Claudia had learned to live with it; the chief, not quite.

"Is the sheriff's crime scene on the way?" she asked. She pushed long fingers through her hair, thick stuff the color of rust. It fell in wayward curls to her shoulders.

Suggs made a sour face. "Yeah, them and the medical examiner. Those clowns just been waitin' for something like this. We'll be tradin' in our blue for their khaki after this one."

The chief's battle with the Flagg County Sheriff's Department was legendary. Every six months, like clockwork, the sheriff made a pitch to the Indian Run Town Council to take over police service. The arguments were sound: Indian Run's police department was small; its equipment was outdated; its officers were poorly trained.

True, all of it. But for all his plodding country ways Suggs was not a stupid man, and until the last year he'd countered pretty well. *Give up your own police, folks, and just watch your property taxes grow wings.* That always shut them up. No one wanted to actually pay for their cops. And besides, crime in Indian Run rarely went beyond a stolen water pump from one of the orange groves or dirty words scrawled on the school walls.

Then faces on the town council changed. People Suggs hadn't grown up with began to control the gavel. Developers looking to buy up another patch of Florida sniffed around, never mind that Indian Run was nothing more than a smudge in the middle of the map. Everybody wanted more cops, and better cops. So after the last go-around, he had hired Claudia sight unseen in a desperation bid to upgrade his department with a bona fide detective—one that until now had never been needed.

Suggs and Claudia moved just outside of the kitchen. Orange and black crepe paper sagged listlessly from tacks in the ceiling in a perfunctory salute to Halloween. A cardboard skeleton, the cheap sort available at drugstore checkouts, decorated the wall below. The garish arrangement would have been visible to trick-or-treaters at the door. A nice touch for the kids.

"Hershey," said the chief, "what've we got here? The sheriff's boys're gonna be all over the place like fleas on a dog. I don't want to scratch in front of 'em."

Claudia shrugged. "It's a little too early to—"

"Hershey, don't bust my chops like that," Suggs said irritably. He pulled at his shirt, already sticky with perspiration. "God knows why in hell you left Cleveland for a cracker town like this, but you did, and you came with enough awards and citations and ribbons to wallpaper a room. So don't tell me you don't have some notion of what in hell went on here."

She waited a beat, gauging the chief's expression, settling him down with her own. Then: "All right. You're right. I do, and none of it's good."

Tall and thin and sharp of elbow, Claudia was neither beautiful nor plain. Her face mercifully lacked the sharp geometry of her body, but it was dwarfed by oversized glasses that gave her eyes an unsettling depth and authority. Those who met her stare pulled away first, shrinking from the penetrating orbs that were sea green in color, the right marginally smaller than the left. Indeed, back in the days when Claudia's daughter, Robin, still spoke to her in a civil manner, she liked to joke that people could walk on her mother's line of vision.

Claudia recognized the power her eyes held, just as she recognized the prerogative of her height. Six feet spoke its own language.

"All right," she said again. "Here's where we are. I did a preliminary poke through the house, and whatever she was killed with"—she shook her head—"it's not here, not now. Could have been a rock, a stick, a two-by-four, anything solid and hard."

A motorcycle rumbled down the street. It slowed when it drew alongside the house, hesitated, then roared away in sudden urgency. Claudia waited for it to pass, mentally calculating the size of the spectator crowd.

"Anyway," she continued, "I've got a couple of uniforms searching the grounds. Maybe we'll get lucky." Claudia glanced at her notes, words crimped tightly on a small spiral tablet. "I also found her appointment book."

"Amen," said Suggs.

"Maybe," Claudia said cautiously. She pursed her lips. "I haven't had time to look at it in any detail, but it's going to be a problem to sort out. The people who came to her for spiritual advice or whatever, they're listed only by initial. No first names. No last names. And if she went anywhere last night, there's nothing written down."

"Some cozy night in," Suggs said.

"I also did a fast interview with the woman who called when the victim didn't answer her phone or respond to the door. They were supposed to meet at seven this morning, hit the road for Orlando by eight. They were going to make a day of it—shopping, that sort of thing. The woman who found the body, a friend named Irene Avery, called the switchboard a little after seven-thirty. Officer Ridley got to the scene first."

Claudia handed Suggs a business card. "I found a batch of these on the coffee table in the living room. Victim's name is Donna Overton. According to Avery, she lived here for some twelve years."

Squinting at the card, he grunted. "The 'Reverend' Donna Overton, certified medium."

"Most of the psychics and mediums—those certified, anyway—call themselves *reverend*," she explained. "A lot of them are spiritualists. I'm told it's a religion."

"Great," Suggs mumbled. "The press'll have a field day with this one. Couldn't be just anyone who gets killed."

Claudia let it pass. Donna Overton was one of about twenty-five psychics and mediums who lived in a six-block neighborhood that pinched off the northwest boundary of Indian Run. She didn't know much about them, except that they'd been a mild curiosity in the early '70s when there were twice as many. Several had moved to a similar community near Deland called Cassadaga, which still attracted a lot of visitors. A few had simply retired. Some continued to live in Indian Run, but most held more conventional jobs and rarely gave readings. She explained that according to Avery the victim had been an exception; Donna Overton's livelihood depended on income from spiritualist counseling.

"This Avery woman, she a medium, too?" asked Suggs.

"Yes."

He rubbed his eyes irritably. "Okay, what else, what else? Give me chapter and verse, Hershey."

"Avery tells me Overton was forty-two and lived alone," said Claudia. "She'd never been married. She has one surviving relative, her mother—and the mother lives in a nursing home somewhere in upstate New York."

Suggs exhaled slowly. "So family—the idea that maybe this was just some kind of domestic thing—that's out."

Claudia nodded.

"What about boyfriends? Was she shackin' up with anyone?"

"Avery says not lately. But there was a guy, someone we'll need to take a look at"—she paged through her notes—"a man named Tom Markos. Avery says he and Overton were an item until about two weeks ago. Markos works at the fish camp. Avery met him once, didn't much like him. Said he looks like a gorilla."

"Yeah, well half the fellas who work over at the camp look like gorillas," Suggs muttered. "Don't mean much by itself."

Claudia looked up sharply. "You know the guy?"

For two years in a row Suggs had taken trophies in the town's annual bass-fishing tournament at Little Arrow Lake. What time he didn't spend at the cramped police department he spent on the lake. So did two-thirds of Indian Run's male population.

"Don't believe I've ever spoken direct to Markos," he said, "but I might could say which one he is. If my recollection is right, he's a big man, hairy, not much the type for sharin' a beer."

Claudia jotted a note. "I'll see if I can round him up today, get him to share information instead."

"Forget about that for a minute," said Suggs. "What about a break-in? A burglar? Some stooge hell-bent on fast income for a drug habit coulda connived his way in. Some of 'em are pretty slick. I'm even starting to hear rumors of drugs bein' sold at the high school. Coulda been someone strung out like a set of Christmas-tree lights."

Already, Claudia was shaking her head. "I don't think so. I can't see that she'd open her door to someone she didn't know, and as far as I can tell there are no signs of forced entry."

"Now hold on a second," said Suggs, his voice incredulous. "How the hell can you tell that? Ridley flexed his shoulders on the damn door to get in. It's hanging from one hinge."

"The hardware's intact," Claudia replied matter-of-factly. "When Ridley got the call he apparently knocked and peeked in windows. When he didn't get a response, he assumed the door was locked and he came through like a battering ram. But the locking mechanism shows the door was open all along."

"Aw, come on."

As if she hadn't heard, she said, "Anyway, unless she'd accidentally left the door unlocked—and Avery says no way—the victim either knew the killer or for some reason believed it was safe to open the door." She adjusted her glasses. The damn things were too tight. "Maybe it was a burglar or someone doped up, but I don't think so. My guess is we won't find anything missing here. Her purse has"—Claudia sought her notes—"ninety-seven dollars and change in it, and a handful of credit cards."

While Suggs thought about that, she glanced around the living room. Neat as a pin. Little to suggest that violence had visited.

"Hershey," said Suggs slowly, "she might not've opened her door to an adult she didn't know, but what about the possibility of a kid? Some damned fool trick-or-treater? Some punks playin' their Halloween roles to the hilt? How about some kids who just didn't like what she was handin' out? Could be more'n one."

Simultaneously, Suggs and Claudia looked toward a half-empty bowl of candy on the coffee table. Overton had provided a nice mix: Mars Bars, Snickers, Tootsie Rolls.

"Maybe, but not a strong maybe," said Claudia. "The coroner will fix a time of death, but I don't think Overton was killed much before midnight, maybe one. Blood's still clotting and rigidity is just starting to settle in. It's unlikely there were any kids still trick-or-treating past nine o'clock, ten at the latest. And I just don't think that's it."

Suggs groped in his pants pocket and pulled out the stub of a Tums roll. He grappled with the wrapper and popped two of the medicinal candies in his mouth.

Claudia watched, waiting.

"What else?" he asked. "Can we at least assume we're dealing with an amateur? There's bloody footprints all the way from the kitchen to the front door. Couple of splotches on the walls, too.

Whoever did this left a trail a blind man would find."

Claudia inclined her head. "I don't think we can assume anything. Crime scene might find prints. Maybe they'll vacuum something we can use. But the tracks and those smudges on the wall . . . ." She shook her head. "No good. They're Ridley's."

"What?"

"Here's the problem," said Claudia. She sighed, thinking about the young officer. She'd spoken to him briefly outside, his boyish face still white. "Bobby panicked. He's what? Twenty-one, maybe twenty-two? Three months out of the academy?"

"Wait, wait, wait . . . what are you tellin' me, Hershey?"

"I'm telling you that Bobby blew in here like a cowboy—maybe showing off for Irene Avery, who was right behind him—then he found the body in the kitchen and went nuts." Claudia gestured at the tracks. "He slipped in the blood on the linoleum, fell, got up, and made a beeline out of here. I'm told that he got outside, heaved his breakfast donut, and yelled for someone to call the cops."

"Oh, hell. That it?"

"Not quite. You see the pair of jack-o'-lanterns Overton had set up on TV trays alongside the walkway to her door?"

Suggs grunted. "Didn't stop to admire the lady's holiday decorations on my way in, Hershey. So?"

"So only the one on the left was still on a tray. The one on the right was smashed to pulp, quite possibly knocked off by someone anxious to get the hell away. There's a beauty of a shoe print, square in the middle of it. And it looks to me like there's a trace of another right under it. Unfor—"

"Well, then, hot damn! The killer left his calling card!"

Impatiently, Claudia shook her head. "No. Officer Ridley left his calling card. On his way out he stepped on the pumpkin right smack over the trace print, which probably *did* belong to the killer, and which we'll probably never get a line on."

A car door slammed outside the house. Voices carried in the early morning air. The crime-scene techs had arrived.

The chief's jaw tightened. "Boy, Hershey, you're havin' a good time with this, aren't you? Far as you're concerned, it's just one big hoot an' a holler. You—"

"Wait a minute. I—"

"No, you wait!" Sweat slicked the chief's face. "Tell the truth, Hershey. You just been hopin' for a chance to show us what boneheads we are out here, what corn-shuckin', tobacco-chewin' boneheads we are. You look at us and you see two-bit security guards who couldn't cut it on a real police force."

"That's ridiculous," Claudia said evenly. "If I believed that for a minute I wouldn't be here myself."

She wondered if that were true, though. Burnout had propelled her from Cleveland. Serendipity and a defeated muffler had stopped her in Indian Run, a tree-and-sky community of eight thousand souls and fourteen sworn police officers.

A mile past the lake, cattle ranchers anchored the western and southernmost reaches of Indian Run, their vast property curling north around the town's small commercial and government district until it abruptly ended where acres of citrus groves began. Scattered residential pockets fanned northwest from the town's center, the newest and most contentious such neighborhood named Feather Ridge. Those who called Feather Ridge home commuted as far north as Orlando for jobs. They built country houses in the mid six-figure range, erected a private school for their children, finagled a small airport, saw to their recreational needs with tennis courts and a membership-only golf course, and periodically upset the balance of Indian Run by pushing for more of the same. Developers loved Feather Ridge's residents; most of Indian Run hated them. And though Claudia didn't live in Feather Ridge, she was viewed with the same suspicion as all outsiders.

From the first day on, most of the officers called her "Stilts" behind her back. Robin had complained that the kids she met wouldn't stop staring, and she cried for a week when she realized the town had no mall. And both of them learned early on that the slightest breeze carried not the scent of confederate jasmine but the stench of cattle.

In a rare and awful moment of impulse, Claudia, at thirty-six with a thirteen-year-old child and a U-Haul trailer in tow, had embraced not the Norman Rockwell village she thought she'd found, but a make-do community where yellow cattle-crossing signs became landmarks for roads that were otherwise unmarked altogether. Still, short on money and long on determination, Claudia tried to make the best of it. She was stuck with Indian Run and it was stuck with her until the end of her one-year contract.

But she said none of that to Chief Suggs. It was personal to him, what happened in the town. And anyway, his campaign to goad her was beside the point. The point was the dead woman at their feet.

When he paused long enough to fumble for another Tums, Claudia pointed at the still form and reminded him in clipped words that he had asked for an assessment.

"Like it or not," she began, "you wanted to know what we've got here, and a big part of what we've got right now is about the most seriously contaminated crime scene I've ever had to deal with in my life."

Claudia thrust a hand toward the door Ridley had broken. It

leaned crazily, letting in a single shaft of light. "It's going to play hell with the investigation," she told the chief, "and yes, the crime-scene techs are going to climb our clocks because of it. Now if that's not what you want to hear, then your best bet is to find someone else to put on this case, or give it up to the sheriff's department."

Dust motes moved lazily through a finger of light. Claudia looked past them and locked eyes with Suggs. He took a long time to respond. "Indian Run hasn't had a murder in four years," he said quietly. "And that hardly qualified. Was just some joker who sliced up another guy over a pool-table fight. I can't even think of anything before that. But now—what you're telling me now—I got myself a psychic killed on Halloween night. To top it off, I got a crime scene with maybe the best evidence stuck under one of my own officer's shoes."

Claudia started to speak, but Suggs held up both hands. "Don't look like I got much choice here, Hershey. Don't know much about homicide. My boys know less." He gave her a long look. "So all right. Do what you got to do. Say what you got to say. We'll go your way for now."

With a snap, she shut her notebook and slipped it into the pocket of her jacket, a fermenting ground for most of her investigations. The jackets she characteristically wore, special-ordered wraps with sturdy bellows pockets and a mid-thigh cut, managed to conceal her revolver and much of the police paraphernalia the job required. Robin thought them tacky.

As Claudia turned back to the kitchen, Suggs stopped her briefly. She turned inquiringly.

"Hershey, I hear-tell you play the oboe," he said. "That true?"

Warily nodding, she conceded that it was. Probably another black mark, and she wondered how he had heard that. Wished it were the banjo instead.

"You play it good?"

"I play it so-so," said Claudia, though in truth she played quite well.

Suggs grunted.

"What?" she said. "What's the point?"

"No point. Everything gotta have a point with you, Hershey?"

"Most things do."

"Well, this don't. I heard it yesterday and so I'm askin'."

"That's it?"

"That's it, Hershey."

With no further explanation, the chief fished a piece of candy from the bowl on Donna Overton's table and went outside. Claudia took one last, lingering look in the kitchen, then followed briskly. The scent of blood would be with her the rest of the day.

CHAPTER 2

FOR THE LONGEST TIME AFTERWARD, it was almost impossible to pull in a deep breath. He sucked at the air noisily, taking it in huge gulps to stem the nausea. And the sweat—it seeped from every pore as if he'd just run a marathon. He could smell himself; swore he could smell her too.

But it was over. She was dead, and he had killed her, and he was glad.

The man let the hours pass into light, burn into the brilliance of afternoon, then fade softly into night. He moved from his chair twice, once to shower and use the toilet, once to eat cold pizza from two days earlier and catch what they were saying on the radio. Then he sat again, just staring. His breath came evenly now and he could think clearly.

The bitch didn't understand. He could see it on her face. Hear it in her voice. And it was amazing, really, that she didn't. How many times had they been over it? How often had they discussed what had to be?

Tilting his head, the man listened to the silence. Then he chuckled. For a minute, he thought he'd heard her again! How ridiculous. He gave his head a shake and laughed aloud. Okay. So maybe he still had a little of the heebie-jeebies in him. Made sense. He hadn't been sure he would kill her. He hadn't planned it at all. But she'd surprised him, all right. He hadn't counted on her coming back. No, sir! Maybe he should have, but he didn't, and so he'd had to kill her dead.

Well. There were things to consider now, weren't there? As good as it felt—the bitch was dead—there were things he had to know, and he played the scene through his mind like film on a reel.

On the plus side, as messy as it had been, he didn't think he'd left anything behind; and thank God, the cops here were all a bunch of Barney Fifes. They lived for speeders barreling through town on the way to somewhere else. Unexpected death? Well, it just didn't happen in Indian Run. They wouldn't know what to do.

Still . . . those machines, that new forensic equipment, it could be pretty sophisticated, couldn't it? Would it find something invisible, or maybe some little hair or something? And what was it the radio newscaster said? That some new detective was leading the case, some woman lieutenant? She wasn't from here, not originally. Would that be important?

Restless now, the man rose from his chair. He set about making dinner. Steak, baked potato. A couple of rolls. It surprised him a little, his appetite returning. But he took it as a good sign. What he'd done, it had been the right thing. The only thing. And the detective, forget it. If she were any good she wouldn't be in a two-bit town like Indian Run. Probably a drunk bounced off a force somewhere else. He'd watch her, find out what he could, listen to what everyone was saying—oh, how they loved to talk in this town—but he wouldn't worry.

The bitch was dead. His biggest worry was over.

The steak sizzled on the broiler. The man flipped it, judging it nearly done. He pulled the potato from the microwave and wrapped it in foil to keep it warm. Then he heated a few rolls and set everything on the table.

Come Monday, he would go about his business like always, like he always had until the bitch opened her mouth, wanting from him, always making demands.

The man paused, a forkful of steak halfway to his mouth. That she was gone, it was partly luck. Just plain, stupid luck; and luck was not the way to make things turn out right. He knew that; he would have to move through his days carefully.

Mulling it over, the man brought the fork closer to his mouth. The meat was medium-rare, perfect. He grunted and opened his mouth, starved. But wait a minute! Wait a minute! What was this? His eyes narrowed and he jerked his hand closer to his vision, dropping the fork. Damn it! A nick on the fleshy part of his hand! He hadn't noticed it earlier.

As if it were on someone else, the man stared at the cut, spellbound. Not a bad cut, but it was there and he didn't remember it. How could that be! His hand began to tremble. Then it shook violently and he began to sweat once more. His stink rose up again.

The bitch had left a reminder after all. She had carved the memory on his flesh. Maybe she would never, ever leave him alone. Not really.

The man retreated to his chair, his supper untouched. He had to think, he had to think. He had to get past this, put his life back where it had been before the bitch had surprised him. She didn't call the shots. Not now. He just had to remind himself that he was in control. Yes. He was in control.

CHAPTER 3

INDIAN RUN JUNIOR HIGH had been around for thirty-five years. Its history showed in the center of the hallway where tile once blue had worn to a matte gray from thousands of footsteps. Wax buildup from optimistic cleanings climbed the walls a good two inches, announcing age like tree rings.

But except for the rapid tick of Claudia's shoes, the hallways were silent at five o'clock. No games on a Monday. No dances. No club meetings.

She swept past a long row of scarred metal lockers, then slowed, looking for room 107. She would have preferred a root canal to the unexpected summons from Robin's algebra teacher. It couldn't be good news and she was tired, two eighteen-hour days into a murder investigation. Where would she find time to swing into the appropriate mother role—whatever the hell that was—when, even when she had the time, Robin responded to mother noises with less enthusiasm than she displayed toward a television commercial?

Just past a drinking fountain, the door to 107 stood open, and Claudia saw a man hunched over a desk in front of a blackboard. He looked up unsmiling when she knocked.

"You must be Robin's mother," he said, rising and formally extending a hand. "I'm Victor Flynn. Thank you for coming."

Flynn stood as tall as Claudia, but was thick and slightly stoop-shouldered, as if mathematics maybe weighed him down. His handshake was firm, but clammy, and when he spoke he revealed uneven teeth that loosed a blast of sour breath. She drew back reflexively.

"Please, have a seat," he said. He had small slate eyes that peered restlessly at Claudia from behind heavy, black-framed glasses. "I know you must be very busy."

The spindly student desks advertised discomfort for all but the most tolerant. She tested one for wobble, then perched stiffly on the edge.

"Mrs. Hershey," said Flynn as he rested a hip on the edge of his own desk, "I asked that you come in so that we can head off what appears to be a problem with your daughter, Robin."

There it was. The kiss of death.

"I'm afraid her grade is slipping rather dramatically," the teacher continued. He fiddled with the stems of his glasses. "I know I don't have to tell you that Robin is a very bright young lady, but what you might not be aware of is that in the past several weeks she just hasn't been working to her full ability."

Oh, shit. Hadn't been aware. Should have been aware, but wasn't aware. Bad mother, bad mother.

"Unfortunately," Flynn continued, "she's sliding into a D and if she doesn't concentrate she'll be looking at an F."

Jolted, Claudia shook her head. Surely a mistake. She could see the kid bent over the dining room table, books spread out, a Diet Pepsi to the side, a fluorescent green pad opened in front of her.

"I don't get it," she said slowly, her spine straightening. "Are you sure? Her report card showed her with a solid B. I don't understand how she could drop that far that fast."

A thin smile split the teacher's mouth. He stroked the insubstantial sideburn above his right ear. He had limp brown hair to match, the sort of hair that would fall out prematurely.

"Actually, I'm afraid your daughter never carried anything higher than a C grade," Flynn said tolerantly. "You must be confusing the B with some other subject Robin's taking."

As clearly as if she were holding it now, Claudia could still see the computerized sheet with gray type. She remembered thinking the printing ribbon should have been changed before the grades were sent out. But as for the grades themselves, well, they'd all been satisfactory, even good. He was asking her to accept the unacceptable.

Still: "You're sure there's no mistake?" she asked. "These things do happen, don't they? I mean, isn't it possible you've confused Robin with some other student?"

In response, Flynn handed Claudia a duplicate of Robin's report card. "I'm sorry. There's no mistake, Mrs. Hershey—or should I call you 'Detective' or 'Lieutenant'?"

What a howl, thought Claudia as she scanned the sheet, her eyes stopping on the C- for algebra. The alteration she had missed on Robin's report card was something she never would have missed in police work. She muttered that it didn't matter how Flynn addressed her.

His hands went back to the sideburns. "I guess this is something of a surprise to you," he said solicitously, "but the truth is that Robin's just not doing her homework regularly. What she does turn in is often incomplete. Consequently, she's doing very poorly on tests."

Claudia hardly heard. She was disappointed; she was angry. Was this Robin's way of getting back at her for uprooting her? Or was this a typical adolescent challenge that had more to do with hormones out of whack than anything Claudia did or failed to do? Were all thirteen-year-olds similarly conniving? She didn't know, and she despaired at how best to deal with it. Clearly, the way she had been dealing with it didn't work.

Since moving to Indian Run she'd given her daughter full rein, trying to let her come to terms with an abruptly different situation in her own way. The biting sarcasm, the scornful looks, the flaunting of household rules, Claudia let it ride. The theory was, Robin would come around. What Flynn was telling her was that she hadn't.

The teacher reached for some papers. He held them out to Claudia. His hands shook slightly. "Um, take a look at these."

She handled the papers as if bacteria crawled all over them. Three D's. Five C's. One B. Two F's. On one paper, a quiz, Robin had doodled flowers. Without looking up, Claudia knew the algebra teacher's ferret eyes were all over her.

"This is just since the last marking period, Mrs. Hershey," he said. "I did make an appointment on Friday to talk to her this morning during her study hall, but she didn't follow through."

Claudia's stomach contracted. She looked up. "She never showed at all?"

"She told me in class this afternoon that she'd forgotten and that she, uh, had band practice after school and couldn't make it later." He leaned forward slightly. "There is no band practice today, Mrs. Hershey. Frankly, I'm quite concerned."

Nodding, she said tersely, "I'm just a bit concerned myself."

What she didn't tell him was that Robin had a tin ear. Not only did she not play an instrument, but she could barely distinguish one instrument from another. The lies were piling up like traffic at rush hour.

Flynn was doing that damnable thing with his sideburns again. Claudia wanted to bat his hands away. "I guess I should thank you for letting me know what's going on," she said. "I'm sure not all teachers would bother."

"Don't give it another thought," he said. He regarded Claudia with a distant smile. "I take pride in my teaching and I take an active interest in my students."

She started to rise, but Flynn was just warming up. He launched into his philosophy of teaching and Claudia tuned him out. Her eyes drifted to the blackboard. Numbers and letters were painstakingly chalked all over it. Most of them were meaningless to her; she remembered algebra as "x equals y" or some such thing. It made about as much sense as Donna Overton's brutal slaying, and Claudia's mind turned to the preliminary reports from the medical examiner and the crime lab.

The Reverend Donna Overton was killed between eleven and midnight, maybe twelve-thirty, by repeated blows to the head from some unknown blunt instrument. According to the medical examiner, death probably closed her eyes with the third or fourth blow, but the killer hadn't stopped there. Nine blows could be distinguished, though the medical examiner speculated as many as thirty had been applied. A few blows had landed on the woman's shoulders, and she'd additionally suffered a broken index finger on her right hand, probably from falling, fighting, or a poorly placed whack by the killer.

The angle of the blows and the blood pattern on the kitchen walls suggested the killer was right-handed, tall, and strong. He'd come at her straight on, and probably quickly; other than the broken finger and overturned table, there were no telltale signs of combat or even serious defense. The killer had come in close, but not close enough—not in any sort of body wrap—for there weren't any tissue or cloth fibers beneath Overton's fingernails, nor was there any blood that hadn't drained out of the woman herself.

And of blood, there had been plenty. It had splotched the walls and pooled on the small linoleum floor. The victim's clothing, a flowing blouse with a bright, flowered print over a black skirt, were drenched to the point that colors were hard to distinguish. Some of the blood on the floor had been diluted by water, likely spilled from a plastic tumbler that had fallen from the table.

Rape was not an issue. The medical examiner's report showed no evidence of vaginal bruising, no deposit of semen.

Not robbery. Not rape. What then?

Flynn's voice intruded and Claudia looked up. That she was his sole audience seemed not at all bothersome to the teacher. He proselytized at length, first about the value of keeping to goals, then about overcoming obstacles by eliminating distractions. His voice rose and fell like a preacher's.

She smiled mechanically, nodded perfunctorily, and blocked him back out.

There was no telling how much evidence Officer Bobby Ridley might have contaminated in his bungling efforts to get in—and out—of the death scene. And what evidence the technicians had carefully bagged and marked suggested little of value. Hairs other than those belonging to the victim were plentiful, but then, dozens of people visited Overton's home for readings. It was likely that one of the hairs belonged to the killer, but just as likely that none did.

The same held true for fingerprints. Most, of course, belonged to Overton. A few on the base of the telephone, the bedroom dresser, and nightstand—and one clear thumbprint on the coffeemaker in the kitchen—screamed the presence of Tom Markos. That stood to reason. He'd been her lover. He could also have been her killer.

The desk creaked when Claudia shifted her weight. Markos was no choir boy. The criminal record he'd compiled over the years was clear on that. But he'd kept to himself since drifting into Indian Run eight months earlier, and questions about him elicited little more than a shrug. So why then had he vanished? Frowning, she made a mental note to try the fish camp once more before the day was out.

". . . and the material we're going over right now isn't all that complicated, actually, don't you agree?"

Damn. Flynn was asking her something now. Grappling to pick up the thread of the conversation, Claudia nodded affirmatively. *Yes, yes, whatever.*

The teacher's eyes narrowed briefly, but then he smiled and slid off the desk. "Maybe I can illustrate the point better than I can verbalize it," he said. He walked to the blackboard, picked up a piece of chalk, glanced over his shoulder at Claudia, and began to scribble. An algebraic equation appeared.

While Flynn nattered on and scribed numbers, she thought about the jack-o'-lantern. *Damn it to hell, Ridley couldn't have blown the crime scene any better if he'd tried.* The dominant footprint in the pulp matched the rookie's shoe. The print beneath was too indistinguishable for a read. At best, she could hope for pumpkin traces on the killer's shoe—if he hadn't tossed it, scoured it—if indeed he were caught.

And what of the black thread a crime-scene tech bagged from the kitchen? It had been snared in a nick in the side of the counter. Did it mean anything? It would have to be matched against all of the clothing in the victim's closet and hamper.

Also inventoried were a heavy-duty staple lying on the counter, a tiny screw caught in a dust bunny between the counter and refrigerator, a beer-bottle cap beside that, and on the floor by the victim's feet a blood-soaked cigarette that hadn't been lit. Overton smoked, and Claudia remembered a newly opened pack on the counter. The brand matched that of a stubbed-out cigarette in a bedroom ashtray.

Elsewhere in the one-bedroom house, the technicians had dutifully catalogued the minutiae of the Reverend Donna Overton's life. The pattern showed a reasonably tidy housekeeper with a fondness for knickknacks—she seemed to favor miniature animal sculptures—cheap makeup, hard candy, coupon-clipping, and romance novels.

In the bedroom, a worn comforter with a flower pattern covered the double bed. Two plumped pillows with matching shams decorated the head; a homemade afghan draped over the bottom. The bed hadn't been slept in that night. The medium's closet held simple clothing from Wal-Mart, Kmart, and an outlet store; her medicine chest showed over-the-counter drugs and a dated prescription for an expectorant. Towels, faded but neatly folded, hung smartly over a rack on a wall beside the toilet.

In a small sunroom adjacent to the living room was a folding table with two chairs, a shelf with more knickknacks, and a single bookcase with titles addressing everything from astrology to Zen Buddhism.

The most expensive possession Overton owned was a thirty-inch color console television with stereo sound—hardly a necessity in the small room. But it looked new and stood like a trophy against one entire wall in the living room. A television guide on top of the console lay open to Friday, the day Overton was killed.

Who are you, Donna Overton, and why would someone want to kill you?

Claudia had seen a lot of senseless, brutal killing, mostly from gunshots—a clean way to kill, and easy. There were stabbings as well and yes, a few beating deaths. Death by knives and beatings shouted rage. Most were spontaneous. But this, this seemed both controlled and, yet, not.

A sudden sound jolted her back to the purgatory of algebra. Flynn was clapping chalk dust from his hands, moving back toward her. She stood when he approached, then involuntarily flinched at the blast of vile breath.

"In Robin's case," he was saying, "I'd be happy to tutor her after school—an hour here, an hour there—because I'm quite sure she can still pull her grade up and maybe even finish with a solid C. If you can just convince her to work a little harder."

Claudia backed out of range. She smiled tightly. "I'll try."

"Good, good!" Flynn enthused. His hand sought his sideburn. "It can't be easy, trying to juggle the demands of parenthood and a job such as yours." He shook his head sympathetically. "This murder—it's all over the radio and TV—is it anywhere near being resolved?"

Everyone wanted to know. The murder ranked right up there with the citrus reports. She gave the algebra teacher her stock answer: "The investigation is moving along."

He nodded. "I understand it's very difficult to make an arrest if a suspect isn't identified within the first twenty-four hours."

"We're working on it." Claudia began to move off.

"That poor woman, she seemed so nice."

She stopped so abruptly that Flynn bumped against her. "Wait a minute," she said. "You knew her?"

"Well, no, not actually. I'd only met her the one time, during the Halloween party."

"Back up a minute, Mr. Flynn." She didn't hear the sharp edge in her voice, but the mother was gone. The cop was back. "What Halloween party? What are you talking about?"

Flynn regarded Claudia peculiarly. "Well, the party where she conducted the séance, of course. I can't believe you don't know."

"I don't know, Mr. Flynn. I wasn't aware of any séance or any party." She called the dead medium's appointment book to mind. Nothing showed she'd gone anywhere the night she was killed. Nothing. "It would have been nice if someone had brought that to our attention."

"I'm sorry. I just assumed the police would've been told. It was quite an experience if you go for that sort of thing." He looked embarrassed. "The fact that I attended a séance . . . well, I hope you don't take that as a reflection of my professionalism as a teacher. I can assure you that—"

"I don't care if you dance naked under a full moon, Mr. Flynn." Claudia hitched the notebook from her pocket. "What I do care about is no one thought that the police might be interested in information about the last few hours of Donna Overton's life. The party . . . tell me about it."

"I . . . well." Flynn cleared his throat. "Lucille Schuster—she's an English teacher here—she had a Halloween party, mostly faculty people. Costumes, the whole bit." He flicked at his sideburns. His eyes looked just past Claudia's. "There were perhaps a dozen of us there. She—Lucille, that is—surprised us with the séance."

"What do you mean?"

"Well, just that Reverend Overton was presented as a surprise. None of us had known she would be there. Oh, I guess Lucille's husband did, but he's a traveling salesman and was still out of town. Anyway, Lucille was tickled with the whole thing. I guess she'd arranged it secretly, thought it would be perfect for a Halloween party. I can't imagine what she must've paid, but it—" Flynn stopped abruptly. "You don't think the séance had anything to do with it, do you?"

"What time did Donna Overton leave?"

"I don't know, exactly." He pursed his lips. "Maybe . . . maybe around eleven? Something like that. It—"

"Where can I find Lucille Schuster, Mr. Flynn?

Flynn gave Claudia directions to the English teacher's house. He apologized again for not having said anything to the police, but said he'd assumed they knew. And then, as she clipped away down the hall, he wished her luck with her daughter.

CHAPTER 4

THE LOCALS LIKED TO JOKE that the only reason Little Arrow Lake existed at all was because God had water left over when He was done putting Lake Okeechobee together. Not sure what to do with it, He tossed it over his shoulder like salt for luck and it landed in Indian Run, where it filled some two square miles in the shape of a foot.

The lake never made it into any Florida tour guides, which was probably just as well since only those intimately familiar with the surrounding geography would ever find it. The lake was more obscured by snarled foliage than a tick on a poodle, and its only access was by a twisted series of unmarked washboard roads. By the time Claudia reached it early Monday evening, her mood was as dark as the soil on her car.

The hour was drawing onto six, rushing the early November sky on a slide into dusk. But if Tom Markos was here, she wanted to be the one to talk to him. Lucille Schuster would have to wait. Robin would have to wait, too.

The air was nippy and still, trapping the scent of fish and woods. Claudia got out of her car and inhaled. Six or seven cars and two pickup trucks were wedged between laurel oaks, but no one was in sight. Fishermen liked to milk every bit of light out of the day, and she assumed they were just leaving the lake.

She picked her way down a sloping dirt path that led to a wood-frame building on stilts. It perched on the edge of the lake as purposefully as a heron, but without the grace. On the far side to the right was a boat ramp. Just beyond that were a number of vessels for rent: skiffs and flat-bottomed bass boats for serious anglers, two canoes for nature lovers. A few fishermen were just tying up.

Claudia watched for a moment, then took the loose steps that brought her to the doorway of the building. Despite the chill, the door was open. The smell of stale coffee and bait wafted out.

A few fishermen stood at a counter, poking through a box of lures. Others huddled at a snack bar, trading stories. A plastic globe with two old donuts in it sent Claudia's stomach on alert, but she ignored it and headed for the sales counter. Eyes followed her.

An old man behind the counter greeted her with the prerequisite curiosity and suspicion reserved for strangers. He wore a sleeveless fishing vest over a plaid shirt. Colorful lures were clipped to his chest like military ribbons.

Seeking a bridge across the skepticism she read in his rheumy eyes, Claudia asked offhandedly how the fish were running. She said that from what she understood, late evening was one of the best times to drop a line.

The old man eyed her dubiously. "If you're thinkin' of going out, I can rent you everything you need and get you squared away on a boat. But you'd be wasting your time right now. You only got maybe a half hour of real light left, at best." He squinted past Claudia. "You by yourself? We don't have no guides."

She smiled. "I'm not here to fish. I wouldn't know a rod from a reel. I'm just trying to find Tom Markos. I stopped by Saturday and Sunday but I guess I missed him."

The old man nodded. "Yeah, Tom, he normally works weekends but he was out with a head cold or something. He's here today, though, working down by the rentals." The old man gave Claudia an appraising look. "He don't get many personal visitors."

"Thanks. I'll find him." She pointed at a lure with a treble hook and a twist of brightly colored feathers. "Nice."

The old man shrugged, then leaned toward Claudia confidentially. "Nice lookin' all right, but it don't work worth a damn. This one's just for show." He winked.

"Ah." She looked at the thing again, then impulsively reached for her wallet. "How much is it?" she asked. What might be too shoddy for fishing would be perfect to adorn a Christmas package. Take the hooks off and it could be laced through a bow. Robin might like it.

"I'll give it to you for a buck-fifty," said the old man. He shook his head. "Like I said, though, it ain't worth a plug nickel."

"That's all right," said Claudia. "I like the colors."

"Women," said the man. He grunted, his suspicion fading to amusement.

After counting out a dollar and a half, she watched the man bury the hooks onto a piece of Styrofoam.

"Ain't got no bags, Miss," he explained, "but that oughta keep you from accidentally stickin' yourself."

Claudia thanked the man and slid the lure in her jacket pocket. She angled toward a door on the opposite side of the building. Another set of wobbly stairs greeted her, and she took them cautiously. They stepped off to an elbow-shaped path that led to the boat ramp.

Markos was an imposing figure, powered by broad shoulders and thick thighs that strained against stonewashed jeans. He was more beard and eyebrows than face, and more hair than head. He knelt inside a boat, fiddling with the engine.

Claudia watched him work for a moment. "Mr. Markos?" she said, pulling her ID from a jacket pocket.

When Markos glanced up, she flipped the ID open, revealing the shield inside. "I'm Detective Lieutenant Hershey. I'd like to talk to you for a few minutes."

"I know who you are," he said indifferently. He turned back to the engine. "I don't have time to talk."

"This won't take long."

"I get paid for doing what I'm doing right now, Miss. Nobody pays me to make conversation."

"I'm here on police business, Mr. Markos." Claudia watched his big hands finesse the engine. "You can work while we talk."

With a savage pull, Markos started the outboard. He looked at her through dark eyes and shouted above the roar of the engine. "Fine. Get on. I got just enough light to take the boat for a run, see that it's working right again."

She hesitated for a second, then stepped into the vessel, a sixteen-footer with two raised swivel chairs. Her leg shook as she stepped over the bait well and sought firm footing at the bow. With barely enough time to settle herself, the boat lurched forward. She grabbed the edges of her seat on either side. The boat shot across the lake, rendering conversation impossible.

Gingerly, Claudia freed one hand long enough to pull her jacket closer around her. Wind whipped her face, pushing hair into her eyes and sending a fine mist across her glasses. She looked down as the vessel skimmed the surface. The boat sat lower in the water than she had imagined it would. Water boiled at the sides. She tried not to think about it.

They moved at a steady clip for ten minutes, whistling past a few anglers on their way in. She was freezing. She tucked her head toward her chest. The air swooped through her jacket collar.

Suddenly, the boat turned sharply right. Water sluiced over the edge. Claudia caught her breath and planted her feet more firmly. She could swim, but not well. And what she couldn't do was arm wrestle an alligator if it came to that. She'd seen one in the distance, gliding low in the water at the edge of the lake.

But as suddenly as the boat had turned, it shuddered, then stopped. The engine coughed asthmatically. Silence fell over the lake.

Claudia exhaled silently and wiped her glasses on a sleeve. They smudged instantly. Experimentally, she tried her chair and swiveled so she could face Markos directly. She could see that he'd been watching her.

"Too much air in the fuel line," he said. He tapped the outboard with a dirty fingernail. "It's like a kid choking on a chicken bone."

They drifted gently in a recess edged by clumps of fringe rush, sword grass and cattails, some of them eight feet tall. Cypress knees jutted irregularly from the water. The cypress trees themselves, towering figures laced with Spanish moss thick as angelhair pasta, screened what little light remained. A crushed beer can announced previous visitors. Something jumped once—a fish, maybe.

Without taking his eyes from Claudia's face, Markos fished a cigarette from his shirt pocket and lit up. He didn't offer the pack to her. "Hope you're not in a hurry, Miss."

"It's lieutenant, Mr. Markos, and I thought *you* were."

He flicked ash into the water. His expression shifted slightly, showing a spark of belligerence. "Not much I can do about it now," he said. "Need to give the engine a rest."

Claudia leaned forward. The boat rocked slightly. "Let's not play games, Mr. Markos. I'm sure you know why I'm here."

He took a long drag on his cigarette. "Donna's dead. I heard it this morning. You're looking to finger me for it."

"I don't know enough to finger anyone, Mr. Markos. I'm here to learn what I can and—"

"And you want to know where I was when she was killed," said the man. His voice dwarfed the space between them. "You want to know did I do it, don't you?" With an expert flick of his finger, he sent the cigarette spinning into the lake. "I didn't."

Claudia measured the steel in Markos's eyes. She wondered how far he'd taken her from other boaters. Voices carried from a distance, but she couldn't isolate the source. Still, they were here now. There might not be another opportunity.

"All right," she said at length. "Let's just back into this, Mr. Markos. Where've you been spending your time from Friday to today?"

"Home."

"Who can vouch for that?"

"No one can say I was, and no one can say I wasn't."

"I can say you weren't there Saturday or Sunday, and you weren't here either."

"I don't answer my door to strangers." Markos busied himself by biting on a fingernail. "And if you were asking around for me here, then you already know I was out sick. And anyway, so what? What's the point? Donna was already dead by then, wasn't she? That's what the TV says."

"The point, Mr. Markos, is that you're lying to me."

"Prove it."

"I might have to."

He looked away. "Donna and I had a thing for a while. Then we busted up, I don't know, about a month ago—"

"Two weeks ago."

"So okay, two weeks ago. And so what? There a crime in that?"

"There's a crime in murder, Mr. Markos."

"Look, Donna broke it off because it didn't turn out to be right. We weren't a good fit."

"How so?"

Markos leered. "I like beer better'n broads."

"Where'd you meet her?" asked Claudia, ignoring the look.

"Outside the grocery store." He foraged through a pocket and produced a pair of nailclippers. "She'd gotten a couple of bags of groceries, and when she was leaving, her car wouldn't start."

"Go on."

Markos worked around his nails, taking his time. "I'd just pulled up and was about to go in. It had been raining and she'd left the lights on. Battery was dead. I had my truck and I gave her a jump. We got to talkin'. She told me her old man used to fish in tourneys. We went for coffee. One thing led to another. We started going out regular-like. And yeah, we slept together."

Holding his left hand out, Markos examined his nails. He started on the right hand. Both hands were dark and scarred.

"You were married once, long ago, weren't you, Mr. Markos?"

Surprised, he looked up. "Something wrong with that?"

"If you knock your wife around—and you did."

"Once is all. She hit me first."

"I see."

Markos leaned forward abruptly, rocking the boat. "I was married to this woman for a year, tops. We were kids. She was wild and so was I. We both drank too much. We were drunk when we went at each other. Later, she called the cops. I spent the night in jail and then got three months' probation. It was just kid stuff."

"Kid stuff?" said Claudia. "Is that also how you explain the bust for assault with a deadly weapon over in Loxahatchee? What was it? Back in 1979? And what about the battery charge eight years later? Was that kid stuff too?"

"So you dug up my sheet." Markos pocketed the nailclippers. "I'm impressed. Even Indian Run's got access to a computer."

"Yes, and it suggests you like to rough people up, Mr. Markos. It also suggests you've had your nose in drug activity."

"Never convicted and I've been clean since '90."

"So you say."

"That's right. So I say."

Claudia studied Markos's face. "Let's try again. Where were you late Friday ni—"

He lunged. The boat dipped violently and she brought her arms up, one hand reflexively reaching beneath her jacket toward the trouser holster that held a Colt .38 Special. She felt Markos fall against her, forcing her to snatch at the side of the boat. Her knee rapped hard against the bow. Water cascaded over the side, stinging her with its icy chill.

She gasped, angling for purchase, and got a lock on the gun. Her knuckles scraped against the frame of the boat, but she slid the revolver from its holster.

At the same instant, he pushed to his feet. He shouted unintelligibly and swung something in an arc. Claudia took awkward aim and, in a heartbeat second of indecision, saw an indistinct form fly from his hand. A snake, long and dark, twisted acrobatically, then hit the water and slithered out of sight.

She exhaled sharply.

Looming above her, his Rasputin face stone-like and dark, Markos said nothing, but his eyes shifted to the gun. Claudia lowered it slowly, catching her breath.

He looked at her dispassionately. "Water moccasin."

He gestured toward a cypress branch parallel to the boat. "Thing was hanging off of there. They move quick, and this one was too close for comfort—mine or yours. They say snakes can smell blood from a hundred feet. Might be the truth."

Claudia's mouth was as dry as old paint. Gradually she eased herself back onto the chair and holstered the revolver. The adrenaline rush left her spent, but she hooked her eyes on Markos and kept them there.

The boat swayed mildly when he returned to his seat. He patted his shirt pocket for cigarettes, then shook his head. "Damn. The pack fell out."

Claudia saw it drifting toward a cluster of sword grass. Darkness was descending rapidly. "Let's get back. The next time we talk it'll be in *my* office, not yours."

Smirking, Markos asked, "Not so keen on fishing anymore?"

"Let's go."

"Suit yourself." He reached down and fiddled with the engine. It spit once, then sputtered to life. They made their way back to the camp in silence. Claudia watched Markos tie up and told him they would talk again. He acknowledged the comment with a shrug.

She irritably picked her way back to the car, tripping once on a tree root. She paused outside the vehicle, peeling off her wet jacket and tossing it in the back. Black with minuscule threads of burgundy, the jacket was one of her favorites. It would run her ten bucks for dry cleaning.

She stowed the revolver in her handbag, thought about the hour, and headed off.

Lucille Schuster wasn't home, but a baby-sitter awed by the detective's badge told her where the teacher and her husband could be found. Claudia stopped for gas, found a phone, and touched base with Robin, then broke every speed limit on her way to Denny's restaurant.

The place was crowded with the dinner trade. She pushed past a line in the waiting area and made for the nonsmoking section. Lucille Schuster's hair was redder than the baby-sitter had described it, and in seconds Claudia descended on her table.

"Mrs. Schuster?" she asked, ignoring the husband.

The woman looked up quizzically. She was in her mid-twenties and had a Kewpie-doll face. "Yes?" she said pleasantly.

Claudia showed her shield. "I'm Detective Lieutenant Claudia Hershey and I need to talk to you about Donna Overton."

Schuster's face drained of color and she looked at her husband uncertainly. "Well, I . . . can it wait?"

"No, it can't."

The man cleared his throat. "Look, Detective, I think—"

"You're Mr. Schuster?" Claudia asked in a clipped voice.

"Yes. Ralph."

"I don't need to talk to you just yet, Mr. Schuster, although I will want to later. Right now, only your wife." Claudia returned her gaze to the teacher. "Let's go. Outside."

Diners around the Schusters' table watched surreptitiously as Claudia strode rapidly toward the door, Lucille Schuster trailing meekly. Someone held the door for them, and she led the teacher outside, out of earshot.

"The police chief in this town takes murder personally. We both take it seriously," Claudia began. She lowered her face until her eyes were level with the younger woman's. "Donna Overton was murdered the night she conducted a séance at your Halloween party. I know you know that."

Lucille Schuster whispered a "yes."

"She may have been killed less than an hour after leaving your home, but apparently you didn't find that interesting enough to come forward and say anything to the police. I hope you have a good reason."

Tears formed in the teacher's eyes. Claudia held up a hand. "Save the theatrics, Mrs. Schuster. I've had a bad day and I'm not in the mood." She watched the woman fight for control, then said, "Why didn't you come forward?"

Schuster waited for a couple to pass them. She looked at the ground and said, "I didn't want the school administration to know I'd had a . . . a séance."

Claudia strained to hear. "Speak up. I can't hear you."

"I said, I was afraid the administration would find out." Her voice wobbled. "The principal is a very straight-laced kind of man. I didn't think he'd find it fitting, you know, that teachers were doing that sort of thing. I mean, there's all this worry over kids these days getting into heavy-metal music and . . . and devil worship . . . that sort of thing. It wouldn't look good."

"So you simply said nothing."

"I'm sorry," the woman whispered. She began to sob. "I'm sorry," she repeated.

Claudia sighed. This was a major screw up. Until now, the investigation had been proceeding with the assumption that Donna Overton had never left her house that night. No one had seen her go or return. Nothing had been written in her appointment book to indicate she'd had an appointment. And now this. The séance may have had nothing to do with the murder. Or everything.

Schuster sniffed. "I . . . uh . . . do you have a Kleenex? I left my purse at the table."

Without comment, Claudia rummaged through her own bag. She pulled a small packet of tissues free and handed it to the woman. She waited while Schuster blew her nose.

"Thank you," the teacher said, her voice muffled in the Kleenex.

"All right. Let's go through it step by step," said Claudia. "You'll still have time for dessert."

Claudia started to grope for her jacket pocket, then remembered the wrap was in the backseat of her car. She dug in her handbag again. The back of an envelope would have to do for notes. She clicked a ballpoint pen open.

The woman began to bawl all over again.

"Oh, for heaven's sake, Mrs. Schuster," said Claudia, "knock it off already. Your tears move me about as much as a dead roach would and I won't stop for them again."

With a snuffle, Lucille Schuster looked up tentatively. She blanched, then pocketed the Kleenex.

Sergeant Ron Peters answered the phone. "Oh, hi, Lieutenant. What's—"

"Ron? Grab some paper. Grab a pen. I've got a lot of information to pass along."

Claudia clamped a hand over her right ear. She was at a roadside phone booth, midway between Denny's and her house. Trucks favored the rural route, and they rumbled along steadily.

"All right, Claudia. Paper ready. Pen ready. Fire away."

With the receiver clutched between her chin and shoulder, she consulted the back of her envelope. It was black with ink, cramped notes marching down, then straight up the margins.

"You're not going to believe this one," Claudia told the sergeant. "There was a little more to Donna Overton's Halloween than trick or treat."

In five minutes, she filled Peters in. There had been twelve people at Lucille Schuster's Halloween party, not counting the medium. Festivities kicked off at nine o'clock, giving guests with children enough time to troll for candy door-to-door. Donna Overton appeared at ten-fifteen, conducted a séance at ten-thirty, and left just after eleven o'clock for her rendezvous with death. The party started to break up at one o'clock. The last straggler left at one-thirty.

The séance—having Donna Overton in—was a spontaneous idea; the teacher had found the medium's name in the phone book and contacted her at seven o'clock that night, tickled at being able to arrange something like that so quickly.

According to Schuster, the séance was a huge success. She described the way lights were dimmed and guests were shushed while the Reverend Donna Overton went into a Shirley MacLaine mode. It seemed like hours were passing, but it must have only been minutes before Overton's head tightened, then suddenly flopped and her eyes closed. Then they fluttered open, whites showing. Guests gasped and nervously looked at each other for reassurance. And then, when Donna Overton began to speak, it was in another voice—something deep and throaty—what guests took to be the voice of someone long departed from the corporeal world.

The performance—or whatever it was—said Schuster, was absolutely spellbinding. And afterward, with the comfort of lights again, there were giggles and nervous titters and the booze flowed. No one was sure if Donna Overton had actually communed with a spirit or if she was just a fantastic actress. But then, no one much cared, Schuster told Claudia. It made for great theater and everyone at the party claimed to have had an enormously good time.

Ron whistled appreciatively. "Unbelievable," he said. "I had no idea this fortune-telling business could get so serious."

A truck hauling livestock barreled past Claudia. *Someone should slap the driver with a ticket,* she thought.

"Look, Ron. Here's what I need next. And I need it fast."

"Ready."

"Schuster says she's absolutely sure no one left the party before one. But I want you and Moody to talk to each of them anyway." Claudia gave Peters the names the teacher had provided. "I want to know their ages, their weight, their height. Schuster said it was a costume party. I want to know what everyone was wearing. I want to know what each of them did immediately prior to the party and immediately after. I want—"

"Whoa, whoa, slow down just a little."

Claudia gave it a beat. "All right. Get each of them to describe the party, down to every tiny detail. Let them prattle on. Get everything you can. And I want to know every single thing that Overton said, whether it had to do with the séance or not. Everything. Find out if any of them knew Donna Overton before that night, no matter how casually."

"Yeah, but if Schuster says none of them left until at least one, and we know Overton was killed between eleven at the soonest and twelve-thirty at the outside, then why—"

"Because, damn it, this is the closest we're probably going to get to the last minutes of Donna Overton's life. Schuster could be mistaken. For that matter, she could be lying. We need every shred of information we can get, no matter how inconsequential it seems."

"Okay."

"More importantly—and I need you to jump on this the minute we hang up—one of the guests, the one named Tom Orben, he apparently brought a video camera and taped the whole thing. We need to see what he shot. We need it now. Unfortunately, Orben's out of town on—"

"Good timing."

Claudia waited for another truck to pass. The phone booth shook. "What'd you say?" she asked.

"I said, good timing."

"Exactly. Anyway, find out from the school principal exactly where Orben is. Lucille Schuster thinks Boston. Find Orben. Get the tape. It's Monday. I want that video on my desk by tomorrow evening, by hook or by crook."

"Maybe his wife is home—"

"Think, Ron! Did I give you two Orben names?"

"Well, no. I—"

"He's single. Lives alone."

Claudia pressed her forehead against the smudged glass of the phone booth. She took a deep breath. Ron Peters was one of three uniformed officers she had pulled for assistance. Suggs bellowed about overtime and the gaps their instant detective status would leave in the patrol shifts. But she was adamant. On her own, she couldn't track every lead, talk to every neighbor, twist every arm that needed to be twisted. Peters was no gem—none of the three were—but they showed instinct the remaining officers didn't. They would have to do.

"I'm sorry," said Claudia. She pictured Peters taking notes, his milky white countenance coloring slightly at the rebuke. "I'm being a bitch. It's been a helluva day, but that's no reason for me to take it out on you."

While Ron murmured something, Claudia thought of Robin. The day wasn't even close to folding.

"I'll call the chief from home tonight, let him know what's going on," Claudia continued. "I'll be in, oh, probably by six. Please get in touch with Carella and Moody now. Let's plan on meeting at eight. Maybe if we put our heads together we can steer this—"

Two cars drag racing flashed past Claudia. Kids, probably. She sighed, registered what the cars looked like, and told Peters to get a patrolman on the road.

"Anyway, Ron, maybe something'll break out of all of this. We've got a few names. We have some interviews under our belts. Now we have the party, and if I'm lucky I'll learn a little more tonight."

"We could use a break," said Ron. "We're getting a lot of calls on this. The mayor's office, of course. Joe Public, scared to death. A couple of reporters. And psychics who didn't even know Overton are coming out of the woodwork, wanting to work with us on this."

"Just what we need." Claudia grimaced. "There's nothing supernatural about Overton's murder, and if we bring in psychics we're only going to feed the hysteria."

Ron snorted. "Just wait'll the press learns she conducted a séance the night she was killed."

"Whoa! The press better not learn it. The less we make of the fact that Overton was a psychic—"

"Medium."

"Right. Medium. Anyway, the less the better."

"Okay. I hear you."

"Yeah, well please make sure everyone else does, too, all right?"

They talked for a while longer, then Claudia hung up. She stood silently in the phone booth for a minute, rotating her shoulders. Tension always started there. Before long, it would work its way into her head.

CHAPTER 5

THE GROCERY STORE was called Philby's—just plain Philby's—and it was the only game in town unless you were of a mind to drive eighteen miles to the Winn-Dixie across the county line. Claudia was not. She had the energy of a dead campfire.

After untangling a shopping cart from the battalion of baskets at the front of the store, she moved robot-like up and down the aisles. In fifteen minutes Philby's would close, but so what? She'd be out in five. In another ten, she'd be home. Lamb chops, a baked potato, a veggie—hell—maybe even some of that Pillsbury dough you could twist into rolls and bake for only twelve minutes.

She didn't cook often, and she didn't cook particularly well. Her daughter did, but heaven forbid the kid would think of throwing something together for the two of them. At thirteen, Robin was playing adolescence by the book. Parents were the pits. Zits traumatized. Boys tantalized.

Oh God, what to do, what to do.

The checkout clerk swept each item across a laser beam with a proud flourish. Modern technology had come to Philby's at the same time Sunday hours did.

"Honey, you look bushed," said the clerk, a round woman named Doris. Her husband managed the bowling alley, where Claudia lately had taken to eating since it was close to the police station.

"A little on the weary side," she acknowledged. She forced a smile.

"My husband, Arthur—you know Art? Works the bowling alley? Anyway, he told me he saw you there at lunch. Said you looked like death-warmed-over then. You look worse now, the truth be told."

Claudia watched a box of cornflakes flick across the scanner. In Cleveland, anonymity was assured. In Indian Run, you couldn't scratch your nose without a third party commenting on it later.

"It's been a long day," she mumbled to Doris.

"You got anybody in jail yet?"

"Not yet."

"Who'd have thought something like that could happen here," Doris said wonderingly.

"It happens everywhere," said Claudia.

"Well, I hope you get someone soon." She hit the total. "Fifty-eight dollars and sixty-seven cents." She took Claudia's money, then began to bag the groceries. "Nobody's gonna rest easy until someone's put away on this."

"We'll find the person. And I'm sure it was an isolated type of thing."

"Hmmph. That's not what they're sayin' on the TV."

Claudia made a face. "Who's saying?"

"Well, you know, the psychics! This TV reporter—I don't recall the name, but was Channel 3, the six o'clock report—this reporter was interviewin' some of the dead woman's neighbors. One of 'em says to the reporter that she had a feelin'—that's how she put it, she had a feelin'—this was just the beginning."

Great. Just great. Indian Run didn't have its own local TV station. Channel 3 was situated in Land of Rivers—a misnomer if ever there was one—some thirty miles distant. The station rarely had occasion to even peek into Indian Run. That it had now meant that Overton's death would spiral out of control soon.

Claudia had hoped—foolishly, she recognized—to keep the story low-key. The town's twice-weekly paper never probed deeply, and with luck the murder would've been too old to look sexy to any of the more aggressive press by the time they saw the *Gazette's* story. That wouldn't happen now.

Claudia helped Doris load the bags into her cart. *For almost sixty bucks there should have been more than three bags*, she thought.

Doris rattled on about the Channel 3 report. "They nabbed Chief Suggs in his office, but he didn't say much." Doris laughed. "That old fart. I love the man to death—he and my Art fish together sometimes—but I gotta tell you, he looked about as comfortable talkin' to that reporter as somebody who'd just had his wisdom teeth pulled."

After mumbling additional reassurances, Claudia said good-bye and pushed her cart to the parking lot. The most the Indian Run Police Department had been able to supply her was a battered Cavalier with more than 87,000 miles on it. The passenger door didn't work at all. The driver's door took muscle. Claudia wrenched it open, pushed the seat forward, and irritably stowed her groceries on the backseat. A slightly damp odor rose from the jacket in the back.

She got in the front, slammed the door, and promptly backed into another car easing out at the same time. Her groceries fell to the floor.

"Shit," Claudia muttered. She climbed back out.

The Mustang she hit was older than the Cavalier. But where the Cavalier had nicks and dents and rust, the Mustang had only smooth lines beneath a brilliant sheen—except, now, for the taillight.

A man unwound himself from inside the Mustang. He scanned

the damage, then pulled thoughtfully on his chin as he watched Claudia approach.

"Now that's too bad," he said. "This car's made it all over the country and just about over every rush-hour interstate you can imagine, and it's never managed a scratch. Figures it would get its first battle scar in a parking lot."

While offering an apology, Claudia fumbled in her shoulder bag for a scrap of paper. She tore off the bottom of the grocery receipt.

"Look, I'm in a hurry," she said. She started to scribble her name and number down. "You can get in touch with me on an estimate. I'll talk to my insurance company. It shouldn't take long to settle up."

"Well, now hang on. Let's see what we got," said the man. He bent down to examine the Mustang's taillight. He shrugged when he straightened. "The light's been knocked out, but that seems to be it, really. My biggest problem will be getting nailed by some gung-ho cop on my way home."

Claudia chuckled dryly. "Don't worry. Lightning never strikes twice in the same spot."

"You lost me," the man said.

"I'm a cop."

"Ah!" The man smiled. "Now there's an irony for you." He stuck a hand out. "Dennis Heath."

"Claudia Hershey."

They shook. Heath's hand was warm and dry. He held the shake a fraction of a second longer than necessary. She saw nicely shaped nails when he released her hand. Her eyes processed the rest of him: hazel eyes, she thought, though it was hard to tell with just the dull illumination from the parking lot lights; thinning hair the color of clay; a square face—maybe some Slav in him; lines around the eyes and mouth that put him at about forty; her height, give or take a half inch; just the tiniest bit of roundness where his stomach met his pants. Claudia didn't think she'd seen him around before.

Lights flickered, then dimmed behind them. She looked back. Philby's had just closed and Doris was coming out. "Oh, goodness, a little fender-bender time, huh?" she sang out merrily.

Claudia sighed and gave a half wave back.

"Any substantial damage to your car?" Heath asked.

"You must be joking."

Heath's smile appeared easily. "Actually, I was." He peered in Claudia's back window. "Bet your eggs are broken, though."

"Worse things have happened, believe me. Here, take my phone number and—"

"Oh, look. Let's just not worry about it." Heath shrugged lightly.

"It's not a big deal in the general scheme of things. It's certainly not major enough to yank in the insurance people. They just look for opportunities to up their rates."

"Yes, but I'm clearly at fault. You have a broken taillight and we're talking about a vintage car. I'll pay for it."

"Really, it's—"

"I insist," she said firmly. She held out the piece of paper. When Heath took it, his fingers glided across her own. His eyes were actually quite nice.

Heath looked from Claudia to the piece of paper. "Nice handwriting," he said.

"You'll revise your opinion when you see it under the light."

"Don't be so sure."

"It's the only thing I *am* sure of today, Mr. Heath."

They moved apart. As she clambered back into her car, she heard Heath call something out to her. She rolled her window down and stuck her head out. She told him she couldn't hear him.

"I said, you'd look better in a Maserati. Or maybe even a refurbished Mustang."

Claudia shook her head and rolled up the window. She drove off, surprised to find herself smiling just a little.

The house blazed with lights and rock music. The throbbing beat sheared the smile off Claudia's face the moment she stepped out of the car, and she looked toward the source.

She and Robin lived in the last house on Daffodil Lane, a name that embarrassed her daughter as much as the house itself. The house was a one-story structure with oversized hallways and odd angles that defied conventional furniture arrangement. It was pale green in its current incarnation, having been through two renovations and one expansion in its thirty-year history. The overall effect was lopsided; Robin groused that it looked like something Alice might've found through the looking glass.

Gritting her teeth, Claudia shoved foodstuff back into the paper sacks. Heath was right—the eggs were broken. She grabbed two of the bags and headed for the front door, fumbling for her keys. As it turned out, they weren't necessary. The door was unlocked. Eight-thirty at night, and anyone could walk in. Robin knew better. Damn it, she knew better.

Tension twisted from Claudia's shoulders straight into her head. The television was on, but of course Robin wasn't there. She would be in her room, plugged into the sound system Claudia had bought with guilt money after the move down.

"Robin?" she called out loudly.

Nothing.

She set the bags aside and headed down the first hallway. It was as long as a tunnel. She called her daughter's name again, louder. Then again. Robin's bedroom door was cracked and Claudia nudged it open.

Her daughter lay on her back on the bed, her knees drawn up, headphones clamped to her ears, oblivious. Her foot tapped to the rhythm of the song.

For a minute, Claudia just stood there. She felt herself soften. Enduring a nine-year marriage to a man with the sensitivity of a tree stump made sense in context with the daughter produced at the midway point. In her most objective moments, Claudia almost felt gratitude, if not for the interior of her ex-husband, then at least for his exterior. Brian's casual good looks were stamped all over Robin. Where Claudia was long and angled, Robin was petite and soft. She had her father's wheat-colored hair and indigo eyes, and a mouth that turned impishly at the ends. Claudia wished Robin would use her mouth to smile more. But she didn't. Holding it back was a good weapon.

Claudia vanquished the memories. She crossed the room and fumbled for the volume control, then turned the music down.

"Hey!" said Robin. She jackknifed into a sitting position, eyes flashing. "You could knock!" she said.

"The door was open and you didn't hear me calling," said Claudia. Not a very good beginning. "Look, kiddo, I've got one more bag of groceries in the back of the car. Why don't you get it while I start dinner?"

"Get a life, Mother! It's after eight-thirty. I already ate."

"Ah, but not lamb chops, I bet," said Claudia with forced cheer. When had Robin started calling her *Mother*? "I'm going to broil them up royal."

"Big deal."

Claudia let it pass. "Just get the bag, will you?"

Robin scowled, then vaulted off the bed, throwing body language like a pugilist. She glowered at her mother and stalked out.

While she was gone, Claudia made for the den. The desk overflowed with receipts, junk mail, a new music sheet, magazines, canceled checks. One day soon, it would have to be sorted.

The report card was sandwiched between the sheet music and a utility bill. She pulled the computer form free and shook it open. She scanned it quickly, then studied the B beside algebra.

Son of a bitch.

Exhaling, Claudia folded the sheet and returned to the kitchen just as Robin pushed the last bag of groceries on the table. Wordlessly, the girl turned and left. Claudia dropped the form on the counter, her mouth rigid.

The books, the magazine articles, the newspaper lifestyle stories—they all advocated restraint in situations like this. Problems were to be addressed thoughtfully. Children should be encouraged to open up. Parents must listen. Communication had to be conducted in a neutral, relaxed environment.

Very well, then. Claudia set about making dinner. She popped two aspirins and uncorked some Chablis. The books were right, of course. Difficulties didn't have to necessitate confrontation. This was hardly a police interrogation.

While the lamb chops broiled, she set the table and called her daughter, inviting conversation. But Robin stayed sullen, spurning idle repartee with monosyllabic responses. By the time they sat down to eat, Claudia had lost what little hold remained on her appetite.

"I don't see why I have to be here. It's too late to be eating dinner," Robin groused. She stabbed a piece of meat and chewed resentfully.

"You wouldn't say that if I'd put pizza on your plate," Claudia teased lightly.

"I would too. Pizza makes you fat. It's nothing but calories and cholesterol."

"Still tastes good."

"Doesn't matter. It's not what's on my plate, anyway."

Claudia sighed and put her fork down. "All right. How about this? Maybe I just want to have dinner with you because I don't think we're talking to each other enough." Claudia thought for a moment. "The irony is, ever since we moved here—at least up until this case—we've had more time than ever to spend together. I'm home at night. I'm here for you. So, why aren't we talking?"

Robin rolled her eyes. "There's not a whole lot to talk about."

Utensils clinked against plates. "You sure?" Claudia asked softly. She took a swallow of wine. "You used to have loads of stories about school. But you hardly say a word anymore."

"Nothing to say."

"Oh, come on. How are your classes coming?"

Robin shrugged. "Okay."

"Just okay?"

"They're okay, all right? They're fine." She pushed a roll into her mouth.

"No major problems?" Claudia persisted. Why wouldn't the kid open up? "Nothing I can help you with?"

Slamming her fork down, Robin said, "What's with the third

degree? I said everything's fine!"

"I don't think so, Robin," Claudia said gravely. She pushed her plate back and regarded her daughter. Then she retrieved the report card from the counter and dropped it beside Robin's plate.

"If everything's fine, then maybe you can explain this," Claudia said. She leaned against the counter, resisting the urge to cross her arms.

Robin glanced at the paper. "It's my report card." The shrug was nonchalant, but her eyes gave her away.

"I know what it is, Robin." Claudia struggled to keep her voice level. "I also know it's been altered."

Pink flames rose in the girl's cheeks. "I don't know what you mean."

"Yes you do."

"I do not."

With unplanned abruptness, Claudia pushed off from the counter and slapped a hand against the table. Plates and utensils clattered. Robin jumped.

"Knock it off! You damn well do know what I mean, and whether you want to talk to me or not, you'd better start trying," she said rapidly, neutral intent out the window. "I mean it. I'm running out of patience fast, kiddo. I want an explanation, and I want it now."

Robin sat upright. Like a bird not yet out of the nest, her mouth closed, opened, closed, and opened. Her eyes acknowledged that calamity loomed, but then, as if she'd made some sort of decision, she took a deep breath and folded her arms across her chest. "As usual, you're making a big deal out of nothing," she said petulantly, tilting her chair back on two legs.

"You call this nothing?" said Claudia. She snatched the computer form and shook it six inches from her daughter's face. "You changed your grade! You lied to me! You call that nothing?"

"It's not like I turned it into an A," Robin said.

"And so that makes it all right?"

"See? It doesn't matter what I say!" She glared at her mother. "You're just going to bitch me out no matter what."

"Watch your mouth, young lady."

"Watch your mouth," Robin mimicked in a sing-song voice. Her eyes blazed adolescent rage. "Why don't you just read me my rights?"

"Don't push me, Robin."

"Or what?" Robin's chair banged back on all fours. "Mother Rambo will—"

"That's it!" Claudia said hotly. She snagged the girl and hoisted her to her feet, an iron grip on each arm. The chair clattered to the floor. "I've had it with you, Robin," she snapped. "You've become a manipulative little brat; and like some kind of June Cleaver, I've been tiptoeing around you and letting it happen. Well, no more! We're—"

Robin scowled and turned her face away.

"Look at me!" Claudia snared Robin's chin and forced eye contact. "You're about an eyelash away from disaster. Keep it up and I swear I'll tattoo a print of my hand right on your butt."

Defiance gave weight to Robin's jaw. "That's ridiculous! I'm too old for that."

"You think so?" Claudia's grip tightened. "Then go ahead. Try it out. Push me once more and see what happens."

Claudia sent up a prayer that Robin would not test the threat. The speech she'd rehearsed was not the one she was giving, damn it. And if Robin crossed the line, Claudia didn't know what she'd do and she didn't want to find out.

But after a moment, Claudia felt her daughter slump almost imperceptibly. Her eyes registered uncertainty.

There is a God, thought Claudia. She released her daughter and gestured at the fallen chair. "Pick that up and sit down. We're going to get through this if it kills us both."

Claudia returned to her own chair. She told herself not to cave in, then looked at her daughter sternly. "All right. I want to know what's going on with you, kiddo. The report card, everything."

An eternity passed, and then: "I hate it here. It's a stupid place. The school is stupid. The people are stupid. Half of them eat brain tumors for breakfast."

"Come on, Robin. You're not making sense," Claudia said. "You've made some friends. You've even got some boy calling you."

"He's a nerd."

"Yeah, well, you spent forty minutes on the phone with that nerd the other night," Claudia reminded her.

"It wasn't that long," Robin mumbled.

"The point is, I think you're going way out of your way not to like it here, and despite your best efforts you're starting to like it, anyway. And that makes you angrier than ever at me."

"That's not true."

"Well, true or not, maybe it's something for you to think about." Claudia watched the girl toy with congealing grease on her plate. "You need to think about a lot of things, Robin, and one of the first is your algebra grade. What you did—for whatever reason—is absolutely unacceptable."

"I hate algebra, and I hate Flynn."

"Well, that's too bad because, like it or not, you're going to encounter a lot more things you don't like in life, and you can't always just close your eyes and hope they all disappear."

"I didn't expect anything to just disappear," Robin mumbled. She plucked at her nail polish, a gaudy shade of maroon with flecks of silver in it. "I just thought I'd do better next time and you'd never know the difference."

"You thought wrong," said Claudia. "Anyway, I expect that grade to come up fast, and I expect you to get it there by concentrating on your homework."

Claudia waited for Robin to say something, but she didn't. "Mr. Flynn told me he would spend some time with you to get you back up to speed. I want you to get with him and make an appointment first thing tomorrow."

"I get the point," she said dully. "Can I go now?"

Water dripped relentlessly from the kitchen tap. Claudia listened wearily. In for a penny, in for a pound.

"There's one more point for you to get," she said at length. "You're grounded—six weeks. No telephone. No television until your homework's done. No one over, and you don't go anywhere."

Horrified, Robin looked up. "That isn't fair!"

"It *is* fair," Claudia said quietly. "Your free rides are over. I've been letting you get away with murder and we both know it." She raised an eyebrow. "End of the road."

For another five minutes Claudia reiterated household rules and expectations, laying down the law precisely the way her mother had and precisely the way she'd vowed she never would. And then she let her daughter make good her escape.

Later, she brooded a while over her oboe, seeking comfort through the familiar weight in her hands. Her long fingers slid along the barrel to the ring keys, solemnly sounding out "Desperate Dreams," and then, "Sojourn of the Moon."

Destiny might have put her in an orchestra pit, a natural extension of a surprising talent discovered in junior high. Things hadn't gone that way, of course, but still, the precision required by the instrument was usually enough to pull her back into orbit during casual play. Twenty minutes into it, however, Claudia returned the oboe to its case. No magic this evening.

Her life was not in a concert hall. Her life was in Indian Run, with a pile of dirty dishes, a headache, a dead woman, and an angry child.

Much, much later, she peeked in on Robin. Sleep demanded a truce, and the girl's face was slack against the pillow. Claudia brushed a hand gently against her daughter's hair, then called it a night.

CHAPTER 6

THEY WERE ALL THERE: Chief Suggs, Sergeant Ron Peters, Officer Mitch Moody, and Officer Emory Carella. Suggs wore a sour face. Only two Tums remained in the roll he'd opened an hour ago, and he eyed the crimped package disgustedly. Then he tossed it on his desk and watched it skitter to the edge.

"What I'm basically hearing is that we're nowhere on this thing," he said. His eyes floated to Claudia's face. "No real suspect. No real evidence. No real nothin'. Overton gets planted tomorrow and she's goin' to her grave without anybody bein' able to say why."

"Maybe not even her," Moody said softly. He tugged at the corner of his mustache. "And for all we know, whoever killed her is in another country by now."

Claudia didn't think so, but she said nothing. Moody had dropped out of law school after three years, aghast at the sluggishness of the legal process. He thought he could accomplish more as a cop, so two years ago he'd returned to Indian Run where he was born, pinned on a badge, and took to the streets. Moody was bright, intuitive, and persistent, but just now he was discouraged. They all were.

"Four days now," said Carella, a bookish officer with a long face and a nasal voice. "We're getting our tails kicked on this thing." He shook a cigarette loose from its pack and lit up. Ash floated to his lap. "I should've listened to my wife and stuck with accounting. Numbers always add up one way or another."

"Yeah, but that's about as exciting as watering your lawn," offered Peters, ever the pragmatist.

Through a shroud of smoke, Carella said, "So who says this thing's been exciting, anyway? We've goosed dozens of people— some of them twice—spun the fingerprints through Clearwater's fancy computer, pulled a partial history on the victim—"

"And we've only just begun," Claudia interjected firmly. She stood to shake the cramp from her leg. "Before we're through with this thing we'll have talked to hundreds of people. Get used to it or bow out now. There's no time to indulge in whining."

No one said anything and the silence made the chief's small office seem smaller yet. She sighed. She longed to bum a cigarette from Carella, but she'd given them up on the long drive to Florida. She also longed for police officers whose experience matched their intellect, but this was it. This was what she had to work with.

"How are we coming on breaking down Overton's client list?" Claudia asked Carella. The medium's practice of scheduling clients by initials only was great for assuring her visitors anonymity, but it was playing hell with the investigation. "We need that appointment book stripped down like a Cadillac in the wrong neighborhood."

Carella pulled on his cigarette. "Yeah, I know. And it's not coming as good as I'd like," he said. "Some of Overton's friends knew flat-out the names of some of her steadiest visitors. We're already talking to them. And a few of the people who saw her for readings have called in on their own. But we still got a cluster of initials we can't match up."

"Shit," Suggs said. "Any one of 'em could be the killer."

Shrugging, Carella said, "Problem is, a lot of people who see psychics—especially on a regular basis—don't want anyone else to know. Figure it makes them look foolish. Short of trying to match initials with names in the phone book for Indian Run—and hell, all of Flagg County—there's not a lot more I can think to do."

"Then do that," Claudia said flatly. "If it comes down to it, get Roselli in records to come up with a computerized listing from the phone company." She studied the twelve-pound bass mounted above the chief's desk. Ugly thing. "He can feed in the initials and run a sort—"

"Damn it, Hershey!" Suggs protested. "You're forgettin' where you are. We ain't got a computer that can do all that."

"Whatever 'all that' really amounts to," Peters added softly.

"Rent a computer if you have to. Lean on Flagg for support. Buy a program. I don't know," said Claudia. "But we can't just sit on our thumbs. We need to have a match for every initial in Overton's schedule."

Carella made a note.

"Meanwhile, shake Overton's friends a little harder. My bet is they know more than they're saying."

The door to Suggs's office opened hesitantly. Officer Bobby Ridley's gaze settled uneasily on Claudia. "Sorry to, uh, disturb everyone, but the video Sergeant Peters asked for? The one from that teacher, fella named Tom Orben?" Ridley held a hand out. "Here it is. Orben returned our call from Boston and told us we could enter his premises to pick it up."

"I hope you didn't bust the damned door to get in," the chief muttered.

Ridley's face colored. "No, sir. Orben, he keeps a key hidden under the third brick leading to his porch."

"Thanks, Bobby," Claudia said. She smiled briefly and took the video. "Good work."

When Ridley left, she turned to Moody. She hefted the video thoughtfully. "Go round up Lucille Schuster, no matter what she's doing. Bring her here. She can ID the people at the séance."

"Bag of popcorn, too?" Moody asked.

The damned fish hanging on the wall looked like it was smiling. "Tartar sauce might be a better bet," Claudia answered.

Moody grinned. He was starting to understand her.

She grinned back. Small victories counted.

The VCR, anyway, was state-of-the-art—the chief's personal machine—and after fiddling with the controls for a few minutes, Claudia slapped the cassette in and pushed PLAY.

They were reassembled again, the five of them, this time in the police station's all-purpose room. The room served as a place to eat and write reports. It also contained the only storage closet sufficiently large to hold evidence, which at the moment was crowded with three bicycles, a water pump, a BB gun, someone's tattered overalls, a handmade bird feeder, and a cardboard box containing some of the Reverend Donna Overton's possessions.

Lucille Schuster sat rigidly on a metal folding chair, her hands knotted together and her eyes straight ahead. Moody had whispered to Claudia that the woman was horrified to be called out of class. She'd whined in Moody's patrol car, but it ended the moment she fell under Claudia's gaze.

Orben's ability with a video recorder would win him no prizes, but the quality of the tape was suitable, and like a relative with an Instamatic at a wedding, he hadn't missed anyone.

Claudia, positioned beside Schuster with a legal pad on her lap and a pen in her hand, perched forward. She ran a hand through her hair. Although she had no great expectations for what the video might reveal, that it contained a snippet of the victim's last hours was enough to make a viewing critical.

The video began with an unflattering close-up of Lucille Schuster's face. Orben shot her dead-on when she opened the door to greet him Halloween night. The red-haired teacher was dressed as Pollyanna—a fitting costume, Claudia thought—and she giggled into the camera, waving self-consciously at Orben as she ushered him into her house. The camera followed her lasciviously, angling at bosom level whenever she turned toward Orben.

More silly footage followed as Orben panned guests and took a lingering shot of the buffet table. Food was artfully arranged between Halloween decorations; plastic forks, spoons, and knives in orange and black lay like railroad tracks on both ends of the table.

"Nice spread," Carella whispered.

"Thanks," said Schuster.

Claudia bet she was blushing, pleased.

In the absence of Schuster's husband, the party worked out as boy-girl, boy-girl. Those in attendance besides Orben and Schuster included Alice and Russell Keefer, she a social studies teacher and dressed as a geisha girl, he an insurance salesman and dressed as a sumo wrestler; John and Julie Kawalski, neighbors who both had dressed as clowns; Elliott and Jane Brown, he a French teacher and she a Spanish teacher—both bowing to their names in outfits appropriate to farmers; Barbara Reed, an English teacher in an Annie Oakley costume; Jennifer O'Reilly, a gym teacher whose feline grace perfectly suited the cat costume she wore; Steve Goodman, a chunky mathematics teacher in an Abe Lincoln costume; and Robin's algebra teacher, Victor Flynn, preposterously dressed as Zorro.

Orben had persuaded someone to take the video recorder long enough to shoot footage of him personified as Batman. He wrapped an arm around the gym-teacher-turned-cat and tried to sweep her off her feet. Both landed in a giggling heap.

"What would your husband have worn if he'd been at the party?" Carella asked Schuster.

"Well, he says because he has lofty goals he would've probably worn an astronaut's uniform." She smiled shyly. "He's really a fun-loving guy. He loves these kinds of parties."

While the video rolled on, Claudia jotted down names and details of those at the party. Now and then she used the VCR's remote control to press the PAUSE button long enough to ask the teacher a question or to get some clarification. She noted who drank what, and who drank fast, who mingled with whom, and who said what. In her role as hostess, Lucille Schuster stood alone in keeping an arm's distance from alcohol.

Orben, bless his heart, had been obnoxiously thorough. He followed people to the bathroom, caught them scratching at the unfamiliar fabric of their costumes, ogled them up close and at a distance, and tuned into as many conversations as he could.

But as entertaining as the opening was, the video drew its heart from Donna Overton's visit. The camera fixed on her almost reverently, following her through quick introductions to the guests and then to the table where she settled in for the séance.

Overton in life displayed a professional demeanor calculated to reduce skepticism without sacrificing the mystic quality she was being paid to demonstrate. She wore no costume and she worked the crowd without props; a warm smile here, a penetrating look there—she radiated knowledge, but in a way that was nonthreatening. And when everyone was settled and the nervous chatter subsided, she moved her eyes from one guest to the next, slowly, curiously . . . piercingly.

Then she began. First, Overton explained that she would attempt to contact "friendly spirits," and she cautioned that even if she were successful she might not know who it was that would respond through her voice and body. Spirits, she confided, had minds of their own. She went on to explain that whatever message a spirit might choose to impart very likely would seem obscure, or perhaps so selective that only one person in the room would understand. She herself, she told the guests, was merely the channel through which spirits elected to communicate.

"It's important for everyone to understand this because, otherwise, some of you will probably be disappointed," she said, her voice soft and convincing. "I have a gift—not a talent, a gift—but just because spirits find me receptive doesn't mean that they're always as cooperative as I'd like them to be. Spirits don't necessarily tell me what's going to happen."

"Can we ask the, uh, spirit questions?" Goodman wanted to know.

The medium chuckled lightly. "You can, but you might not get an answer, or at least not anything that makes sense. The truth is, sometimes what they say just sounds like a lot of gibberish." Shrugging modestly, Overton continued, "Still, they almost always convey something, and if what they tell me is useful to someone in this room, well, then I'll be happy to have served some purpose beyond entertainment."

After that, Overton requested that the lights be dimmed. Schuster raced to the wall switch. All but illumination from a hall light and street lamp outside the window died. Faces were cast in shadow.

Overton nodded her approval and asked everyone to join hands. A self-conscious rustle followed, but Orben's camera, equipped for available light conditions, rolled on.

"This is almost spooky," Chief Suggs said in a stage whisper.

Carella grunted affirmatively, and Claudia felt her own muscles contract in anticipation.

"Just wait," Lucille Schuster said breathlessly.

Claudia glanced over. For the teacher, the point of the video had become a celebration of a masterful party coup. Claudia suspected that the death of Donna Overton merely increased the status of the party.

For long minutes, nothing happened. Orben took a chance and quickly panned the table. The geisha girl's mouth was an oval. The clown couple clenched hands tightly and gave each other looks only intimates could interpret. Annie Oakley's eyes betrayed a creeping anxiety. Flynn's face was inscrutable—perhaps calculating the mathematical possibility that a spirit could be summoned, Claudia thought without humor—while Pollyanna herself worked to hide a nervous giggle. The others wore similar expressions, all of them intersecting on a plane of anticipation.

Suddenly, Overton's body turned rigid. Her spine straightened so completely she appeared to be off the chair, and her hands dug into those of Annie Oakley and Farmer Brown. The gunslinging Barbara Reed caught her breath audibly; Brown's face seemed to shrink.

"Wow," said Moody. "The special effects are almost as good as something straight out of Hollywood."

A moment later and just as abruptly, Overton's head lolled recklessly and her eyes closed. She moaned. Someone at the table reflexively moaned simultaneously. Then slowly, in seconds measured by heartbeats, Overton's head straightened to something of a normal position and her eyes fluttered open, revealing only the whites.

Gasps accompanied the demonstration.

Then, in a voice startlingly old and weary, which came from somewhere deep within Overton's diaphragm, the medium began to talk. The words at first were halting and thick, as if Overton had been drugged.

"Never . . . the right thing," the voice began. "Try, try, try . . . have to try again. Have to try until you get it . . . right."

A shiver sped along Claudia's arm. The woman was good—very, very good. Claudia could only imagine what the experience must have been like for those buzzed with alcohol and without the safe filter that the tape provided now.

The voice repeated the same admonition in slightly different words, then took on a sharper, clear edge. Overton inched forward, but her eyes remained white and dead.

"You know what you've done to me and you know that I know. You know . . . that it was . . . the wrong way." A shrill laugh pierced the quiet. "You can't stop me, though. You've tried for a lifetime, but you'll never stop me. I'm with you always . . . you know that, don't you?"

A minute passed, maybe two. The video picked up restless movement, but it strayed too briefly from Overton's face to reveal what anyone may have been thinking.

And then: "One day, we'll be back together. It's for . . . the best. You need me. I need you." The cackle again. "But don't ever think that I'm not with you now."

Another silence fell, this time broken by Russell Keefer, the sumo wrestler. Gently, he asked Overton—the spirit—who she was.

The answer was immediate and, it seemed to Claudia, almost angry. "You know me, you can't pretend you don't! You know where I walk and that I walk alone. You thought you were glad, but you're not . . . ."

"I don't understand," Keefer persisted.

"You know me!" the voice shouted, and Overton stood so suddenly that her chair nearly toppled over. Her eyes snapped open wide. She raised a quivering finger that roamed across the table, aiming first at Keefer, then lingering briefly at others.

It was impossible to discern whether the accusing finger was actually meant for anyone, though nearly every guest that Orben managed to capture on tape reacted as if it had been personally intended.

"Oh my God," Julie Kawalski whimpered. She buried her face in her husband's shirt, a frightened clown who'd lost her balloons.

"Relax, honey," John Kawalski said. He rested his chin on his wife's head. "It's just a show, remember?"

Flynn's eyes opened wide. They never left Overton's face, but he wrenched his hand free from Jennifer O'Reilly's and toyed with his sideburns. His mouth parted slightly.

Jane Brown said something in Spanish; it may have been a curse.

"It's lonely where I am, you know," the voice continued. It was slipping back to its earlier, weary state. Overton sat. Her eyes closed again. "It's . . . not a bad place, but it's . . . very, very, lonely. And quiet. Birds don't sing here. They would, if you had only . . . listened. If only you'd paid more attention."

For another two minutes, the voice carried on about loneliness and isolation, about being right and being wrong, about mistakes, and once, fondly, about good times.

"You loved the bread, remember? And on wash day, you always wanted to leave the sheets to dry longer than they needed to. They were so clean. They smelled so good. You were . . . good then. You were almost perfect. You could have been perfect. Try harder. Try harder. Don't disappoint me again. You'll never be without me. I love you. It's not so bad. I'm here for you. I . . . love you anyway."

That was it. That was all. Just a bunch of nonsense. Orben's camera dogged Overton's face until her posture relaxed and her eyes opened. The medium blinked, looked around, and smiled kindly.

"I see we got someone," she said softly. "Judging by your faces, it was someone befitting Halloween night."

A flurry of comments followed:

"Do you know who the spirit was?"

"How did you feel?"

"What did the spirit mean?"

"Boy! It all seemed so real!"

Overton laughed delightedly. "I'm sorry. I have no idea who came calling, folks." She looked around the table helplessly. "It's just as sure a bet that it was no one anyone here knew. Could've been someone who died two days ago or two centuries ago."

Orben chuckled. "Well, it was a lot of bang for Lucy's buck," he said. "I thought we might have to summon the paramedics. Damn, if you didn't have us going there!"

"It always wears me out," said Overton.

Indeed, the woman did look exhausted. With the lights back on—and with them, a reassuring return to the land of the living—Overton's face seemed pinched. She was damp with perspiration.

The whole episode lasted less than fifteen minutes, though it seemed a great deal longer. Except for Flynn, whose face still seemed frozen, the spell was broken. Julie Kawalski surrendered her husband's arm. He gaped at the red mark where her hand had clutched him.

Guests began to move around, to reach for booze. They'd just been to hell and back and had plenty to talk about. The pitch rose rapidly. Laughter replaced gasps. Words such as *illusion* and *great theater* could be heard through the din.

Orben got someone to handle the camera once more so he could get himself on tape standing beside Donna Overton. He held two fingers behind her head and made noises from the movie *Jaws*. Then he retrieved his camera and followed the party chatter, finally zooming in on Overton as she collected her fee from Lucille Schuster and said her good-byes.

At first, their conversation was difficult to follow because of all the background noise. Claudia heard someone bellow that the ice was running low. She heard a woman shriek "Hey, watch it! Your drink's splashing on my costume!" A guffaw followed.

Just as Claudia irritably wished Orben would move in a little closer, he did. The tape danced momentarily while Orben elbowed nearer to the two women.

"Thank you, dear," Overton was saying to Schuster. "It was great fun—you throw a marvelous party. I'm just sorry I couldn't produce someone famous—although, who knows? Maybe we did have someone famous."

Overton rummaged through her purse, produced car keys, then rooted through her bag some more. "Damn. I don't suppose you smoke?" she asked her hostess.

"Sorry, never picked up the habit." Schuster frowned, apparently a little put off that the soft-spoken medium was guilty of so vile a habit.

The video carried Orben's voice from offstage: "I do, but only after." His giggle was lewd, and full of booze.

Overton chose to overlook the comment, said a final good-bye, and left. The video abruptly segued to Jennifer O'Reilly, who was putting on a cat act of a suggestive nature.

There was more, but all of it was increasingly disjointed. Orben evidently kept turning the camera off and on, with longer and longer moments between taping. His last shot showed the door frame leading to the kitchen, and then a bit of the ceiling—liquored videography that no doubt explained his waning enthusiasm for Pulitzer material.

All in all, Orben had encapsulated a solid forty-eight minutes of the party. The focus wasn't bad until the end. The lighting was excellent considering the circumstances. Each of the guests had a chance at amateur stardom.

But other than the séance itself, there wasn't a thing to connect anyone at the party to the Reverend Donna Overton.

Claudia thanked Lucille Schuster for her time and called for a patrolman to drive her back to the school. The others drifted from the room. Suggs, crabbing about a waste of time for a lot of mumbo jumbo, patted his pockets for Tums, shot Claudia an annoyed look, and left without another word.

Well, sometimes it was just like that. Claudia took a moment to stretch, get another cup of coffee, and check her desk for messages. Of those, there were plenty, and she dismissed most. More intriguing was an oblong package loosely wrapped in stiff brown paper. Cautiously, she pulled the paper free.

"I'll be damned," she said to herself. She held up a carton of eggs from Philby's. Then she unsealed an envelope and shook open a piece of paper. At the top was a message: "Something tells me you're eggsactly my speed, Detective Hershey." Below the words was a detailed cartoon showing her and that guy, Dennis Heath, outside Philby's. Both their bodies were exaggerated in size so that they loomed over the vehicles, which nestled bumper to bumper in the parking lot. Smashed eggs and fallen groceries showed every-where.

Claudia glowered in the drawing; Heath looked at her adoringly. His phone number was carefully penned at the bottom of the cartoon.

"What do you have there?" Peters asked, looking over.

"What? Oh, nothing. Just the usual," Claudia said. She busied herself with some clutter on her desk, trying to shield the package from his view.

As unobtrusively as possible, she rewrapped the package and tucked it beneath her desk by her handbag. She pocketed the cartoon and returned to the all-purpose room.

Her notes were still on the chair. Claudia scanned them quickly. She'd filled three sheets on the legal pad. Pushing Heath from her mind, she picked up the remote control, rewound the tape, and watched it again.

CHAPTER 7

THE MAN WATCHED DISTRACTEDLY, his big feet propped on the coffee table. He hated television, but he knew he had to stay in touch right now. He had to know what was being said.

Indian Run didn't have its own local news station, but a reporter from Land of Rivers stood at the entrance to the police department, a microphone with the number 3 clutched importantly in his hand. He stared into the camera, effecting a somber expression. He introduced himself as Eric Morley and announced to viewers he was bringing them a live report. The kid looked like he was barely out of college.

Beside him and just within camera range was a reporter from the *Indian Run Gazette*, some middle-aged yahoo who the man had seen more than once staggering out of the bar beside Philby's. He held a notebook poised in one hand, a pen in the other. The man couldn't recall the reporter's name.

Good. A kid and a drunk were the only ones there. The man clapped two fists together, smiling. Didn't they get it?

Morley chirped background details, trying to make them sound new: the victim's name and address, the time the body had been discovered, that an investigative team had been assembled under the direction of Detective Claudia Hershey, who was expected to emerge momentarily. He made much of the fact that the victim had been a medium.

The man scoffed. Morley nattered on exhaustively, but the story was cold. The kid was just trying to milk it, make it sound like something was up.

After a few minutes the scene shifted to a previously shot segment in the victim's neighborhood. The man rolled his eyes. Channel 3 had run the same piece on its noon report. The camera panned on Donna Overton's house, then focused on two neighbors who Morley interviewed in a low voice that failed to suggest much sympathy. Filler, that's all it was.

The man impatiently shifted his weight into the couch. He held the remote control forward, about to flick the TV off, when suddenly the broadcast segued abruptly back to the police department. The detective's face filled the screen. The man lifted his legs off the coffee table and sat upright.

Claudia Hershey was just leaving the police department when Morley ambushed her and thrust his microphone under her chin. He spit out questions: *Did the police have any suspects yet? How about a motive?*

The detective stopped briefly. She looked tired. She shaded her eyes against the setting sun, which only in the last hour had flickered into life. "I have nothing new to offer," she said evenly. "I told you Saturday and I'll tell you again now: We're investigating a number of possibilities. As soon as I have something concrete I'll have a formal statement. Now, if you'll excuse me."

"But, Detective!" Morley yipped. "This is already Tuesday. Shouldn't there be something by now? The residents of Indian Run are understandably anxious and—"

Her mouth set tight, Hershey brushed past Morley, who stood at least five inches shorter than she. But like a puppy mistaking her action for some game, he trotted after her. Four feet into the chase, he accidentally clipped her heel with his shoe.

Whirling, the detective faced the reporter and leaned down. With her face inches from his, she said, "I don't think you heard me, so let me repeat myself. I have nothing to say right now. When I do, I'll issue a statement. Now step back!" She nodded cordially toward the *Gazette* reporter—who hadn't said a word—and moved briskly to her vehicle.

Morley, his face bright pink, turned back to the camera. For a moment he said nothing, seeming to be listening to a plug extending from his ear. He smiled uncertainly. "That, uh, was Detective Lieutenant Claudia Hershey. She'll be . . . we'll have an updated report, uh, as soon as we can."

The segment faded into a commercial about dish soap.

The man laughed out loud. This was good, this was good. The cops didn't know jack shit. What was he worrying about? He'd been right all along. And that cop Hershey—he'd been right about her, too. She was nothing special. Just poking around.

The man flicked off the television and rose. Although he'd eaten just an hour earlier, he felt hungry again and considered putting a sandwich together. Yeah, maybe that and then company.

He headed toward the kitchen, then wheeled abruptly. He cocked his ear, listening. For a moment he thought maybe he hadn't turned the television off. But then he saw a shadow.

Wait a minute! Was that her? Watching him all along?

Perspiration broke out on the man's forehead. He looked into the darkness of the hallway. Thought he heard her whisper something. No! He *did* hear her whisper!

Damn it! How could that be?

He clamped his hands over his ears.

"Get out!" he bellowed. "Get away from me! I don't want to hear any more from you. I won't listen!"

But he couldn't tune her out. She was pointing at him now. Accusing him. Carrying on again. Oh, how he hated her.

Why wouldn't she leave him alone? Hadn't she done enough? He stared hard into the blackness of the hallway, watched her advancing.

No. Forget it. She was trying to wreck his life and he couldn't listen to another word. He wouldn't. She couldn't make him, not anymore.

Breathing hard, the man lumbered toward the front door. He threw it open and stalked out. He closed his ears. He didn't look back.

Best just to get away. Had to get away. Had to make her go away.

CHAPTER 8

"TAKE A LOOK AT THIS." Emory Carella dropped a sheaf of papers on Claudia's desk. "A little gift from the gods."

Without looking up, she rapidly flipped through the papers. Bank statements, most of them. "Okay, Emory. So what am I looking at here?"

Carella beamed. "Our Reverend Donna Overton? All-around nice lady, Sunday-go-to-church type?"

"Yes, yes, yes." She impatiently pointed at a chair beside her desk. "Sit. Tell me what makes you think she isn't."

Whenever compressed, the cushion in the chair gave off a gasp of air like flatulence, usually good for a snicker or locker-room observation. But Carella was too pleased with himself to notice. He leaned toward Claudia, his hazel eyes bright behind wire-rimmed glasses.

"Look," he said excitedly, poking the bank statement on top. "Take a gander at the deposits made to our late medium's account."

She followed Carella's knobby finger. Listed among nine deposits to First Indian Bank was one for $2,000. The other eight were for a variety of amounts, everything from $45 to $355. Altogether, Donna Overton had deposited $3,505 during the statement period.

"Okay, but—"

"Wait, wait! Now look!" Carella flipped to the monthly statement below it. "Look at this baby," he said, pointing to another $2,000 deposit. Like the first statement, the remaining deposits were of varying amounts, and none greater than $265.

"You with me?" Carella asked. He peered into Claudia's eyes, then flipped to the next statement before she could respond. "Check it out. Another $2,000 entry! And it gets better. The previous two months, she had nice, even $1,000 deposits. All of them in cash, all around the fifteenth of the month."

Claudia didn't need a degree in accounting to see where Carella was headed, but she let him go on.

"Here's the deal, the way it looks to me," said Carella. He jabbed the air with a finger. "Oh—and first of all—I pulled bank statements going back two years, okay? Okay. The lady's tooling along, not doing doodly-squat in deposits until, bam, June. That's when the first $1,000 entry shows up. Then July, bam, another $1,000 entry. And hey, at this point she's already just about doubled her deposit income, okay? Then comes August, September, and October: $2,000 cash deposits around the fifteenth of each of those months!"

Carella leaned back in his chair. He propped one leg over the other. "You see what I'm seeing?"

Like a spring flying off a pen refill, Carella leaped from the chair before Claudia could respond. "The woman's monthly income, if that's what we can assume her deposits were, usually floated in at about $1,500, maybe $1,600," he said, then snorted. "Big deal. In fact, her other financial records show she could barely keep up with her bills, mostly Visa. Then all of a sudden, here come these gigantic entries. Visa and her other bills get paid off, and the lady buys herself a $2,800 TV set, complete with stereo sound."

Claudia remembered the set. A beauty. Something that belonged in a bigger house.

"It's like, where the hell does this sudden infusion of money come from?" Carella asked. He sat again. The chair farted. "She's not getting any kind of Social Security. No pension. Nothing except what looks to be income from readings, or whatever they're called. So where does a lady who charges twenty-five to fifty bucks a pop to gossip with spirits suddenly get big bucks like that?"

"Hmm," said Claudia. She plucked a rubber band from her desk. She stretched it between her forefinger and thumb, took aim at the crusted coffeemaker across the room, and let go. The rubber band pinged off the carafe. She smiled at Carella. "Come on, Emory. Let me buy you a tube steak at the bowling alley. I like the way your mind works."

"I think I just died and went to heaven," said Carella. He sprang from the chair again and gave a little war whoop. Then he cupped his hands around his mouth and yelled, "Yo! Someone take notes! Detective Hershey just gave me a compliment."

By Indian Run's standards, the bowling alley was a hot spot. Beyond the leagues that clogged the twenty-eight lanes most evenings, the alley drew a steady lunch and dinner crowd. The bar, a dimly lit room with two pool tables and a dartboard, likewise did well.

Claudia and Carella anchored themselves to stools at the snack counter and ordered chili dogs and fries. Country music turned low filtered through a ceiling system. It was only eleven o'clock and just three lanes were busy. She swiveled around to watch for a minute.

"I used to bowl in a league in Cleveland," she told Carella.

"Yeah? You?"

Claudia gave Carella a look. "Come on. Am I that much of a square peg? Anyway, anyone who grows up in Cleveland learns to bowl. I think it's practically a requirement for residency."

"So were you any good?"

"Not bad. I carried a 170 average."

Carella whistled. "I'm not in a league, but every now and then the wife and I bring our kids in. We got twins—girls—and I swear they're better than me."

"Oh, yeah? How old are they?"

"Eight." Carella lifted a hip and dug out his wallet. He showed Claudia snapshots of his daughters, munchkin-faced blondes, one with a gap in her front teeth. "Amy and Jessica. Angels."

"Cute kids, Emory."

"Yeah." Carella smiled fondly. "Janice—my wife—she's going to bring them Saturday to the mother-daughter tournament here. You oughta bring your daughter."

She smiled. "Robin's thirteen. She wouldn't be caught dead doing anything with kids younger than her."

"That's no problem," said Carella. "They have two groups. One for eight to twelve, one for thirteen to sixteen. You oughta bring her. She'd have a ball."

It was hard for Claudia to imagine Robin having a ball doing anything with her mother. The girl hadn't been mouthing off since their confrontation. She simply wasn't saying much at all, and what little she did offer was punctuated by exaggerated sighs.

Claudia turned back to face the counter. "I don't know. She's—"

"Hey!" The chief's voice boomed in her ear. "This a private party or can anyone with a badge take up space?" Suggs sat heavily on the stool beside her. He twisted a napkin from the dispenser and wiped his brow. "I was on the horn when you two sneaked out, but Officer Randall was good enough to tell me y'all were headed here and that you were buying, Hershey."

"Well, I—"

"Good!" said Suggs. He beckoned to Maura Taylor, the young woman working the grill. "Hey, hon, put on two more dogs, huh? And put 'em on Lieutenant Hershey's bill.

"Actually," he continued, "I followed you over here because I hear-tell somethin's breakin'. That right, Hershey?"

Surprised at the chief's good humor, Claudia briefed him quickly on Donna Overton's financial statements, letting Carella detail the numbers.

"Whew. That looks to be somethin', all right," said Suggs. He mopped his brow with another napkin. "Shit," he muttered. "Either I gotta lose some weight or I gotta move somewhere where the temperatures don't go past sixty." He looked at Claudia. "Where else this thing headin'?"

"I've got to take another look at Tom Markos," she said. "Moody talked to him this morning but didn't get anything more than I did originally. But I think he's holding back something. Maybe it somehow ties in with the deposits Overton was making."

"Worth a look-see," he said.

Claudia shrugged. "We're also still adding names to our list, names of people who visited Overton on a regular basis. It's a slow process. Anyway, I've talked to a few of them but need to get out to more. Moody and Peters are going to work the list with me."

"Yeah, and the sooner the better," said Suggs. "I took half a dozen calls between yesterday afternoon and today. Psychics givin' us 'tips.' And I gotta tell ya—I ain't too impressed. There's nothin' consistent in what they say."

"Peters says he caught a couple of calls like that, too," said Carella.

"Hershey," said Suggs, "you gotta start talkin' to the press, too. That business outside the station yesterday, well, I don't have to tell you how agitated that made the Channel 3 guy."

"Morley's a dunce," Claudia said. She frowned, recalling the episode from the evening before. "He's fishing."

"I know. It's that whole business about it bein' a dead psychic—"

"Medium," corrected Carella. "Psychics just get hunches. Mediums, they talk to the, uh, spirit world. They—"

"Yeah, well, whatever," said Suggs. "Point is, the guy's leanin' on us. And we got a call from *The Miami Herald*, too. You saw the first story they printed. Didn't have much. But I think this guy's gonna drive on over here in person pretty soon if we don't shut him up with somethin' fast."

"All right," said Claudia. "I'll call him when we get back. I'll give him something, but it can't be much." She shook her head and took a swallow of Diet Pepsi. "The last thing we need is to let the killer know what we know about him. Not that we know much yet."

Their chili dogs arrived and they let talk slide while they ate. She felt buoyed by what Carella had learned. They didn't know the killer. But they knew a little, maybe, about why someone would want Donna Overton dead. Money was a popular component of a lot of murders.

"You know, Hershey, whilst we're busy chasing down the scum that whacked Overton, a lot of other things are startin' to slide." Suggs took a swipe at his chin.

Unbelievable! thought Claudia. "Damn it, Chief! Murder takes a priority," she said. "The rest has to go on the back burner."

"Yeah, yeah, yeah, don't get your underwear in an uproar. Believe it or not, I'm not raggin' on you. And I'm not gonna pull anybody off the murder." He snorted. "Give me *some* credit. But there's one thing I want you to have a look-see at anyway—"

Suggs held up a hand when she began to protest. "Just hear me out. What we have is a kid, girl 'bout fifteen, maybe sixteen, who overdosed this past weekend on some heavy-duty drug. I'm not sure what, but I understand she was mainlining. Now maybe that's everyday stuff in Miami, but other than poppin' kids for an occasional joint, the heavy shit just don't happen in Indian Run. Or at least this is the first I've heard of a kid goin' over the edge. Anyway, the kid spent a couple days in the hospital but she's back home now. I want you to talk to her."

"But I can think of three or four officers who could probably handle—"

"No. I want you, Hershey. Number one, you're the bona fide detective here. I wanna know where in hell the kid got her hands on the stuff. Someone's routin' that crap through my community. Number two, you got a daughter close to that age. And like Robin, the kid's got only her mom, so my thinkin' is you'll probably connect with the kid better'n anyone else—"

"Don't assume that," she said.

"Number three, I want you to do it, so do it."

Carella studiously cleaned his glasses.

Suggs squinted at Claudia. "I mean, you did handle drug cases up there in Cleveland, too, didn't you? You didn't have your nose in a homicide every minute of every day."

She glowered at him. Oh, yes. She'd handled drug cases. Too many. Drugs were just another form of murder. "They weren't my specialty," she told the chief reluctantly, "but yes, I handled them."

"Good." Suggs downed the last of an iced tea. "Ah, that cooled me off some." He pushed his weight off the stool. "Just give it a whirl, all right? Talk to the girl. Give it fifteen, twenty minutes. That's all. If you don't get nothin', we'll come back to it later."

"All right," said Claudia with a sigh. She felt the first bit of fatigue settling in around her shoulders. "You have the particulars with you?"

"On my desk. I'll give 'em to you when we get back. Oh. And leave the girl here a nice tip, huh? Cops got a bad rep for not payin' their own way."

As they were leaving, she took a look at the bowlers. She watched a man pick up a seven-ten split. The guy with him gave him a thumbs-up.

Well, hell. Why not? Claudia took another five minutes to sign herself and Robin up for Saturday's mother-daughter tournament.

CHAPTER 9

HIGH HEELS WERE OUT. So was anything slinky or lacy, not that Claudia owned anything like that to begin with. Her style leaned toward non-style, which meant her closet held precious little beyond the jackets she favored, slacks, unadorned blouses, and a couple of sturdy sweaters.

Once, she had overheard herself described by Robin to a friend. It was about three months after their move from Cleveland. Her daughter was lying on the floor, legs stretched up to the couch, and she was twisting knots into the telephone cord. The knots drove Claudia wild.

"She's no fashion plate," Robin had complained. "She always wears the same things, and her wrists show when they hang out of her jackets. She looks like a stork."

Claudia would've paid to hear what the friend said to that because a moment later Robin laughed delightedly. "Yeah. She's got a rep for being tough on the streets. I think she flosses her teeth with razor blades."

Kids could wound.

After poking around the closet for five minutes, Claudia finally settled on conservative gray slacks, a white blouse, and a rust-colored jacket trimmed in navy. She would have preferred the black jacket, but it still lay rumpled in the backseat of her car where she'd tossed it after the wet lake ride with Tom Markos. Probably smelled of mildew by now.

Well, for better or worse, this was it. She squared off with a mirror and inspected herself. Jeez. She looked like she was dressed for work, but never mind. At least her wrists didn't show, and anyway, she was too far along in life to make herself over for anyone.

Of course, this whole business of going out on a date was ridiculous to begin with. For one thing, Claudia was out of the loop. For another, she was five days into a murder investigation. If she was going to devote her energy to anything but that, she should devote it to her daughter.

She pulled a brush through her hair, wincing at a tangle. She glared at herself in the mirror, then conceded a tiny smudge of lipstick.

A date, for heaven's sake. Where was her head?

Scoggin's restaurant handled absurdly large crowds on weekends, partly because the menu was reasonably inexpensive and the food not bad, but mostly because other than the bowling alley, a few greasy spoons, and the Denny's on the edge of town, Indian Run didn't have much in the way of eateries. But it was Wednesday night, and when Claudia pulled into the parking lot there was only a handful of cars, for which she was grateful. Her plan was to get in and get out fast. Dinner and done. She didn't know how she'd been sucked in by that silly cartoon.

Dennis Heath stood at the entrance to Scoggin's. He showed Claudia a wide smile and said by way of greeting, "You walk fast. I don't get through the drive-in window of McDonald's that quickly."

She smiled and shrugged self-consciously, *aware* that she felt self-conscious. "I practiced strolling once, but it made me feel like I was on drugs." She shrugged again. "Just doesn't come naturally to me, I guess."

The door was double-wide and built of sturdy mahogany. Dennis eased it open and waited for Claudia to go ahead of him. He didn't try to hold her elbow or put a hand at the middle of her back. She liked that about him.

· They sat at a round table by a window that looked out onto a modest garden with a winding walkway. A cluster of queen palms and a few cypress trees with gnarled roots were backlit by spotlights. Someone had planted hibiscus and other hardy plants that stood up to the cold. Here and there, a few concrete benches beckoned.

"I always ask for this seat," said Dennis. "When I look out there I'm reminded of one of those little plastic globes with a village inside. You know, the sort of thing you can turn upside down and shake snow onto."

Personally, Claudia didn't see it. But maybe she'd been in Florida longer than Dennis. She asked him.

"I've been here five months," he said. "I came down here originally to settle my aunt's affairs—she died and left a house just outside Feather Ridge—but once I took a look around I decided to stay. I figured I could work here just as easily as Chicago and without those freezing winds and ice."

"What is it that you do?" Claudia asked politely. The conversation was going to be one of those 'let's get to know each other' deals.

"I sell eggs."

She almost believed him, but then he laughed and said, "No, actually, I draw for a living. Freelance, mostly."

"I should've guessed," said Claudia, chuckling. "Your cartoon was terrific. Me, I couldn't color in the lines when I was a kid and I can't draw a straight line now."

A waiter in shiny black pants, a white shirt, and black bow tie appeared to take their drink orders. After some debate, Claudia asked for a glass of burgundy. Dennis ordered a Scotch, neat. They settled back into conversation.

Dennis did more than draw. Using a variety of art mediums, he freelanced for a greeting card company—everything from schlocky sentimentals to studio cards—occasionally did magazine and book covers, and now and then managed a cartoon sale to *The New Yorker*. But his belated passion, he explained, was breaking into comic books.

"There's a pretty good lock on the market and the competition is unbelievable," Dennis explained, "but if I can develop a new character—something that'll appeal to the young teen set—I might be able to get a bite for myself. I'm toying with some sketches now."

"Maybe you'd like to talk to my daughter sometime," said Claudia. "Robin's thirteen. She's a walking encyclopedia on what's in and what's out."

"Sounds like an invitation," said Dennis.

"Could be." *Where was this coming from?*

The waiter set their drinks on the table and took their food orders. Before Claudia could think of what she was saying, she told Dennis that she'd love to see his work. And then she told him about opening his package in the office, which seemed to lead directly into an exchange of histories.

Just like that, she mused. She had waltzed herself right into the standard dating-game gambits. Worse, she couldn't seem to shut up. Their meals came—blackened grouper for him, prime rib for her—and she hardly noticed. She gorged on conversation as if it were a delicacy she might never have again.

He'd been married for four years, this Dennis Heath, freelance artist with just the slightest paunch and hair that went every which way. No kids, no regrets, no real needs beyond a beer in the refrigerator and a comic book character that would spin the world on its axis.

How wonderfully uncomplicated. How refreshingly everyday. Listening to him, telling him about herself, Claudia didn't feel like a cop and she didn't feel like a mother. She certainly didn't feel like someone who flossed with razor blades. Murder was just a fuzzy concept, and she was grateful that he never brought it up.

After dinner, Dennis ordered fresh drinks. Claudia planned to protest, but she didn't. Nor did she protest when he touched her hand and suggested a stroll in the garden.

"You forget, Mr. Heath, that I don't stroll," she said as they walked to the garden door.

"Could be a problem," said Dennis. He laced his fingers through hers. "I walk with the speed of mollusk."

The early November air was cool and the concrete benches like ice, but after a few rounds of the garden Claudia and Dennis sat. They grinned at each other stupidly.

"This feels like high school," she said.

"If it were, well, I guess I'd just about be getting to the part where I put my arm around the girl. Like this."

Claudia felt Dennis's arm close around her shoulder. "That's about how I remember it," she said softly. "And I think it's my cue to do this." She snuggled against him, liking his warmth.

A minute passed, maybe more. Insects did their night dances, sending out a spiral of sound. A breeze rustled the tree leaves.

"You wear braces?" Dennis asked.

She chuckled. "Not for a very long time. Do you?"

"No."

"Should I be relieved?"

"Yes, absolutely. No danger of getting stuck together. Mom and Dad'll never have to know."

They kissed, a little like high school. And then they kissed a little like grown-ups.

Only later, when Claudia was driving home, did it occur to her that they sat there necking in front of the garden window where anyone could see.

CHAPTER 10

PERIWINKLES IN RAINBOW COLORS graced the short winding path to the home of Mary and Benjamin Curtell. The flowers provided the only colorful note to an otherwise increasingly gray day. The morning had abruptly turned to chill, teased by gusty winds that bore in from the north.

Claudia shuddered a little and paused outside her car to button her jacket. She hadn't grown accustomed to the weather swings that tickled Florida in the winter.

A woman fiddling with the flowers looked up as she approached. She smiled quizzically and stood, brushing her hands together to shake off some of the soil.

"Hi," she said. "Can I help you?"

Claudia automatically took measure of the woman: short and slight, shoulder-length raven hair with a dramatic silver tangle at her forehead, dark eyes under thick brows, delicate features, and skin so white and clear that it looked porcelain. The juxtaposition between light and dark, heavy and delicate was startling. She put the woman's age at thirty, idly wondering whether the woman's moods mirrored the contrasts in her appearance.

With a perfunctory smile, Claudia introduced herself. The woman in turn gave her name as Marty Eckelstrom.

"I'm investigating the murder of Donna Overton," said Claudia. "I was told that Mary Curtell was friendly with her. This is her residence, isn't it?"

"It is, but I'm afraid she's out just now. She and her husband are grocery shopping." Marty glanced at an oversized watch on her wrist. "They should be home any minute if you'd like to wait."

"All right."

"Come on in," said Marty. "I'll throw on a pot of coffee. No offense, but you look like you could stand some." Marty smiled sheepishly. "Sorry. I have a bad habit of saying the first thing that pops into my brain. A family trait."

Without comment, Claudia followed the woman to the door. It was two doors down from Donna Overton's and was similarly small and unpretentious. "Are you Mrs. Curtell's daughter?" she asked.

"No. She's my aunt, my mother's sister. My home is in California, but I'm staying here for the winter, working on my Ph.D."

"Oh yeah? What in?"

"Cultural anthropology."

Once in the kitchen, Marty gestured for the detective to pull up a chair at the table.

"Doesn't seem a likely place for academic pursuits," Claudia observed. She watched Marty wash her hands, then wrestle a coffee filter free from a new box. "The only place of higher learning here is the Indian Run Junior College, and frankly, I think the public library in town is bigger than what the college offers."

Marty put the filter in the basket and measured coffee with a plastic scoop. She chuckled lightly. "Fortunately, I don't need much of a library at this stage in my research. My dissertation involves response to psychic phenomena, and I'm doing the fieldwork for it now."

"I take it psychic interest runs in the family, too?"

"Interest, yes. Ability, no." Marty filled the coffeemaker with water and pushed a button to start it. She turned toward Claudia and leaned on the kitchen counter. "I can barely tell you what happened to *me* yesterday, let alone what might have happened to *you*. And if a spirit voice suddenly decided to communicate with me, I'd probably think I'd left the radio on in another room."

Claudia smiled politely.

"Anyway," Marty continued, "my mother was a practicing psychic until she died, and her mother, too." Marty shrugged. "Even without their gift, I guess it's not surprising that I developed an interest. And frankly, staying with my aunt gives me an in for my research that would be hard to come by without a connection. Most psychics and mediums are pretty defensive about their work—you can understand why—but my aunt's well-thought-of here and I'm making good headway."

"What exactly are you doing?"

Marty shrugged. "Exploratory research. Mostly, I just listen. I sit in on a lot of readings, interview the practitioners, interview the clients, that sort of thing. I'm not trying to make an argument for the validity of psychic phenomena, but for the power of its influence."

"When you say *power* do you mean positive or negative?" asked Claudia.

"Goes both ways," said Marty. "It's not up to me to judge, just to present the research." She grinned. "I had a helluva time selling the idea to my Ph.D. committee. My subject matter doesn't have much of an academic ring to it."

Marty poured coffee. "Cream or sugar?"

"Neither, thanks." Claudia blew on her coffee, thinking. "Miss Eckelstrom, I wasn't looking for you when I came here, but if you've been talking to psychics and clients, you could be an awful lot of help to me."

The woman shook her head emphatically. "Please call me Marty; and I'm sorry, but no way. I'm only allowed the freedom I have because I promise confidentiality."

"But you're not bound by law like a doctor or lawyer."

"I'm bound by ethics."

Claudia regarded the younger woman thoughtfully. "It would seem to me you're also bound by morals," she said softly.

Marty stiffened. A long silence followed. Then: "That's a cheap shot, Detective. It's also a gross simplification of—"

The door opened and a large woman sailed in. Bangles on her wrists clanged like rigging against a mast. She carried a paper shopping bag bulging with foodstuff. Behind her, a man her size followed, likewise laden.

"Ah, here they are," said Marty, relief evident in her voice. She rose to help with the groceries.

"You're a good girl," said Mary Curtell. She then turned to Claudia.

The woman's expression was inscrutable, but Claudia immediately felt the sharp pull of her eyes. Strong eye contact, she thought, must be a trick of the trade.

"Detective Claudia Hershey," the psychic said.

Claudia lifted an eyebrow.

A smile played at Curtell's lips. "Nothing psychic on my part. The murder is the talk of the town, and I saw you on the TV news Tuesday evening. It didn't take a sixth sense to guess I'd be one of those you'd eventually be coming to see. We're a small community and I know the police've been talking to others."

Claudia stood and extended a hand. Curtell's grip was firm.

"You're taller than you looked on TV," she mused.

"I told you bluntness runs in the family," said Marty, forced gaiety in her tone.

Benjamin Curtell moved toward Claudia and shook hands. "Yes, and it was tough enough with just Mary here." He then gestured at Marty. "It's a hoot having two from the same bloodline under one roof. Talk about odd man out."

Claudia smiled politely. Except for their dark hair, there was no physical resemblance between Marty and her aunt. Mary Curtell was round and fleshy, as was her husband for that matter. She carried her weight gracefully, but it cost her. She was breathless and perspiring from carrying the groceries in, and she sat heavily in the kitchen chair Marty had vacated.

The Curtells and Marty bantered good-naturedly while groceries were put away, then Benjamin and Marty excused themselves.

Directing her attention back to Mary Curtell, Claudia said, "As much as you may have expected my visit, I'm sorry I have to intrude on your day. If there were another way—"

"Detective Hershey, you aren't one for small talk." She smiled, not unkindly. "You give off purpose like body heat and that's fine. I'm right at home with directness; maybe you guessed."

Claudia leaned back in her chair. "All right. Can you tell me about your relationship with Donna Overton?"

"You know, I just can't get over that . . . the murder."

Claudia waited. Everyone had to get past this part.

Curtell shook her head slightly. "She was a marvelous woman and I doubt you'll run into anyone who will tell you otherwise." The woman's eyes misted. "She was also a friend."

"I'm sorry," Claudia said softly. "I know this is difficult." She waited a moment, then said, "Mrs. Curtell, obviously we're looking at a lot of possibilities. And we're talking to many, many people. But because you were friendly with Donna Overton, maybe you can tell me something of her life. The more we know about her, the closer we may be to finding whoever killed her."

Curtell shook her head. "I just can't imagine that anyone who knew Donna would kill her. What for? She wasn't powerful. She wasn't rich. She—"

"Mrs. Curtell," Claudia said gently, "we've learned she did have more money than might have been typical of people in your line of work. Recent money."

Surprise registered in Curtell's eyes. "I find that hard to believe." She shook her head. "She was always behind in bills. I mean, like anyone, making payments was a . . . a favorite topic of conversation."

Claudia studied the woman. "You must have known about the television she bought. It's a very expensive set. Didn't you wonder how—"

Curtell shook her head emphatically. "No, no, she told me she pushed her Visa to the limit, that she needed something to lift her spirits," she said, smiling. "No pun intended. Anyway, unless your name is Donald Trump, pushing credit to the limit is pretty much the way of the world."

"The TV was bought with cash. She'd also paid off all of her bills."

A radio played in the background. Something classical. Claudia tuned in briefly, trying to identify the music while she gave the woman time to assimilate what she was hearing with what she thought she'd known of her friend.

"I don't know what to say." Curtell closed her eyes. "I can't think where she would've gotten that kind of money."

"Mrs. Curtell, what do you know of Tom Markos?" Claudia asked.

"Why? You think he . . . ?"

Claudia waved a hand. "I don't think anything right now, but obviously we'll be talking to everyone who was closely associated with Miss Overton. I understand she and Tom Markos dated."

Curtell sighed. "Nicely phrased, Detective." She looked squarely at Claudia. "I didn't much like him. Too . . . I don't know . . . rough for my taste. But Donna thought the sun rose and set with him. At least for a while."

"What happened?"

"That . . . I don't know. One day, he just wasn't coming around anymore. Naturally, I asked Donna about it. But she didn't want to talk about him."

"Nothing? She said nothing at all?"

"Nothing I thought revealing."

"Think back, please. It could be important."

The refrigerator cycled, humming noisily. Claudia waited.

"She said . . . she said he wasn't what she thought." Curtell shrugged helplessly. "But that was it."

"What do you think she meant by it?"

"Well, I don't know. She just suddenly seemed disappointed. I guess at the time I thought maybe she'd learned something about him that she hadn't known before. She had told me that when he was younger he was often in trouble. I don't know; maybe there was an ex-wife or something."

Claudia nodded. "One more thing, Mrs. Curtell. You may know who some of Donna Overton's repeat clients were. We're compiling a list—again, we need to touch base with anyone connected with her life—and you might be able to make sure we aren't missing anyone."

"Well, we traded stories about visitors, but very rarely did we exchange actual names."

"But you do know who a few were?"

When the woman hesitated, Claudia said, "Please. Everything is important right now."

"This is confidential, right?"

"Absolutely."

Curtell drummed her fingers on the table for a moment, then reeled off three names. She watched the detective jot them down on a small note pad. "I know you're duty-bound to check into all of them," she said. "I do understand. But, well, I can tell you right now you won't find your murderer on that list."

Claudia looked up sharply.

"I don't know who killed Donna, but it wasn't a client, at least not a regular."

"How do you know that?"

With a dismissive wave, she said, "I just know, and you can believe that or not. She was killed by someone in this town, Detective, but not by someone she knew. I've never felt more strongly about something."

Claudia cleared her throat. "In other words, what you're telling me, it's a psychic impression."

"That's right."

"I see."

"No, you don't," said Curtell. She locked onto Claudia's eyes, all business again. "I don't have to be psychic to know you're a skeptic, Detective. That's all right. I wouldn't have expected otherwise. But at the same time, you need to watch out for being too closed-minded."

Claudia inclined her head a bit, then took a sip of her coffee. *So that's how they did it*, she mused. Lots of solid eye contact; no beating around the bush. It wasn't hard to understand why people open for the experience—maybe even desperate for it—responded willingly, likely even with awe. She almost smiled. Hell, it was a little disconcerting.

She directed Mary Curtell through a few more questions, none of which elicited anything useful.

It was going on two o'clock. Claudia stood. "Thank you, Mrs. Curtell. I may be in touch again. And no, I won't overlook your impressions."

"Oh, sure you will—for a while."

As Claudia turned toward the door, Curtell put a hand on her shoulder. "Detective Hershey, you have a daughter, do you?"

Claudia paused, and tensed slightly. "I do, yes." Then she shrugged, thinking. "Me and a lot of the adult female population."

"Right, right," Mrs. Curtell said impatiently. Her eyes bored into Claudia's. "I don't mean to step into your business, but there's trouble in her path, Detective."

For a second, Claudia just looked at the woman. Then, unbidden, a spirited laugh slipped from her throat. "I'm sorry, but any trouble in my daughter's path right now would have to be me," she said. "We're at the stage where we conflict now and then."

Damn if the woman didn't have her going for a minute!

Claudia arranged her face into something neutral. "I'm sorry," she repeated. "It's not you I'm laughing at. I'm really not. In fact, your observation—"

"It's a little stronger than 'observation.'"

"Yes, well. At any rate it's very apropos to my circumstances at the moment. My daughter and I are busy working out her adolescence, and we have different ideas on how it's all supposed to come out."

Mrs. Curtell looked at Claudia thoughtfully. She didn't seem offended, but her eyes were speculative. "I'll call you if I think of anything else that might be helpful."

"The flowers look great," said Claudia. She smiled at Marty Eckelstrom. "It would seem you have several talents."

Marty looked up but didn't stand this time. "Periwinkles are about as hardy as they come," she said, her voice guarded. "I can't really take any credit."

Claudia squatted. "Marty, I need your help on this case."

"I told you. I can't. You're asking me to violate not only the integrity of my research, but to flaunt the trust I promised everyone who's talked to me. I just can't do that."

"You can. I'll protect your confidentiality."

"I'm sorry, no."

"I'm sorry, too, but yes." Claudia's voice took on a sharp edge. "A woman has been brutally slain. Are you hearing me? It doesn't look like robbery. It doesn't look like something domestic. And although we're checking a lot of angles, it's very possible that whoever killed her was connected somehow to her psychic work. Maybe a client who didn't like what she was saying. Maybe someone who felt ripped off, or cheated. Murder is almost never random, Marty. There's a reason, and I intend to find out what that reason was. When I know that, I'll know who killed her."

Marty brushed a clod of soil off the walkway.

"I'd rather you cooperated voluntarily," said Claudia. "But even if you don't, I'll force your hand on it. Everything in this community is police business right now, and if I have to I'll use legal tools to make you cooperate. I'd rather I didn't have to go that route."

Marty snorted. "Great."

They stood simultaneously. Claudia felt her knee pop, whether from giving short shrift to her exercises or rapping it on the bass boat, she didn't know.

"How long will it take you to get your research notes together?" she asked the younger woman.

"I don't . . . ." Resignation crossed Marty's face. "Not that long, but I have to be somewhere in"—she checked her watch—"twenty minutes. I also have to call my Ph.D. committee." She gave Claudia a sour look. "I'd also rather not make an issue of this in my aunt's home or the neighborhood."

Claudia quickly calculated how long it would take her to make the remainder of the stops she had scheduled. She also wanted to catch up with Sergeant Peters before the end of the day, see what the others had come up with. If Carella had made further progress, some of what he learned might mesh with whatever Marty Eckelstrom could relate. Talking to the girl who'd overdosed would have to be put off until the next day.

"I don't want this to wait, but I'm going to be running most of the day," said Claudia. She groped in her pocket for a pen and her notebook, then tore out a sheet of paper. She scribbled on the paper and handed it to Marty. "This is my home address. Can you come by this evening, say around nine? I know it's not much of a concession, but if it'll make you more comfortable with the confidentiality, I can at least keep you away from prying eyes here and at the police station."

Wordlessly, Marty pocketed the piece of paper.

Even with the dishes washed, the smell of spaghetti clung to the air. Claudia wrenched the kitchen window open and returned to the barstool at the counter separating the kitchen from the dining room. Her case files were opened, but her eyes were surreptitiously cast at Robin, scrunched over homework at the dining room table.

She watched for a while, sipping Diet Pepsi and listening to the skritch of her daughter's pencil. The television would ordinarily be on, but of course TV was verboten until homework was finished. Without its chatty backdrop, every other sound seemed amplified. Claudia heard herself swallow. She heard a neighbor dragging a trash can to the curb. She heard the damnable ping of water dripping from the kitchen faucet.

"That drip-drip-drip is making me crazy," Claudia said at length. "I don't know how you can concentrate."

Nothing, not even a look.

"Doesn't bother you?"

Robin took her time responding. "No."

"Probably just needs a new washer."

Nothing again. Claudia had to hand it to her. The kid was good.

Claudia untangled her feet from the barstool rungs. A half hour remained before Marty Eckelstrom was due. Time enough to fix the drip.

The tools and fix-it paraphernalia were jumbled in an old rubber dishpan in the storage closet off the front hall. The tangle gave Claudia pause, but the idea of sitting in Robin's sullen silence even one more moment goaded her on. She hoisted the pan and carried it to the kitchen sink.

The faucet was old, its chrome dulled by years of service. Claudia examined it briefly, then sorted through the pan. She'd never actually fixed a leaking faucet but had watched her ex do it once. How hard could it be?

She picked a wrench from the pan and found an opened package of various sized washers. One of them was bound to fit. Then she set to work. But getting the faucet handle off was a joke; the wrench slipped repeatedly, bruising her hands. The packing nut was worse still, and by the time Claudia freed that, fumbled a new washer into place, and began to replace the assembly, the doorbell was ringing. The phone shrilled at the same time.

Damn.

"Grab the phone, will you, hon?" Claudia asked on her way to the door.

"I'm not allowed to talk on the phone, remember?"

She shot Robin a look. "Just get the blasted thing." She watched her daughter amble to the counter toward the phone, then hurried to the door.

Marty Eckelstrom nodded acknowledgment. She carried a beat-up attaché case and a worn legal folder that bulged in the middle. Somehow, she looked smaller than Claudia remembered.

"Thanks for coming, Marty," Claudia said. She ushered the younger woman in.

"I don't recall being left with much choice," said Marty. But her words were without rancor and she smiled slightly. Her eyes fell curiously to the wrench in Claudia's hand.

"Just finishing up a minor plumbing job in the kitchen," Claudia explained. "Come on. Can I get you something to drink? Iced tea? Coffee? A glass of wine?" She waved the wrench. "Shouldn't be but another minute with this thing."

"No problem."

Introductions were made, and while Claudia mixed iced tea and fought with the faucet, Robin and Marty chatted lightly. Robin's dreaded algebra book made a good prop, and Claudia listened in, now and then taking a peek.

"I resisted any type of math until I got to college, and then I had to take some kind of flunky course to catch up," said Marty. She tapped Robin's algebra text. "Algebra was one of the worst."

"Makes me want to heave a lung," said Robin with conviction.

"I mean, it's not like it helps me tie my shoes or anything. And the teacher I have is the grossest thing on the face of the earth."

"Yeah? Then just wait'll you get to physics," said Marty. "The teachers don't get any better and the subject'll put you in the hospital."

"Fantastic. Something else to look forward to."

They both laughed, and a few minutes later Claudia realized that despite Marty's claims to the contrary, she knew her way around numbers. Claudia could hear her guiding Robin through a few problems and felt a stab of jealousy.

With a final twist, Claudia locked the faucet handle back in place. She stepped back, drew a hand across her forehead, and examined her handiwork. She turned the water on, then off. Then on, then off.

"Voilà!" she said triumphantly.

Marty and Robin looked up, and at that moment the faucet let loose a drop. Another fell, and then another. In seconds, the drips were as insistent as before, maybe worse.

Claudia cursed silently.

"Here, let me give it a try," said Marty. She slid off her chair and took Claudia's wrench. "What I didn't tell you before is that I had three older brothers. They taught me how to climb trees, aim a good punch, play football, and fix faucets."

"Yeah, but this is the house Jack built," Robin muttered, giving Claudia a look.

"We'll see," Marty said. She undid Claudia's handiwork in minutes and took off the offending washer.

"I don't get it," said Claudia. "The thing is brand new. Right out of the package."

Marty held the washer at eye level. "Wrong size, is all."

"It looked like a perfect fit!"

"They can fool you," said Marty. "Where's the old one?"

Claudia searched the countertop and found it under some coiled twine that she'd pulled from the makeshift toolbox.

"Until you get one that fits just right, sometimes the old ones will do if you just turn them over," Marty explained.

She anchored the worn washer back on, then reassembled the faucet and turned on the tap. When she turned it off, the dripping was gone.

"Presto-chango, no more drip." Marty smiled at Claudia. "That won't last forever, but it'll hold until you have a chance to get to the hardware store."

"Wow," said Robin. "Is there, like, anything you don't know how to do?" Her eyes pitched admiration.

"Plenty," said Marty, laughing.

Claudia thanked Marty and sipped at her iced tea. She would give anything for the unaffected laughter her daughter was giving so freely to a stranger.

"Hey, kiddo," Claudia said, forcing lightness into her tone. "If your homework's all done why don't you hit the hay? I've got a lot of work to go over with Marty."

"What? It's not even ten o'clock," Robin protested.

"I know what time it is."

She slapped her algebra book shut, collected her folders and pencil, and after favoring Marty with a tight smile, stalked off.

Claudia winced.

When Robin reached the hall, she turned around. "By the way, it was that new boyfriend of yours on the phone," she said. "That Dennis guy."

"Heath, and he's not exactly a boyfriend." Disconcerted, Claudia shot a half smile in Marty's direction. "He's just a friend."

"Whatever," Robin said. She rolled her eyes.

"Am I supposed to call him back?" Claudia asked.

"He didn't say." Without another word, she turned the corner and disappeared down the long hall.

Claudia had walked into the middle of family tension often enough to know that Marty couldn't help but feel the charge between mother and daughter. But Marty negotiated the awkwardness easily, filling the silence with pleasant chatter as she sorted through her attaché case.

Finally, they got down to business.

"I might as well tell you up front that I'm not any more thrilled about getting involved in this than I was when we spoke this afternoon," Marty said.

"Understood."

"Even with confidentiality, the integrity of my research will automatically be compromised—not to mention my word." Marty clasped her hands together. "In fact, I spoke to my Ph.D. committee, and the reality is that they'd just as soon see me go to jail as give up anything."

Marty paused and made a face. "There's a very good chance that not only will I have to forfeit everything I've done to date—two years of work—but that I won't be able to conduct research like this ever again without this breach being thrown in my face. Probably, there isn't a university anywhere that'll give me the time of day."

"Well, I'll talk to whoever—"

Marty waved a hand. "Don't bother. The cards aren't in, but if it comes to it, then that's just the way it'll have to go down. I'm not

the first to face a situation like this and I'm sure I won't be the last."
She sighed. "I'm not being noble. The truth is, I think it'll be easier
for me to live without a Ph.D. than to live with the idea that someone killed that woman and is freely moving around. I don't suppose
it's out of the question that the person could kill again."

"Actually, that's not likely the case," said Claudia. She paused to
remove her glasses and rub the bridge of her nose. "The killer probably had a singular motive related exclusively to his relationship
with the victim. That's almost always true. But whether that person
gets caught, it's a matter of time, Marty. The longer it takes us to
get a bead on the guy, the greater the possibility that he'll never
get caught at all."

"That's almost an invitation to back out," said Marty softly.

"No. But I know this is hard for you. You deserve to understand
what the perspective is."

"Okay. Let's get this over with then, shall we?"

Two hours later, Marty left. Claudia methodically wiped the
rings from their iced tea glasses off the table and dimmed the lights.
She fooled around with her oboe for ten minutes, then settled in
with it on the couch and let its brooding notes take her away for a
while.

Later, twelve-thirty, maybe one—time was losing meaning—she
forced herself through a brief round of stretching exercises, then
fell into bed.

Thank the Lord for Marty. Finally, Claudia thought she had a
solid lead.

CHAPTER 11

YEARS BEFORE HE NEEDED IT, Richard Andrew Matheson built a three-story brick house in a Tallahassee community known for attracting powerbrokers whose influence reached as far south as Key West. It was a spacious house with expansive rooms and all the accouterments money could buy: tennis court, sauna, stables, pool. It cost a bundle, but he never lived there. He rarely even visited—not in those early years.

Where he spent his time was on his ranch in an unincorporated patch of Flagg County, a somewhat more modest spread from which he could comfortably oversee his vast citrus operation and spin money he didn't need with the right combination of shrewdness and ruthlessness. For someone who had never finished high school, Matheson had done quite well. He knew it. He liked it. He guarded it fiercely.

For an outside observer, it almost might have seemed surprising that a man of Matheson's wealth and addiction to power didn't naturally gravitate toward politics. He could have afforded an aggressive campaign; and especially during the early '70s, when Florida's economy was sputtering to a stop, timing for a newcomer was surely on his side. Voters were screaming for fresh blood to represent them. But Matheson was, at heart, uncomfortable with the sophisticated veneer of wealth. For him, it was an effort to talk to people whose education clearly exceeded his own. He knew he didn't sound polished. Indeed, as bright as he was, he agonized over the cracker twang he could never quite erase, sure that it reduced him in the eyes of those whose wallets he matched. It took an iron will not to flash his temper on those occasions when he suspected someone of looking at him with condescension.

So no one was more surprised when political powerbrokers began to cozy up to him—looking not for money, but for "a man of the people," at a time when economic conditions made politicians without an accent suddenly suspect. Matheson was intrigued, but skeptical. For at least eighteen months, he kept his distance. He had money, a wife who still looked good on his arm, the welcome distraction of women even more attractive, and land he could call his own. And still, the powerbrokers came at him. They worked on him as diligently as Jehovah's Witnesses.

Look, they told him, at how well Bob Graham did. A millionaire, and no bones about it. But the man managed to get elected governor—southern twang and all—because people wanted precisely that kind of politician. Matheson's education—or lack of it—would be an asset. People would identify. People would vote for him, and Tallahassee desperately needed someone around whom voters would rally. The state's capital had taken it on the chin.

Of course, they weren't proposing that Matheson go all-out and run for governor. At least not yet. But over time, a state seat? A slot on the right committees? They told him it would be easy.

The whole notion began to have some appeal. In truth, Matheson was beginning to get a little bored. The more he prospered, the less he felt the thrill of achievement. A deal was a deal was a deal, and no one much cared except for other rich people.

He agreed to test the waters. Speechwriters flew into action. Image makers chose his clothes—a nice mix between wealth and down-home, country spun. A public-relations firm saw that his face became recognizable outside of Flagg. The powerbrokers made sure he and his wife got connected to just about every community event that made it into the papers.

Matheson stopped being bored. He started to like it, and then he started to love it. He won election as a state representative twice, redecorated the Tallahassee house, spent time in it during legislative sessions, and imagined himself there permanently in the next year. One term as state senator and, well, who knew what might come next? It was all a lot easier than he ever would have imagined. He created a political agenda for himself that was every bit as impressive as the agenda he'd created in business.

Claudia's eyes burned. She'd been reading yellowed newspaper clippings about Matheson for an hour. What they didn't tell her, Chief Suggs did—mostly truth, partly folklore.

She stood and stretched, reaching for the Styrofoam cup beside her. It was empty again, and that was probably just as well. If she was to catch Matheson and his wife before they went about their day, she needed to move now.

Officer Mitch Moody, his uniform shed for a suit, waited patiently, tugging on his mustache. Claudia signaled that she would be just a minute, and hit the ladies room. Tumblers turned in her mind. Matheson—or rather his wife, Eleanor—was the wildcard in the deck. Maybe it would play. Maybe not. But that the name was among clients reluctantly given up by Marty screamed significance.

Lysol clung to the air and Claudia didn't dally. She emerged and started toward Moody.

"Whoa, whoa, Claudia! Lieutenant!" Emory Carella skidded into view, his tie flapping over one shoulder. "You got just a minute?"

"Make it fast, Emory," she said.

"Okay, here's something that ought to tickle your interest. You know all that door-to-door canvassing we've been doing?"

Claudia nodded.

"Yeah, well, it wasn't amounting to much until last night when I did a follow-up with one of Overton's neighbors." Carella distractedly straightened his tie. "But this woman, Stella Barr, mentioned that about a week before she was killed, Overton fired her lawn boy because she'd caught him spying in her bedroom window. I got one of the patrol guys to pick the kid up. He's in the back, waiting to talk to you. Name's Billy Pyle, nineteen years old. Works for Bindle's Lawn Care."

Moody joined Claudia and Carella. "Does the kid come with papers?" he asked.

Carella grinned. "While patrol was picking him up, I ran a computer check. Three priors, two for indecent exposure and one for fondling himself in an adult theater."

"Just your garden-variety pervert," Moody observed.

Anxious as she was to get going, it didn't sound like talking to Pyle should wait. "What's your make on him?" Claudia asked Carella as she set her handbag on a desk.

"Hard to say. The guy's the size of an ox, but when he opens his mouth the IQ of a moth floats out. Of course," Carella said quickly, "it could be he's just jerking me around. I only talked to him for maybe five minutes."

A parade of potential suspects had crossed through the Indian Run Police Department since the murder investigation began. Anyone who may have had business with the dead medium received at least cursory scrutiny. Those with any sort of police record at all merited far closer attention. Pyle fit the bill. Although Pyle's profile ran to sexual deviancy and Overton had not been raped, he had reason to hold a grudge.

Claudia told Moody to hang loose, and followed Carella to a makeshift interrogation room converted from a supply closet for the duration of the investigation. The room had just enough space for a card table and two metal folding chairs. Billy Pyle sat motionless on one, his hands curled protectively around a faded baseball cap on his lap. He looked up blinking when Claudia entered.

"Hey, Billy," said Carella, "how's it going?" When Pyle responded with a blank expression, Carella said, "This is Detective Lieutenant Claudia Hershey, the one I told you about. She wants to talk to you for a minute."

Pyle must have weighed close to 250 pounds. Beneath a bristled flattop, his face was soft and his eyes wide. He wore a torn T-shirt so stretched across a massive belly that it was threadbare in the middle.

"How do you do, Billy?" she said. She gauged the vacant expression, the droopy eyelids, and slightly opened mouth. "Do you know why you're here?"

"Uh-huh," said Billy. His voice was thick, and with little inflection. He pointed at Carella. "He told me you wanted to see me. Do you want me to cut your grass? I'm real good."

Claudia and Carella exchanged looks. "No, Billy," said Claudia. She pulled up a chair and sat beside him, offering a smile. "I cut my own grass when it needs it."

"Oh." The boy looked disappointed and puzzled.

"But I'd like to know about some of the grass you have been cutting," Claudia continued. "You used to take care of Donna Overton's lawn, didn't you?"

Billy Pyle nodded vigorously, animation lighting his eyes. "Every week. I'd cut it every week. She liked the way I cut her grass and I was always on time. You can ask her. She thought I did a good job."

Claudia watched Pyle's face. "You're not cutting her grass anymore, though, are you, Billy?"

"Not anymore," he answered, looking down.

"Why not?"

"I don't know," said Pyle in a halting voice. His fingers, stubby appendages with folds of flesh at the knuckles, methodically traced circles over the top of his cap.

"You sure you don't know?" Claudia asked softly. When he shrugged, she said, "Is it because you peeked in her window?"

Almost shyly, Pyle said, "Maybe."

"Is that why she told you she didn't want you cutting her grass anymore?"

Pyle nodded glumly. "I think so."

"Did that make you mad, Billy?"

"A little mad."

"Just a little?"

"A little." Pyle pinched his forefinger and thumb together to demonstrate how much. "Like that," he said.

"What did you do when she told you she didn't want you coming around anymore, Billy?" When he didn't respond at first, Claudia touched Pyle's wrist. "You were a little mad. What did you do?"

"I . . . I said a bad word."

"What bad word, Billy?"

"I don't want to say. It was bad. My mom used to get mad at me when I said bad words. She's dead now."

"It's okay," Claudia said reassuringly. "We won't tell anyone. What was the bad word?"

Pyle looked beseechingly at Carella. "Do I have to say? I'm not supposed to use words like that."

Nodding, Carella said, "Go ahead, Billy. Nobody will ever know except us and we won't tell."

"Well, I said . . . I called her a bitch. But I didn't mean it! I didn't mean to say it!"

The air in the small room didn't circulate properly. Someone needed to install a fan. Claudia took her glasses off and wiped her cheekbones under each eye. When she put them back on, she leaned in closer to Pyle.

"Billy, when you said that word to Donna Overton, did she say anything back to you?" Claudia tilted her head, watching the boy's face. "Billy?"

"She said I should go away and never ever come back." Pyle licked his lips. "She said I shouldn't look in windows like that."

"And have you stayed away?" Claudia persisted.

"Yeah," he replied softly.

"You didn't say anything else? You didn't do anything? You didn't hit her?"

"No!" Rabbit-like, Billy Pyle looked frantically from Claudia to Carella, then back again. "I would never hit her!" he said. "She's a nice lady. Maybe one day she won't be mad at me anymore. And then I can cut her grass again. Do you think she'd let me cut her grass again? I cut grass real, real good."

Claudia smiled. She patted Pyle's hand and sighed. "Thanks for talking to me, Billy. Good luck with your lawns."

Outside the room, Claudia told Carella to have Pyle driven home.

"You don't think we should push him a little?" Carella asked. He looked disappointed. "I mean, that kid's big enough to bring down an elephant! What if he went nuts when Overton canned him? He might've. He might've without even knowing it. Look at his priors. Don't you think he's got some basic problems? Maybe gets out of control?"

"I think this," said Claudia. "He bears a couple of more checks. See if he's been peeping in other windows. And talk to the lawn service that he works for. But is he a killer?" She shook her head. "I doubt it. He doesn't even know Overton's dead, and I don't think he's smart enough to lie."

"Maybe he's just slick," Carella insisted.

Claudia gave Carella a dubious look. Her instinct was rarely wrong, and it told her now that the hulking teenager spilling off a metal folding chair was a wrong turn. But experience counted for more, and it told her not to dismiss even remote possibilities out of hand.

"All right, Emory. Check him out," Claudia said while she collected her handbag and jacket. "But tread carefully and don't hold him anymore today. If you push him now with nothing against him but his size, a nickel-dime rap sheet, and a small-potatoes grudge, we'll have every civil rights lawyer screaming for our throats. They'd claim we took advantage of someone who's maybe just a hair this side of retarded, and they'd be right."

The Matheson estate was on the outskirts of Flagg County and was accessible by a quarter-mile, winding, paved road. A canopy of trees gave it shade. A mailbox in the shape of a house stood at the end. Claudia thought it must be nice to put that much distance between a home and junk mail.

Moody whistled appreciatively as he navigated his car around a circular driveway. "Could just about put a third-world village in there," he said.

"And then some," she murmured, mentally calculating that the two-level ranch home boasted some eighteen thousand square feet. Nice. She could hide in one room here and never hear Robin's stereo on the other side.

"A lot of windows to wash," Moody remarked.

Claudia clucked. "Nothing like a little reality check, Mitch. Thanks." She unstrapped her seat belt and got out.

The threshold to Matheson's house was of marble. It led to a double-wide teakwood door, intricately carved with a forest scene. Stained glass paralleled each side of the door. She pushed a bell. She bet it was solid gold.

A woman dressed in a maid's uniform opened the door.

"Good morning," said Claudia. She smiled. "We're here to see Mr. and Mrs. Matheson."

The maid looked from Claudia to Moody, then back. "No solicitations allowed here—there was a sign by the gate—and deliveries go around back."

"We're here on police business," said Claudia. She opened her identification wallet, watching the maid's eyes widen at the sight of her shield. "Please let the Mathesons know they have company." She paused, as if pondering something. "Actually, we really need to see just Mrs. Matheson."

The maid's face radiated curiosity, but she said nothing as she ushered them into the foyer—as large as Claudia's living and dining rooms put together.

"I'll be just a minute," she said, moving off.

It was more like five, long enough for Claudia and Moody to peer into a vast room to the right of the foyer, a room she took to be where most entertaining was conducted.

"Could play basketball in here," Moody observed.

The room held three impressive sets of furniture carefully grouped to allow for casual conversation, a white baby grand piano, a wet bar built into one wall, and a fireplace that took up two-thirds of another. Claudia knew zip about art, but she imagined that the oils she saw, nicely framed and backlit, were originals worth more than the annual payroll at the police department. She lingered at the piano a moment, running her long fingers over the keys. She and Moody returned to their places in the foyer seconds before footsteps heralded the arrival of the Mathesons.

Although Claudia had seen newspaper photographs of Richard Andrew Matheson and had a verbal description of Eleanor Matheson, both were a surprise. He was outfitted in rugged denim jeans, polished boots, and a long-sleeved cotton shirt that revealed thorny gray hairs at the neck. He was fifty-eight but looked a decade younger. Muscles pushed at his clothes. His face, though burnished by sun, showed few wrinkles, and his hair was thick, full, and conceding gray only at the temples. Clear blue eyes in an even-featured face boasted good health.

Claudia looked him over carefully as she extended a hand and introduced herself and then Mitch Moody. While Moody made nice, she studied Eleanor Matheson.

The woman was her husband's junior by ten years, but despite a practiced elegance she looked a decade older. She was thinner than fashionable, and weary lines pulled by gravity fanned out from her eyes. Others radiated from her mouth. The skin at her neck seemed weighted by just a single gold pendant. She blinked incessantly.

Before Claudia could explain the nature of their visit, Richard Matheson seized control. His voice boomed a welcome, as if it were perfectly natural for two police officers to appear at his door, unannounced, at eight-thirty in the morning.

"I was just saddling up my horse—Razor's his name—for a morning ride. Like to do that as often as I can." Matheson thumped his midsection. "Riding's what's kept me in shape all these years." He offered a genial smile and said, "Well. What brings you two out? Is the PBA campaign already under way?"

What a crock. The Police Benevolent Association's annual solicitation campaign didn't extend door-to-door, and Matheson knew it.

"I'm investigating a homicide, Mr. Matheson," Claudia said evenly, her eyes sweeping over the couple. "An Indian Run woman named Donna Overton was killed a week ago in her home. I'm sure you've read about it."

"Oh, right . . . yes, of course!" Matheson tapped his head with a thick finger. "I should have figured as much when you said you were with the Indian Run Police Department. And you know, I remember thinking at the time how tragic that something that, uh, brutal had come to Indian Run of all places."

"Murder happens everywhere," Claudia said. Her eyes hooked to Eleanor Matheson's face. She looked waxy and faint. "And murder investigations often cross jurisdictional lines."

"Well, I don't see how I can be of any help—"

"Actually, I'm more interested in talking with your wife, Mr. Matheson." Claudia turned squarely to the woman. "I understand you knew the victim, Mrs. Matheson. You might be able to help."

"Come on, Detective!" Matheson said quickly, his voice amused. "Eleanor's not the sort who'd spend time with women like that."

"Eleanor might not be, Mr. Matheson, but Eva Matterly is." Claudia shifted her eyes to Matheson's wife. "That *is* the name you used when you saw her, isn't it?"

Matheson put a hand on his wife before she could speak. "Let's continue this on the veranda," he said. His eyes darted to his wife. Claudia saw his fingers press into her arm.

Matheson turned Eleanor toward a wide hall. Claudia and Moody exchanged glances and followed. French doors led to a spacious outside patio that overlooked a wide expanse of carefully cultivated lawn. Beyond, Claudia could see the beginning of Matheson's orange groves. Potted plants in handsome ceramic floor vases pinned every corner of the patio, which extended to the pool.

Matheson gave an order to his maid. He steered his wife to a seat around a glass table, then gestured for Claudia and Moody to sit. He lit a cigarette with an engraved lighter, then settled into a fourth chair. Buying time. Figuring angles.

"Should give these things up," Matheson said. He waved the cigarette distastefully. "It's not a matter of health in my case, but you know, it's not good anymore to be seen in public with a cigarette. A quarter of America still smokes, but no one likes to acknowledge it."

Claudia nodded. She ached to bum one.

Matheson carried on about cigarettes. He told a story about starting off with hard-core Camels. Smoke rose around his face like dry ice. She noticed that he directed most of his comments to Moody, who tapped a pen against the table edge.

The maid returned with a pitcher of orange juice and chilled Waterford glasses. Matheson thanked her and poured for everyone. "Truth be known," he said, "the country'd go to financial hell in a handbasket if everyone gave up cigarettes tomorrow. 'Course, no one wants to think about that."

Time to get down to business.

"Mrs. Matheson," said Claudia, "records indicate that under the name of Eva Matterly you'd been seeing Donna Overton for readings once a week for seven months, almost eight. For the first three months you paid her forty-five dollars a visit. For the last four months you paid her sixty. She was obviously important to your life. I'd like to know—"

"Look here," Matheson interjected. "I can't see how any of this has any bearing—"

Claudia's hand went up. She faced Matheson. "Please. The question is for your wife, Mr. Matheson. I'm talking to everyone who had contact with the victim. It's routine procedure."

A mourning dove cooed. Matheson shook his head irritably. "That whole psychic stuff. It's just a bunch of crap, Detective."

"Evidently your wife doesn't agree."

"A lot of people visit psychics and mediums," Moody said gently. He rolled the pen back and forth across the table, then set it aside and smiled sympathetically at Eleanor. "Who's to say there isn't something to it?"

Eleanor Matheson twisted a diamond ring around her finger. She blinked furiously but sought Moody's eyes. "It's . . . for me, it was . . . well, Reverend Overton was almost like a . . . a friend."

Matheson scowled.

"My husband doesn't understand," she said quietly. "I guess a lot of people wouldn't. And maybe it *is* foolish, seeing a medium. But I . . . Reverend Overton was so refreshing, compared to the people I ordinarily associate with. You see, I'm on a number of community committees. And, well, given my husband's position, naturally we host political parties with some frequency." She shrugged helplessly. "I can't explain it. It's just that Reverend Overton was someone I could trust in a way I really can't trust other people."

"It's not so foolish to want a friend, Mrs. Matheson," Moody said. "Everybody needs someone to talk to." He smiled easily. "My wife would go nuts if she was stuck with just me to talk to. Don't get me wrong; we love each other. But I don't exactly trade recipes with her and she doesn't exactly cling to every word I have to say when I get on a roll about the latest football game."

"What hogwash," Matheson muttered. He drained his orange

juice.

Claudia watched him. "Do you have a problem with that, Mr. Matheson?"

"I don't have a problem, Detective," he said. "Not with friendship. But we're not talking about friendship, no matter what Eleanor would like to believe. We're talking about fortune-tellers who feed off weak wills, who, who . . . summon voodoo spirits." He lit another cigarette. "*That* I got a problem with."

Eleanor winced. "She didn't always summon spirits, Richard, especially in the last couple of months. Sometimes we just talked. She was a good listener."

"Yeah, I bet she was," Matheson said bitterly.

Obviously, it wasn't new territory for the Mathesons. But Eleanor's voice had little fight in it.

"All right, all right," said Matheson. He took a long drag on his cigarette. "What exactly do you people want? Believe me, I have business a lot more pressing than my wife's fascination with some foolish woman who talks to ghosts."

"You don't need to stay," Claudia reminded him.

But he didn't leave. He pushed his chair back and put a booted foot across his knee, then sighed elaborately and tilted the chair back.

"Mrs. Matheson," Moody said, "what kinds of things did you and Reverend Overton talk about? And did she ever seem nervous to you, especially in the last couple of weeks?"

Eleanor picked up Moody's pen. She toyed with it distractedly. "We talked about our lives, mostly mine."

Her husband smoked furiously, all cordial pretense gone. Veins stood out on his forehead.

"It wasn't anything important, really. Just talk. Sometimes she gave me advice. She'd tell me I needed to relax more, to let myself be more open."

"My wife also sees a shrink," Matheson said. His chair slammed back on all four legs. "Didn't know that, did you? Didn't know that she relies on drugs for depression—"

"Richard—"

"What, Eleanor? It's okay to tell them that you sought advice from a crooked medium, but not okay to tell them that you need a shrink, too?" His eyes flashed darkly. "The shrink, I'll go, even at his outrageous fees of a hundred-and-fifty bucks an hour. But at least what goes on in his office is private. The law sees to that."

Bingo.

"We're not interested in your private life," Claudia lied. "This is just part of an investigation. Whatever your wife tells us is confidential." She watched Matheson for his reaction. "No one really cares—"

"Detective," he said, his voice rising, "don't patronize me. I'm not a stupid man. When the media learned about Nancy Reagan's sessions with a psychic, the entire country cared! It just about ruined Ronald Reagan. Shit, we're talking about the man who was president of the country! And how will history remember him?" He thumped his forefinger on the glass table. "I'll tell you how! As the man who ran the country through his wife—which was actually through a ridiculous psychic! And it doesn't matter a hoot or a holler that it wasn't true!"

Moody's soft voice followed. "I think you're exaggerating—"

Matheson stood abruptly. "We're done. This interview is over. You want to talk to me more—or my wife—get a subpoena. And give it to my lawyer. I'll even give you his damned name." He began to root through his pockets. Moody handed him a pen and a piece of paper.

Matheson scrawled something on the paper and slammed it with the pen to the table. "Here," he said. "I've got better things to do with my time." He turned. Stepped away.

Claudia and Moody rose. Eleanor remained seated. Her eyes blinked like a venetian blind being adjusted. An egret took flight a short distance off. Magnificent. But she didn't see it.

Last shot. Claudia began to move off, then: "Just another question or two, Mr. Matheson." She called out to his back. "Thirty more seconds."

"See my lawyer."

"Did you ever meet Reverend Overton yourself?"

Matheson stopped, half a dozen paces away. He half-turned. "Don't be ridiculous." His voice was low, on fire.

"Did you ever give her money yourself?"

"Get off my property!" he said, whirling.

Claudia smiled grimly. She moved closer to the man, out of earshot of Eleanor. Left three steps between them. Watched closely. Felt Moody in her shadow. "Are you having an affair, Mr. Matheson?"

Sweat poured from the rancher's face. "I'll have your freakin' badge, Detective." His fists balled up, but his hands stayed at his sides. "I . . . you . . . ."

Moody inched closer.

"You won't find work in a dime store if you even think about that line of questioning again," Matheson hissed. He glared at Claudia, shot the same dark look at his wife, turned back. "Don't underestimate me."

"I don't think I am, Mr. Matheson," Claudia replied evenly. "We'll see ourselves out."

She nodded at Moody and they left. They stepped through the French doors. They were halfway to the foyer when they heard a glass shatter.

Moody hesitated. He looked at Claudia.

"Don't worry about it," she said. "He's got a few things to work out."

"Mrs. Matheson . . . ."

"She'll be all right. He won't dare touch her." Claudia nudged Moody forward. "He knows we're keeping an eye on him."

A few clouds were starting to gather. The groves looked darker. It was hard to see the fruit.

"That got a little hot," said Moody. He started the car. "And, I don't know, think we really learned anything?"

"Well, we got plenty to think about," said Claudia. She wrapped the seat belt around her.

"I couldn't believe you hit Matheson with that business about an affair."

She shrugged. "Just a shot in the dark."

"Yeah, well, that was a big one."

"Not really. Matheson despises his wife. It doesn't take a big leap of imagination to assume he's playing around—or did. Not the kind of thing he'd want leaked to a medium."

"Hell, I got the impression he's terrified just at the thought that someone'll find out Eleanor's been seeing a medium at all! Sure would play hell with his climb to Washington."

"Uh-huh. Kind of a double whammy for the old goat. Maybe enough to pay off Overton."

Moody steered onto the highway. Matheson's groves began to recede. Traffic took on a city tone. "Enough to kill her?"

"People have killed for a lot less."

"You think his print on the pen will give us a match at Overton's house?"

"I don't know. Worth the check, though."

Taking one hand from the wheel, Moody tapped his pocket. "Turned out to be easier than I thought. I was worried I'd have to try and sneak off with their orange juice glasses. Would've been hard to conceal."

Only half listening, Claudia nodded. She played the conversation with the Mathesons back. She watched their faces, as if they were on a movie screen. Matheson had money. He had connections. All of it had made him powerful. And it had made him dangerous.

CHAPTER 12

HER NAME WAS SHAYLA KINCAID, but Claudia bet the girl couldn't even spell it. Or wouldn't care to. She was stick thin and pasty. Her light blue eyes watched the detective disinterestedly. No matter the question or attempt at conversation, she hadn't spoken a word since Claudia sat down at the foot of her bed.

"She's been like that since we brought her home from the hospital," Elaine Kincaid whispered, as if her daughter were asleep. She hovered uncertainly at the bedroom door. "I haven't been able to coax her out of her nightgown. Maybe that's to be expected. The doctors said she'd probably be withdrawn."

Claudia motioned for Mrs. Kincaid to leave the room. When she was sure the woman had gone, she lifted the girl's right arm and looked at the soft spot in the crook of her arm. Discoloration, old. Same with the left.

The girl watched but didn't react. Claudia pursed her lips, studied the kid. Shayla had long blonde hair that needed a good washing. Tangles bunched at the ears. Then, saying nothing, she pulled the cover down and pushed Shayla's nightgown up past her knees. She reached for the girl's right leg. Shayla stiffened and pulled back. But just as suddenly she let go. The marks were behind both knees, too. One behind the left looked new.

Fantastic. The kid had been out of the hospital less than a week. She was shooting up already. Somebody was fueling her, and with more than cocaine.

Sixteen years old. A baby, really. Just a baby.

Claudia covered the girl and leaned forward. She took Shayla's hand. Dry as desert sand.

"Talk to me, hon," she said to the girl. "This can't be what you want."

Shayla blinked, looked away.

"You almost died, Shayla." She squeezed the girl's hand. "You know what that is, to be dead? To not ever open your eyes again?"

It was useless, of course. The girl was beyond caring. Claudia patted her hand and let it go. She stood, walked around the room. Everything was white, clean looking. The room was spacious. A couple dozen stuffed animals with marble eyes decorated the dresser, the bed, a bookcase. A shelf held a trophy for track. Almost two years ago. A lifetime.

Claudia opened drawers, rooted through the closet. She examined each stuffed animal, looking for ripped seams that might signal a depository for drugs. She walked the room. No sign that carpeting had been pulled up. On her hands and knees, she peered beneath the bed. Rolled the girl one way, then the other, exploring between the mattress and bedsprings.

Nothing. She hadn't expected to find anything here, and she didn't.

Discarded on the floor were some folders and books. Government. Calculus. English. Claudia bent down, picked them up. She flipped through a few pages in the calculus book. Paged through the folders. "Buddy" was written everywhere.

Claudia knew Shayla was watching. She turned to the girl and held out a folder. "Who's Buddy, Shayla?"

Shayla closed her eyes.

Elaine Kincaid rubbed her hands together. She didn't know who Buddy was, she said. Shayla had never mentioned him. No, she hadn't noticed the name on the girl's school books. Couldn't remember ever really looking at the folders. There hadn't been much reason to.

"I don't know, Detective Hershey. I've tried to give her everything." Mrs. Kincaid shivered lightly. She was thin, but not emaciated like her daughter. "I've denied her nothing. I just don't understand how she ever got involved with drugs." Her voice dropped to a whisper. "I didn't see it coming." The woman began to weep.

Claudia waited. They almost never knew how it began—the parents—and Claudia believed them. She'd seen drugs get into kids from good homes and bad. Black kids, white kids, poor, rich. Drug influence was not discriminating.

"Mrs. Kincaid," Claudia said gently. "Your daughter needs to be in a treatment center. "The hospital wasn't enough. It only got her past the hump." She exhaled. "Shayla's on drugs right now. If she doesn't get help soon, she'll be dead before the year is out."

"No! How can you . . . she's been here since she got home. She, she . . . ."

Claudia shook her head. "Somehow, she's been out, Mrs. Kincaid." She told the girl's mother what she'd seen. "Probably through a window. It happens all the time. What's important is you need to get her in a treatment center. Today, if you can. Don't wait for this problem to go away."

There were more tears. Claudia guided the woman to a chair in the living room. She sat beside her. "Can you give me names of any of your daughter's girlfriends? Who does she hang out with?"

"Nobody, at least not now," said Mrs. Kincaid. She sniffed. Her eyes were red and wet. "For a while, she was friends with a girl named, uh, Tess. Tess Van Owen. But I don't know. Shayla hasn't mentioned her in maybe a month. Possibly more."

Claudia wrote the name down. She talked to the woman for another ten minutes and gave her the name of a treatment center in Flagg. She made the woman promise to make the call. Told her she would check back the next day.

As she prepared to leave, Mrs. Kincaid grabbed her elbow. "Detective," she said softly, "Shayla's not a bad girl. She really isn't." Mrs. Kincaid shook her head. "She's . . . she used to be an A student. Athletic, too. Very, very good."

Claudia put her hand on top of the woman's. "I don't doubt that for a minute, Mrs. Kincaid. Not for a minute."

When Claudia had been in high school, she'd once been abruptly called to the principal's office without any explanation. It was the day she'd been spotted smoking in the john and also the day she learned she had outscored the rest of her class on college-prep exams. So it could have been good news. It could have been bad. To Claudia on that day, it didn't matter. The not knowing was enough to twist her stomach into a fist. By the time she got to the principal's office, marching silently behind the man's secretary, she felt like throwing up. Her voice wouldn't work. Her legs trembled. She studied the principal's shoes when he came out from behind his desk.

Tess Van Owen was nothing like that. She had no idea why Principal Mitchell Hightower wanted to see her, but she'd been in and out of his office so many times for minor infractions that it was just a game. She didn't look at Hightower's shoes. She matched him eyeball for eyeball, her ruby lips curled in arrogance and feigned indifference. She paid no attention to Claudia, whatsoever.

Hightower had told Claudia what to expect, and the man knew his students. Tess Van Owen was, he said, a spitfire. She was also one of the most brilliant students to ever walk the halls of Indian Run's high school and she knew it.

"Don't expect her cooperation, Lieutenant Hershey," Hightower cautioned. "Tess is academically exceptional. But she also hates authority, and she goes as much out of her way to bend rules and cause trouble as she does to ace every exam ever put in front of her. She knows the Kincaid girl, yes." Hightower shrugged. "Chances are excellent she also knows this Buddy character you're trying to find. But she won't help you."

Big surprise, thought Claudia. "Well, maybe I'll get lucky," she told Hightower. "Meanwhile, just follow my lead, all right?"

Hightower welcomed Tess to his office, then gestured at Claudia. "This is Detective Lieutenant Claudia Hershey, Tess," he said pleasantly. "She's looking into some drug activity and thought you might be able to, uh, help."

Tess looked bored. She rested a hip against a bookcase, and turned an insolent eye toward Claudia. The girl wore huge loop earrings—two in each ear—and they rattled when she moved. Her hair was dark and cropped short in an expensive style. She wore black body stockings under a short lime green skirt, and a black sweater that fell off one shoulder. Desert boots completed her outfit.

Yup. One tough cookie.

Claudia opened with a slight smile, then briefly explained the focus of her investigation. Tess didn't bat an eye. She didn't smile back. She drew a stick of gum out of her pocket and put it in her mouth, tossing the wrapper on the bookcase.

"Tess," said Claudia carefully, "an investigation like this tends to go in a thousand directions. But I understand that you were friends with Shayla Kincaid."

"So what?" said Tess. The girl shrugged and studied her nails. They were long and painted fluorescent green to match her skirt. "Lots of people know Shayla."

"Then lots of people also know Shayla almost died last weekend," said Claudia.

"She turned into a doper."

"And you don't care about that?"

"Not my problem."

Claudia moved closer to the girl and leaned against Hightower's desk. "Well, you're right about the first part," she said. "Shayla turned into a doper. You're wrong about the second part. It *is* your problem because I'm making it your problem."

Tess looked at Hightower. "Do I have to put up with this shit?"

Embarrassed, Hightower said, "Come on, Tess. That kind of talk doesn't do anyone any good. And I should think you'd want to cooperate. Shayla was your friend."

"*Was* is the operative word," Tess said sullenly.

Claudia nudged the girl's foot with her shoe. "Hey, listen up," she said sharply. "I don't really care how close you were to Shayla," she said. "And I don't have a lot of time to put up with your smart mouth. The point is, you knew Shayla, and that means you probably knew the guy whose name is plastered all over her notebooks. Buddy."

Recognition flickered in Tess's eye. But she shook her head lazily. Earrings jangled. "Never heard of him."

"I think you have."

"Well, BFD. Think what you want."

Tess turned to go, but Claudia blocked her way. "I'll ask you one more time. Who's Buddy, Tess?"

Glaring, Tess answered, "I told you, I don't know."

"You *do* know," said Claudia, thumping a finger on Hightower's desk. "And you'll share it with me here, now, or I'll haul your little butt over to the juvie center in Flagg and we can talk there. There is such a thing as obstructing a lawful investigation, and that's what it looks to me like you're doing."

Hightower flinched and shifted his weight uncomfortably.

Tess shot him a disdainful look and snorted. "I'm leaving," she said. "This is total bullshit." She turned a haughty eye to Claudia. "You can't make me say anything."

Claudia almost let her go. She'd had it with kids this week. First Robin. Then that rag doll, Shayla. And now this girl. No adult waged war more effectively.

But just when Tess Van Owen was nearly home free, she foolishly miscalculated both timing and proximity. The girl was turning through the door, sailing back to class, probably off to hold her friends spellbound with the story of what had just transpired. Her step was jaunty, her head held high in triumph. And then in careless afterthought, her hand swept fast and low behind her back in an unmistakable middle finger salute.

In two decisive strides Claudia closed the gap between them. She grabbed Tess by a shoulder and spun her around, then expertly turned her against Hightower's desk. In a moment, the girl's hands were snared behind her back. In less than thirty seconds her wrists wore handcuffs.

Tess's earrings clattered on the surface of Hightower's desk. She yelped in surprise.

"When you live on the edge, you run the danger of falling off," Claudia said brusquely. She pulled Tess upright and faced her. "Let's go." She started to duckwalk the girl toward the door. The reaction she expected wasn't long in coming.

"Wait a minute, wait a minute!" Tess squeaked. She pushed against the detective's body, an ant trying to budge a grasshopper. "Buddy—he's Robert Lindstrom—that's his real name."

Claudia slowed, but her grip stayed firm on Tess. "I'm listening. What else?"

"Well, I mean, I don't know him, not really. I just, like, know who he is," Tess said. The words rushed out. "Please, I was just fooling around, that's all."

"Fooling around?" Claudia snapped. "Flipping the bird at a law enforcement officer is your idea of fooling around?"

"I'm sorry, really. Let me go, please? My parents'll kill me."

"One can only hope," Claudia muttered. But she removed the handcuffs. Ha! The girl's eyes were fixed on the detective's shoes!

Claudia studied the girl coolly. "All right," she said. "Let's hear it—and no more of your so-called 'fooling around.' I want everything from A to Z."

Tess swallowed her gum. "Buddy used to hang around here," she said. "I think he went to school over at Vo-Tech. But he dropped out. He started to show up here maybe a couple months ago. He'd just hang out."

The tremble in Tess's hand was almost imperceptible when she reached for another stick of gum. Claudia noted it and waited for the girl to go on.

"Shayla got to know him in the parking lot. Buddy has this car, see, a big old bird. I don't know what kind. I think Shayla liked that." Tess looked uncertainly at Claudia's face. "One time, Shayla introduced me to him, but I didn't like him. I told her that and, I don't know, the more she saw of him the more I, like, backed off from her."

"Go on," she urged.

"Anyway, he worked at a McDonald's for a while. But he got fired. Then he worked at the fish camp part-time. Last I heard, he worked at some garage. I guess he's, like, just making the rounds, you know?"

There wasn't a lot more to tell. Robert "Buddy" Lindstrom worked solo in drugs, at least as far as Tess could tell; she never saw him hanging out with other guys. She hadn't seen him lurking around the school in a couple of weeks.

"So you stopped hanging around with Shayla about the time Buddy cozied up to her, is that it?" Claudia asked.

Tess nodded. "I don't know. She just got weird." Tess's voice dropped to a whisper. "I couldn't even talk to her."

Nothing surpasses teenage hurts, Claudia thought. "You know, maybe it wouldn't hurt if you tried again. Shayla's going through some really hard times. She's going to need a friend."

Her observation didn't call for a response and she didn't get one. She glanced above Tess's head at Hightower. The principal stood as rigid as a steel girder.

"Mr. Hightower," Claudia said calmly, "I think Tess can go back to class now."

Hightower waved Tess away. The girl moved toward the door.

"One more thing," Claudia called after her. When Tess turned back, she raised a stern eyebrow. "You're bright, but you don't have a lick of common sense. Show that finger to the wrong person one day and you just might find it broken. Believe me, there are people out there even tougher than you."

Tess left a little less conspicuously than before.

Hightower sat heavily. "I don't think I could do your job, Lieutenant Hershey." He popped a peppermint candy in his mouth.

"I don't think I could do yours, either, Mr. Hightower."

On her way out Claudia thought again about her own long walk to the principal's office. It was the cigarette, of course. And there'd been hell to pay when the principal ratted to her parents.

CHAPTER 13

THE BOWLING BALL WAS A FOURTEEN-POUNDER, spackle green and threaded with minute scars from three years on a league in Cleveland. But disuse over ten months gave it a heavier feel, and Claudia hoped she wouldn't make a total fool of herself when she hurled it down the lane.

The Seventh Annual Indian Run Mother-Daughter Tournament was apparently a crowd-pleaser. Saturday morning, nine o'clock, and every lane was filled. Every entrant arrived with a cheering section. The high-pitched warble of female voices pulsed like arteries shot with caffeine.

Robin hadn't wanted to come, of course. Bowling was dumb. Her mother was the enemy. But nearly an entire week of being involuntarily rooted to the house eventually gave the tournament a diversionary appeal. It was better than nothing; Claudia was better than no one.

Emory Carella bounded into view, his grin a full half-moon. "Hey, it's the good lieutenant! I didn't recognize you at first without a jacket flapping at your legs."

Claudia wore jeans and a peach sweatshirt. She shrugged. "I know. It's so seldom lately that I'm not dressed for work that I almost feel like I'm undercover."

"Yeah. Nice to have a day off, huh?"

"Half a day, anyway." Claudia told Carella about Shayla Kincaid. "I got a couple of uniforms looking for this Buddy character. So if they round him up I'm going to have to talk to him. Couple of things on the Overton case I want to check out, too."

"Can you believe it's a week since the high priestess of the spiritual world was found dead?"

Claudia was spared a response when an attendant at the desk began to bark rules for the tournament over a loudspeaker. There would be three games, scratch scores for the older division; handicap scores for the younger. Highest series in each division would win fifty dollars. Second highest, twenty-five. Third highest, bowling alley T-shirts. Five minutes to roll-off.

"Pretty straightforward stuff," Carella observed. He looked around. "Where's your daughter?"

"Still looking for the perfect ball, I guess," said Claudia. She slipped into bowling shoes. They felt tight. "She refused to believe me when I told her she wouldn't find a six-pound house ball."

Laughing, Carella wished her luck and bid her farewell. "I have to check on my own little darlings," he said. "We're on lanes 23-24. Stop by afterward so I can show them off."

"You bet."

Claudia surreptitiously did a few deep-knee bends and stretching exercises. She couldn't hear her joints pop over the din, but she felt them. The regimen of exercises she forced herself through daily had fallen by the wayside with the death of the medium. The aging process was unforgiving, she thought grimly.

Robin skittered to the bowling circle just as the announcer declared a ten-minute practice session. "You'll never guess who's here," she told her mother breathlessly.

"Who?"

"Shannon's on lane four and Holly's on lane seven." Robin's eyes sparkled. "They got stuck going too!"

Ah, so that made it all right. Mothers all over town were dragging their daughters out for a good time. It was working so well that Robin had forgotten to be resentful.

"Maybe we can, you know, get pizza with them afterward," Robin said hopefully. "They're all going. I mean, it's like part of the whole tournament gig. They'll think I'm a geek if we don't."

"Oh, well God forbid." She smiled. "Sure. Pizza sounds fine."

Robin swooped off to tell her friends. Claudia waited, foregoing the practice rolls; and then the serious business of bowling began.

Tournament rules called for mothers to bowl first. Claudia hefted the ball experimentally. She eyeballed the pins, crooked teeth sixty feet down the lane. To accommodate her long strides, she positioned her feet as far from the release line as possible, judged distance, and pushed forward.

The ball left her hand early, slithered to the right, and clipped four pins. Overcompensating on the second throw, she hooked the ball too far to the left. Three pins fell.

Oh yeah. This was bowling, all right.

With a wobbly approach, Robin threw a gutter ball. She giggled self-consciously, then followed with a second ball that took two end pins out.

"We have to do this how many times?" she asked her mother. "Maybe we should just jam now before anyone sees how awful we are."

"Speak for yourself, kiddo," Claudia retorted. She retrieved her ball from the return, calculated speed and distance—and threw a seven-ten split. Her second ball chipped the seven pin by a breath.

Robin laughed delightedly, then threw two more gutter balls. But they both got better. Claudia finished with a 148; Robin with a 91.

By the third frame of the second game, they'd made friends with the mother-daughter team on the adjoining lane. Banter fell as easily as a spring shower. Once, Robin even permitted Claudia to demonstrate technique. No sour face. No sarcastic bite. Just Claudia's long arms against Robin's, her hands braced against her daughter's.

After the second game, Claudia gave her daughter a fistful of dollar bills and sent her for sodas. Then she sat at the scoring table to double check the figures—computer scoring had not yet made it to Indian Run.

Not bad. A 173 for Claudia. A 118 for Robin.

Someone whistled appreciatively behind Claudia. She turned to see Dennis Heath smiling down.

"What are you doing here?" she asked, a slow grin rising.

Dennis lightly worked his hand beneath her hair. His touch was warm on her neck. "Just slumming," he said. "Actually, I'm into action. This looks like the right place for that." He leaned over her shoulder and squinted at the score sheet. "Is this to be believed? Four strikes in a row?"

"Nothing to it and it only cost me one fingernail. Of course, there was nothing to the three open frames either."

"I think I'll stick to fishing," said Dennis.

"Oh, no. Don't tell me Indian Run's in your blood already."

"Must be. Worse yet, my money's in Indian Run."

"What do you mean?"

"I mean I just bought a bass boat."

Claudia groaned. "Tell me you aren't serious."

"When in Rome . . . ."

"I don't believe it."

"The truth is stranger than fiction." Dennis uncrinkled a brochure and dropped it on the scoring table in front of her. "It's a beauty. Picked it up at a dealership bright and early this morning and put it in the lake forty minutes ago. You and your daughter— if you'll come—are my first guests. The fish are my first victims, I hope."

The brochure showed an eighteen-foot tiller craft with a sharp nose and an outboard engine that looked like it meant business.

"I've had one experience out on the lake and it wasn't something I care to remember," said Claudia. She handed the brochure back.

"Then you obviously weren't out with a skilled fisherman," said Dennis. "Besides, I'll pout if you don't come with me," he persisted, affecting a hangdog expression. "That would be bad. Pouting makes hair fall out faster." He tugged at a lock. "You won't want me bald."

"The real question is whether I want you with fish," she said.

A cheer rose from two lanes over, and someone whooped with laughter.

Claudia looked at Dennis skeptically and said, "Don't expect me to bait my own hook and don't hold your breath for me to clean anything that winds up on the end of it. And don't even imagine that my first excursion will be today. I've got work to do when this thing is over."

While they haggled over details, Robin surfaced at Claudia's elbow. "Drinks are on the table behind us," she said, her eyes making a critical sweep over Dennis's face.

"You must be Robin," Dennis said, smiling.

"And you must be the boyfriend."

"Is that good or bad?" Dennis asked.

"Guess that's up to my mother." She scowled at Claudia. "We bowling or what?"

"Lighten up, Robin," Claudia warned.

Some of the reserve slipped back into Robin's posture. "Nice to meet you," she said to Dennis. She didn't look at him. Then she turned away and busied herself wiping down her ball with a rag.

"The kid's crazy about me," Dennis said. He winked at Claudia. "Must be my eyes."

"I'm sorry, Dennis. She's just a little difficult these days."

"She's a teenager. That's her job. Besides, if she doesn't fall in love with me, I'll make her fall in love with my boat. I bet I can entice her if I let her invite a boy sometime."

"Banish the thought!" Claudia smiled wanly. "I don't think I'm ready for that. Motherhood's a trial as is."

They talked of meeting for drinks later, and Dennis left.

Claudia watched her daughter polish the ball with a rag. "You know, it wouldn't have killed you to be nice," she said a moment later.

"What do you mean? That *was* my nice."

Claudia's brow furrowed.

Robin exhaled dramatically. "Oh, all right. He just took me by surprise, is all. He seems okay."

"He *is* okay." Claudia picked up her ball and moved to position. The third game was getting under way. "And you were downright rude."

"Look, I'm sorry, okay?"

Claudia lowered the ball and turned toward her daughter.

"Really," Robin said softly. She twisted a lock of hair into a cable. "Sometimes my mouth just motors faster than my brain."

"Can I be hearing right? Is this something like an apology?"

Slumping in her seat, Robin rolled her eyes. "Can we, like, not make a big deal out of it? I mean, we're holding up the game."

"Right," said Claudia. "The game." She turned away to hide a grin. Then she let the ball go. It curved slightly right, came in crisply on the Brooklyn side, and scattered all ten.

There was joy in Mudville after all.

Their balls could do no wrong. By the end of the seventh frame it looked as if Claudia and Robin actually might come out of the tournament with cash prizes. Mother hadn't left an open yet. Daughter hadn't thrown a gutter.

So what if Marty Eckelstrom had shown up in the fifth to cheer them on, out of breath and apologizing for being late? So what that Robin had quietly extended the invitation and "forgotten" to mention it to Claudia? Hell. Kids her age sometimes got smitten with adults whom they perceived as having all the qualities their own parents lacked. Everyone knew that.

Claudia's response was to bowl her brains out. She headed into the eighth with a 181 and a spare to back it up. But the self-satisfied smile she bought with a strike slid away when she turned around. Mitch Moody stood rigidly behind the bowler's circle, his expression solemn.

"Big problems, Lieutenant," he said to Claudia when she was within earshot. "We got another body, just one street over from Overton's. This one was a medium, too."

CHAPTER 14

DEATH HAD BEEN SWIFT AND EXPERT. Irene Avery, modestly attired in a granny gown and clutching a blood-soaked pillow, lay supine on a twin bed. Her face was gone.

On the twin bed four feet away lay her dead dog, a small thing concocted of wiry fur and a spatula tail. Between the beds on the floor was the baseball bat that had killed them both.

A neighbor, concerned when Avery failed to retrieve her morning paper, made the grisly find.

Claudia grimly took it all in. She remembered from one of the interview reports that the dog's name was Ginger, though everyone knew Irene called it Honeybunch. The dog had received all of the love Irene could no longer affix to her husband, who had died of a heart attack two years earlier.

Probably, the dog's ticket to death came first, perhaps when it perceived a threat to Irene. And the killer hadn't messed with it long. Except for one crushed eye and the tongue that lolled from its mouth, the dog's face was plenty recognizable.

While Moody silently watched, Claudia examined the woman's body, first from one side of the bed, then from the other. She'd been in and out of the room three times. The crime-scene techs and medical examiner had come and gone. Two attendants from the morgue stood impatiently in the wings; they hadn't eaten lunch yet.

"What do you think?" asked Moody. "We dealing with a copycat killer, some nutcase who read about Overton in the paper and wants in on the action?"

"No." Claudia straightened. "I think we're dealing with someone who wants us to think that." She gestured for the attendants to take the body.

"But other than the fact that she was beaten to death," Moody said, "nothing's the same. We've got forced entry through the jalousie windows." He followed Claudia outside the house. "Mrs. Avery was killed in her sleep. The guy left a bat. Everything's wiped clean of fingerprints. And looks like her wallet was cleaned out; not a folding bill in it. The whole thing just doesn't feel the same."

"Yeah, it does," said Claudia. "The guy who killed Overton was in a rage, out of control. This time, he was thinking."

Moody and Claudia walked toward their cars. "So maybe the killer figured Mrs. Avery knew something about Overton that he thought she would be telling us, something worth shutting her up about?" Moody said.

Claudia didn't answer at first. She wrenched the door to the Cavalier open and got in. "Whether that's it or not, Overton's still the key. He was messy with her, real messy. But he was also lucky and he knew it. That's why he didn't take chances on Avery. That's why everything's so clean. What we have to do is pick apart this guy's luck by going back to square one. Either we're missing something altogether or we have it and just don't recognize it yet."

The mood in the tiny police station was somber. The story of Irene Avery's death was on the radio within two hours; it would be on the TV news at six and detailed in all the morning papers. One dead medium was news. Two dead mediums was sensational. No one would be able to put a finger in this dike.

Chief Suggs sat heavily in the chair beside Claudia's desk. No one cracked a smile when the seat farted.

"You want the good news first, or the bad news?" Suggs asked. He propped his right ankle over his left knee and briefly inspected his boot.

"Does it matter?" Claudia asked.

"Probably not."

"Then just spill it."

"All right. The lab looked for a match on prints at Overton's house and what Moody got off the pens at Matheson's house. Neat parlor trick, but that's about it."

"I think I know what's coming next."

The chief nodded. "Yup. I bet you do. Eleanor Matheson's prints are there, which we expected. But Richard Matheson's ain't. If her no-good, rich husband ever paid a personal visit to Donna Overton, he didn't leave any evidence. That's the good news."

"That's good news?" said Claudia.

"Yup. It's good news because the bad news is that our friend Tom Markos seems to have disappeared. The guys out at the fish camp say he was due in about noon but never showed. So in my mind, we've pretty much eliminated one suspect and made a heavy case on the other."

"Anyone check Markos's trailer yet?"

"Come on, Claudia. You know we ain't got no probable cause to enter." Suggs patted his pockets, found the Tums. "On the other hand, we just happened to find ourselves a, uh, concerned neighbor who wasn't as mindful of legal dos and don'ts."

She smiled tiredly.

"This neighbor says the coffeepot was still on and a half-eaten sandwich was parked on the kitchen table," the chief continued. "Baloney and cheese, I think he said. Also, buncha clothes seem to be missing from the closet."

"A hasty departure," Claudia mused.

"Uh-huh. That's how the concerned neighbor saw it."

"We got an all-points out?"

Peering at his wristwatch, Suggs said, "As of about fifteen minutes ago. My guess is when we pick this piece of horseshit up, we're gonna find the scent of blood on him. Is that your read, too?"

On the surface, it was a tidy fit. Markos was a cartoon thug. He knew the police were looking at him, hard. And if he killed Overton to shut her up about something, it made sense that he might kill Avery too, worried that she knew the same something.

But what was the something? Where was the motive?

"Well? Hershey? You got an opinion on this or not?"

Claudia steepled her fingers. "Chief, my opinion is so half-baked it's not even out of the oven yet. Markos? I don't know. It's too easy, too—"

"Oh, come on! Markos has to be sweatin' things big time, or why else would he take off?"

"Because he heard Avery was killed and he's running scared," Claudia said promptly. She paused while a group of patrolmen passed her desk. "Sounds like Markos left his lunch on the table, maybe right after the first radio report," she continued. "He knows we'd look at him first, so off he goes. He might have other things to hide. Ex-cons do it all the time, whether they're guilty or not. When things heat up, they run. Period."

Suggs pulled a rumpled handkerchief from his pocket and vigorously blew his nose. "Damn it all, Hershey, you're turnin' out to be a disappointment all over again." He peered at her over the top of the handkerchief. "The trouble with you is you can't see the forest for the damned trees. You want to make like this is some big deal, some Cleveland Mafia thing. You was hopin' Matheson was our pigeon because it'd make big headlines and—"

"That's ridiculous," Claudia said stiffly.

"Yeah? Well, I'm not so sure, Hershey." He glowered at her. "All I *am* sure of is that Markos is scum. My money's on him all the way. I'm puttin' a warrant out for his arrest and I'm gonna leak his name to the press vultures."

"I really think that's premature," said Claudia.

"Of course you think it's premature, Hershey." Suggs jammed the handkerchief back in his pocket and stood. "You wanna think the case can't go down without you bein' the moving force behind it. But it can, and it will. With or without your approval, we're gonna nail Markos, prove he done it, and see that he fries."

The police radio crackled in the background, wheezing routine calls as if the day were just any other. An old lady caught shoplifting at Philby's. A jimmied padlock on the boarded-up country-western bar across town. An officer going 10-7 for a coffee break. A motorist needing assistance on Arrowhead Road.

With a practiced ear half-tuned to the indistinct chatter, Claudia leafed through reports, taking another look at Overton's life and death, watching for a connection to Avery's last day. She warned the dispatcher not to interrupt for anything not related to the case.

Once, exasperated, she left and bought a pack of cigarettes. Screw it. The nicotine would give her brain locomotion. Later, she called Robin to say she'd be late, late, late. The kid murmured sympathy, then told her they'd won T-shirts from the bowling tourney. Would've been a cash prize if Claudia had been able to finish out the last two frames.

Oh, and Marty Eckelstrom? Boy, a righteous lady all the way! Did Claudia know that Marty used to play drums in high school? And wow, wasn't it cool, what she was studying now?

Yeah, cool, Claudia thought dully. Marty stands in on the pizza bit after bowling, and drives the kid home. All of a sudden, the sun rises and sets around her. The drummer gets pizza and Robin's adoration. The oboe player gets a dead body and the chief's contempt.

Claudia hung up and blew a smoke ring. Well, good. Let's see Marty top that. Then she started in on the reports again.

The hours floated by. Carella, Peters, and Moody were scattered through the psychic block, talking to neighbors, hoping someone had heard something. Uniforms were scaling the streets, looking for witnesses. But a baseball bat makes little noise. And a woman bashed in her sleep doesn't yell out.

At nine-thirty, Claudia gave it up. She slid reports into her briefcase and stopped by the dispatcher's desk for messages. She knew there would be a lot, and there were.

The night dispatcher, a stoic middle-aged woman named Sally, presented a cluster of pink telephone message forms. She watched silently as Claudia scanned the sheets. Four calls from Channel 3, two from a *Miami Herald* reporter, one from *The Tampa Tribune*, one from the *Orlando Sentinel*, two from the Associated Press, one from the weekly. They were lapping up the Markos angle, quoting "a reliable source."

"Give these to Suggs," Claudia told Sally.

"I did, and he gave them back. Said for me to tell you to 'handle 'em.'"

"Great."

Claudia sifted through the others. Tom Orben wanted his video back. *Yeah, when hell froze over,* she thought. She told Sally to put him off; the video was potential evidence.

Another pink slip: The algebra teacher, Victor Flynn, called to discuss Robin's progress. There were early signs of improvement. Claudia shook her head. This he felt compelled to pass along on a Saturday?

"Maybe he has the hots for you," Sally commented.

"Oh, now there's a fun thought," Claudia said.

Sally laughed. Then she explained that Flynn had been at the school catching up on work when he heard about the Avery murder; he told Sally he thought the news would cheer Claudia up, given "the tough day she must be having." He was disappointed that he couldn't talk to her personally.

Crushing the message into a ball, Claudia looked at the next slip. Someone—a Madam Suarez—called to see if the police might want assistance. Her fee was very reasonable for investigators.

"She's out of New Orleans," Sally explained. "I've read about her in the *Enquirer*. One of those psychics who's always getting press. One of the things she makes a lot of noise about is Elvis. Says he's still alive, being held prisoner somewhere in Central America."

"Tell her when she produces Presley's body we'll be happy to talk to her," said Claudia. She handed the message slip back to Sally. "No, wait a minute. Don't say that. Just say we'll . . . think about it. The psychic community might not understand my wit."

The last message was from Dennis. It said, "I'm smiling cartoons for you. Keep the faith."

Claudia tucked the message in her pocket, ignoring Sally's steady look. This was one she'd answer herself. Then, steeling herself, she went back to her desk and made the calls to the media. She danced around the Markos business, telling each reporter nothing but making it sound like she had, and assured all of them exclusives the moment something broke. Not a very original dodge, but it would work for a while.

It was quarter to eleven when she finally went home.

CHAPTER 15

THE MAN RAN HIS FINGERTIPS along the rough bark of the branch. If it came down to it, the branch would do just fine. He nodded and got down to business, hardly working up a sweat. He liked the idea of using a branch. It couldn't be traced, for one thing. For another, it was natural.

Pulling the saw against the branch, the man gave great thought to his circumstances. So far, he'd done well, and he was only doing what had to be done. If he could just resist the panicky feeling that sometimes threatened to overwhelm, he would continue to do well. In daylight, that was easy. He could review his actions clearly, think rationally.

It was only at night when shadows fell that he jumped at every little noise. It was only then that he wondered whether he'd over-looked anything. In those moments, those dark slivers of time, all that saved him from losing control was the reassuring thought that in the end, he was doing everyone a favor. If nothing else, *that* mes-sage was loud and clear.

Alone on the land, the man threw back his head and roared, tickled at the notion. He was doing them all a favor!

And God Bless America, it was still possible to get away with murder. Or at least what the law of the land defined as murder. Fortunately, they were stooges, all of them, even Hershey. The cops were all lined up like ducks crossing from one pond to the other. Hershey was right there in the middle. For that matter, if it came down to it, she might even be useful.

The man paused to wipe his brow. He looked around the vast property. Look at this, for instance. Here he was, right out in the open, the most obvious place in the world, and no one was look-ing. No one would even think to look here. The man was reminded of a baby playing peekaboo. If the baby couldn't see you, then you couldn't see it.

The branch eventually gave in to the man's will. He knew it would. He hefted the thing, feeling the weight. He looked around and swung it a few times, hard. Perfect. Better than the bat. He was aware of the irony, that it was a branch from an orange tree. Just the right touch for Indian Run.

One thing, for sure. He would do what he had to do. For himself. For everyone. It was all a matter of being in control, and it was a lesson worth repeating. Hadn't he learned that from the best?

The man eyed the tree, then hacked off several more branches. Why not. This was what being in control was all about. He was thinking good. He was following his own instincts. Really, he was just about untouchable.

CHAPTER 16

THE CHURCH OF THE AWAKENING SPIRIT stood box-like on overgrown St. Augustine grass threaded with weed. Trees stood in random clusters here and there. Adjacent was a small graveled parking lot, two-thirds of which was filled. Psychics and mediums had turned out in force for Sunday services. In a moment, they would be coming out.

Leaning against her car, Claudia smoked a cigarette. When the killings were solved, she would give them up again.

In less than two weeks it would be Thanksgiving, and increasingly it looked like the murders of the mediums would still be served up as news along with turkey. More than a week had passed since the discovery of Irene Avery's body; two since Donna Overton's.

Claudia dispiritedly tapped ash to the ground. The investigation was going nowhere. No latents in Avery's house. No line on the baseball bat. No physical evidence that amounted to anything. Between the two mediums, more than fifty clients seeking spiritual advice had been interviewed; an easy two dozen, more than once. The FBI's Behavioral Investigations Support Unit in Quantico, Virginia, was slowly putting together a psychological profile on the killer. Of course, Claudia thought bitterly, it wasn't a priority case; the killer hadn't killed often enough to merit the attention of a Ted Bundy. Only the notoriety of their profession gave the dead mediums access to the FBI's vast computer network and expertise.

At five after ten, the plain wooden door to the church opened. People started to emerge. Most were women. They spoke in low tones.

Claudia watched for Mary Curtell. The way Marty told it, although her aunt was certified only as a psychic, not a medium, she nevertheless subscribed to the religion and philosophy of Spiritualism. Believers accepted that spiritual life transcended death and that a greater intelligence beyond the corporeal world prevailed. They also, of course, believed contact with the spirit world was not only possible, but provable.

"As far as they're concerned, Spiritualism is perfectly in sync with Christianity," Marty had told Claudia. "They'll tell you that it advocates adherence to Christ's lessons and that Jesus was actually the greatest psychic teacher ever to live."

At Claudia's dubious expression, Marty shrugged and added, "Hey, I'm just telling you what I know. And don't walk yourself into a debate. Believe me, the Spiritualists know the Bible and they can point out references in a heartbeat."

Claudia crushed her cigarette under her shoe and started forward when she spotted the round psychic. They made eye contact. Claudia didn't know how much of this whole psychic business she bought into. Certainly she didn't buy Madam Suarez's brand. But could there be validity elsewhere? Maybe yes, maybe no. Hell, who was to say?

In her characteristically blunt fashion, Curtell said, "I'm flattered, Detective Hershey. Anyone else would be looking for God at a church, but here you are looking for me."

The two exchanged wry smiles.

"There's a small picnic area on the north side of the church," Curtell said. "It's not much, just some trees, a few tables and benches, and a rusted barbecue grill, but we can sit and talk."

When they were seated across from each other, Claudia explained that her visit was unofficial. Their talk would not go on a report.

"Frankly, I'm running a little counter to some of the thinking on these murders," she told the woman. "There's a push for the investigation to continue full tilt in a direction I think is premature."

Curtell nodded. "It's a small town, Detective. Word is filtering out that the chief is gunning for Tom Markos and you aren't."

No longer surprised at the speed with which news traveled, Claudia merely shrugged and said, "Something like that. We've been all over the board on this one. But because Markos took off, the chief is convinced he's the best suspect, maybe the only one."

"Sure, and it makes sense," Curtell continued. "Anyone who knows that Donna was sleeping with Markos would come up with the same thing. Who's kidding who? Markos is bad news." The psychic waved at someone in the parking lot, then turned back to Claudia. "But he didn't do it. I told you before and I'll tell you again, whoever killed Donna was not someone close to her."

"Look," said Claudia, "I've been inundated with calls from psychics and clairvoyants and mediums and astrologers and whatever. People from all over who claim they know who killed Overton and Avery. Some insist it is Markos, and they know how we can find him. Others say it's someone else and they can help us track him. I even got a call from that Madam Suarez . . . ."

"The Elvis connection," laughed Curtell.

"Right."

"And what you're hearing isn't making a lot of sense, am I right?"

"They're speaking in tongues," said Claudia, "and I don't have time to track down leads based on . . . you know. The switch-board's going nuts. It's not unusual for police to get calls from psychics who want to help, but because the victims are psychics themselves—"

"Mediums."

"—mediums, everyone and his brother is coming out of the woodwork."

"And you want me to help you sort things out?"

Claudia watched a few stragglers pulling out of the parking lot. "I want you to distill what you're hearing from the psychics in this community, from the ones who knew the victims themselves."

"The case must really be going badly, because for you, this is really reaching." Curtell cocked her head. "I don't mean that unkindly, but you're as much a skeptic as the day you showed up at my door."

"Maybe a little less so." Claudia watched the woman's face. "Without at least some ambivalence I wouldn't be here now."

For a long time the psychic said nothing. She picked at a jagged splinter on the bench. Her eyes were steady when she looked up. Her voice was soft.

"Your killer has a fixation with hands. Either that, or they at least represent something to him. Don't ask me to explain that. I can't. It comes from a highly regarded medium in the community, but I won't give you her name; she's terrified. I will only tell you that I believe her."

Reflexively, Claudia drew her cigarettes from the bellows pocket of her jacket. She held them up. "You mind?"

She waved a hand. "Go ahead. Just don't ask for my psychic impression of your lungs."

Claudia smiled thinly. No one could ever leave it alone anymore, this whole thing about smoking.

While Claudia put a match to her cigarette, Curtell continued. "There's more, Detective Hershey. And what I'm about to tell you comes from me."

"All right. Thank you."

"I keep seeing ash. And I keep seeing light coming from a small window." The psychic shrugged. Her eyes narrowed, as if she were privy to some private viewing. "The ash, the light—somehow they're connected to Donna's house. But I don't know how."

Claudia bit her lip to conceal her disappointment. It was turning out to be a bust after all. Hands, ash, light. Shit. She might as well be watching Donna Overton going into a trance on video again.

"Both could be symbolic," Curtell said slowly. "The ash, especially. It could be representative of something." She shook her head vigorously. "But they're fundamentally important. Somehow."

Thunderclouds were building in the distance. This had been a mistake, coming out here, one of those desperate measures. Maybe Suggs was right. Maybe stubborn pride—something—was pushing all reason to the back of her mind. Claudia watched the clouds shifting, growing darker. What did she have to show that Markos didn't do it? That he didn't kill both women?

"Go back to Donna's house. Look again." Curtell stood. She dusted the seat of her skirt. "I'm not asking you to abandon the reality you cops steer with. But a look beyond that won't hurt you, either."

"One more question," said Claudia, smoke slipping from the side of her mouth. "Of all the things I've heard, just now and from the psychics who've been calling in, no one yet claims to be, uh, in touch with Donna Overton's spirit. Can't the mediums, you know, log in?"

"Things are always black and white in your world, aren't they, Detective?" Curtell sighed. "It's not that way in the spiritual world, I'm afraid. Shades of gray dominate."

They walked together to their cars. Claudia thanked the woman several times, trying to compensate for the doubt she knew she was projecting. Whatever Mary Curtell was or wasn't, her instincts were good.

"By the way," Claudia said, "that trouble you mentioned with my daughter? Well, we're pretty much working things out. I think maybe what you said may have prompted me to stop being such a weasel with her."

The psychic looked up sharply. "Whether you believe me or not with what I've just told you, don't brush aside what I said about your daughter."

"I'm not, I—"

"You are. You're trying some flattery on me, but it's coming across as patronizing. I can live with that. I don't even dislike you for it. But you won't be able to live with yourself if your disregard for what I say turns tables on you."

"Well, then, what exactly are you saying, Mrs. Curtell?" Claudia irritably stubbed out her cigarette, reached down, and pushed the butt into the pack. "What am I supposed to make of it?"

"Your daughter's on a path. It leads into woods. It's dark, and she's walking into it. I keep seeing the light fading behind her—"

"Oh, come on."

"—and something is in those woods, waiting. Something evil. She's in trouble."

That damnable chill crawled along Claudia's arms again. Damn psychics.

"Call me if you see any more," the detective said at last. She heard the sarcasm in her voice, couldn't help it.

"You'll see before I do," said Curtell. Her eyes held Claudia's. Then finally, she struggled into her car, looped the seat belt around her waist, and drove off.

Claudia watched the departing vehicle. A mockingbird started up somewhere. Turning, she looked for the bird in a clump of trees. Didn't see it.

How ridiculous that it should feel like an omen.

CHAPTER 17

EXCEPT FOR A CROOKED STRIP of yellow crime-scene tape still across the front door, padlocked by the police and repaired just enough to make it close, nothing announced that the serenity of the small house had been shattered two weeks earlier. No reason to guess that it would be on the market for an eternity, eschewed by buyers who would not want the ghost of Donna Overton competing with their dinners or nights around the TV.

But that's how it would be. The Reverend Donna Overton might have found peace, but her house never would. And the most that Claudia could hope by now is that the house might still yield secrets the dead medium would not.

It wasn't much of a hope. Whatever wasn't discovered during the initial crime-scene investigation wasn't likely to be discovered now. Claudia knew that. As assigned homicide investigator, she herself had directed the crime-scene technicians' efforts in the slow, methodical fashion that in Cleveland had provoked heated exchanges with every new murder she caught.

She took too long. She wanted too many surfaces dusted for prints, too much area vacuumed, too many photographs taken, and way too many items bagged for analysis.

Give it up, they would tell her, the doily under the lamp had nothing to do with the shotgun wound in the victim's temple. But she would make them bag the doily anyway, and then she would hound them to make her case a priority, to get the evidence scrutinized and put on a report ASAP. Sometimes they did. Sometimes they didn't. Mostly they did, though, because Detective Lieutenant Claudia Hershey had a rep for seeing things no one else did.

But Overton's house . . . she'd missed something. She felt it, even without Mary Curtell's stern admonition to go back. It might have been because the crime scene had been botched from the get-go. Or maybe because that damned Suggs followed her like a bloodhound, resentment etched in his eyes.

Well. It didn't matter. Monday had fallen with no new leads, and so here she was, back again, pulling the tape off the front door and letting herself in for another look. Her instinct and the psychic's impression were too much to ignore, no matter how clearly logic laughed.

The house was chilly, even though the air outside fanned a pleasant warmth, Florida's siren call. Claudia lingered just inside for a minute, taking in the quiet setting, letting her eyes filter things in a way she couldn't when men in uniforms were crawling all over it.

She tried to envision Donna Overton returning from the séance, then took the steps she imagined the woman had taken. Kitchen, bathroom—no, probably bathroom and then kitchen. She'd poured herself some water. She'd gotten her cigs out.

Then what? Had the doorbell rung? Did someone knock? Claudia furrowed her brow, recalling the medical examiner's report. Because the blood on the floor had been diluted, presumably the water hadn't been drunk, at least not most. And the cigarette found on the floor hadn't yet been lit. It looked more and more as if the woman hadn't been home more than perhaps five or ten minutes before someone came to the door.

Had the killer been lurking behind a bush, just waiting? Claudia shook her head irritably. It seemed unlikely, too risky. No one would have known precisely when to expect Overton in because the invitation to conduct the séance had been spontaneous. Her closest friend hadn't even known about it. Did that mean, then, that someone had followed her home?

Methodically, Claudia moved through each room. She went through every closet, every cabinet, every drawer. She looked through an old family album. She flipped through the pages of romance novels tucked here and there, hoping something would flutter out. And though she'd done it before, she groped beneath cabinet bottoms, table bottoms, the down side of any surface to which something important might have been secretly taped.

What she wanted was something that didn't fit, and she found it in the bathroom forty minutes later.

Nothing jumped out immediately. That was the stuff of television drama. Claudia's cursory inspection showed what she remembered: a half-empty bottle of Bayer aspirin, Kaopectate, a box of Band-Aids, a sampler bottle of Scope, Dactril, Triaminic, Sudafed, Maalox, dental floss, a Bic shaver, three nail polishes, cheap vitamins high in vitamin C, a dated prescription for an expectorant. Not much else.

But the cabinet itself—how could she have missed it? One of four screws that held the cheap box to its recessed wall compartment was missing. The three that remained appeared loose and scarred, as if a screwdriver had fiddled at them often.

Why would that be?

Claudia looked closer. Minute shavings from around the screw holes dusted the compartment. She straightened. A red flag and she'd missed it.

It took some doing, but the screws were loose enough that with just her fingers she was able to remove them. She placed them on the bathroom sink. Then she took the medications out and put them to the side as well. The cheap cabinet itself pulled free from its cavity as easily as a rotted tooth from a socket.

Hello. Stashed in the recess, which had been crudely enlarged, were tidy two-inch by two-inch plastic bundles of a white powdery substance that Claudia figured for cocaine. Beside it were a dozen toy balloons. She opened one and carefully poured out a powder with a slight brown tint. Heroin. Had to be. Maybe imported from Mexico.

Well, Chief Suggs, here's your drug source, Claudia thought grimly. *Here, Mary Curtell, here's your ash. And here,* she reluctantly told herself, *was a damned fine reason for Tom Markos to kill the Reverend Donna Overton.* The resourceful ex-con had probably been running an operation from her house. What a perfect setup for a man whose own home would always be a favorite target for police.

Maybe Overton knew, and Markos was feeding her money—all those neat cash deposits—to keep quiet. Maybe she'd gone along, then got nervous. Maybe they'd had an argument, and she'd threatened him with exposure. He'd come back, and he'd killed her.

But then: Why not take the damned drugs? Was he scared off? Panic-driven enough to leave the drugs behind? Would he do that?

Another scenario: Markos was running his drugs from Overton's house, but she didn't know. Maybe suspected, but didn't know. She got whacked before he could retrieve the drugs. The cash deposits, they could still represent hush money from Matheson, who had his own reasons to keep the medium quiet.

A final scenario: Overton herself was running drugs, a little sideline to spiritual advising. For that matter, maybe her clients were after more than spirits.

Nah. No way did that play.

Claudia pulled her notebook from her pocket. She glanced out the narrow bathroom window. Clouds were starting to build again. The blustering clouds the day before hadn't spilled a drop. Now, they were trying again. She watched for a moment, then shook them off and prepared to inventory the cache.

The house was silent as stone, so devoid of sound that when she clicked her pen open she heard the spring wheeze. And then she heard something else, a faint but distinct scrape immediately behind her.

She whirled, just in time to see a shadow flash at the window. Dropping everything and cursing, Claudia ran. She bruised her elbow rounding the front door, then galloped like a madwoman around the side.

Someone was vaulting the chain-link fence a hundred feet behind Overton's house, and she rocketed after him. Her shoes thumped resolutely against the ground, calling cadence in time with her breath. She could do this; she could catch the son of a bitch. Pump the legs. Swing the arms. Pump the legs. Swing the arms. Time the breaths, and pump the legs, swing the arms.

Boosted by adrenaline, she felt speed on her side up until the fence, a nasty thing five feet tall and laced with a thorny vine. Part of the vine was dying, and where it had browned, the thorns rose like rusty nails. Claudia paused, losing precious seconds looking for a toehold. There was none. She fumbled at the greenest leaves, swore, and started to negotiate the barricade. The first leg over was easy. She almost lost her balance on the second. A jagged piece of metal on the fence snagged her jacket; she pulled furiously at it and heard it rip. A thorn tore at her skin; the cuts would pester like hives later. But then she was over, and as she dropped to the other side, Robin's words came to mind: *Mother Rambo.* Claudia pinched out a hollow laugh and picked up the pursuit, trying to settle back into a rhythm.

Pump the legs. Swing the arms. Pump the legs. Swing the arms.

But breathing hurt suddenly, and the bastard was fast. He tore between two houses, leaped another fence, sprinted three blocks up the sidewalk, then stopped suddenly and turned to check the distance between them.

Claudia's lungs doled out breath in gasps. Shit! How long had they been running? Five minutes? Ten?

While he paused, she bent forward unsteadily and braced her hands on her knees, sucking air, vowing to give up cigarettes, wondering how she still managed enough oxygen to play the oboe.

The sprinter was young and lanky, dressed entirely in black. He stood similarly hunched, maybe just as winded, the fight sucked out of him. Across the distance they stared at each other like comic book gunslingers. Dogs began baying. A block over, a lawn mower started up.

Grudgingly, Claudia straightened and rasped at him to stop— "police, freeze," all those things—but the words were a spur. He bolted across the street and into a copse of trees.

Where were the neighbors? Was anyone dialing 911?

The stitch in her side stabbed like a shard of glass. A blister rubbed mercilessly against her shoe, and her legs threatened to buckle. All the while she pushed herself back into an unsteady gait; she told herself no way, not now, oh no. Every breath had to be measured. Every pounding step sent a jolt clear to her jaw. They were both moving more slowly, true, but the gap was clearly widening.

Claudia gave it another two hundred yards, then abruptly shifted to a walk. Screw it. Heaving and clutching her sides, she watched the man recede into shadow like some dream phantom. Let it go. She had the advantage of longer legs, but he had the advantage of youth. Time to give it up.

And had the son of a bitch not tripped, he would've made it.

He went down hard, skidding on damp leaves. The fall stunned him, and he lay frozen. Claudia watched disbelieving, then shrieked commands at her legs and accelerated one last time. Just as he began to find his feet, she pitched herself on top of him, knocking the wind out of both.

Wheezing, she straddled the punk and grabbed a fistful of hair. She yanked his head backward. Leaves stuck to his chin and mud smeared his cheeks.

"Don't even think about moving," Claudia whispered hoarsely in his ear, the most she could manage.

Without letting go of his hair, she withdrew her revolver, then groped stiffly through her pocket for handcuffs. Aw, hell. Somewhere along the line they'd been jarred out of her pocket.

Wobbling slightly, Claudia somehow got them both on their feet. She held her gun on the kid and demanded his belt. With some difficulty, she wound it around his wrists and secured his hands behind his back, then patted him down. Her efforts produced a pocketknife and a crumpled marijuana cigarette.

The boy eyed her sourly.

"Here's the plan," the detective said. She grimaced, trying to work a charley horse out of her left calf. "We're going to walk very slowly back, but before we do I want to know who the hell you are."

The boy looked to be seventeen, maybe eighteen. His hair was greasy and as black as his clothes. A clot of dirt stuck to his right ear. He looked at Claudia from beneath hooded eyes, then shrugged. "Go play with your gun. I ain't gotta tell you nuthin'," he said. "I know my rights."

"Yeah?" she pushed the youth against a tree. "You also know what carpenter ants are, kid?"

He just looked at her.

"I do because I had them in my kitchen once. They're big buggers, the size of paper clips. And they're called carpenter ants because they eat wood. Raw. The only thing they like better is flesh." Claudia looked just above the kid's head. "They can strip a rabbit in ten minutes. Don't know how long it takes to peel skin off a body, but maybe we can find out."

Looking above him once more, she said, "There's a little trail of the big guys making their way down the tree to your face right now."

Squirming, the kid tried to crane his neck to see. Claudia wouldn't let him. She showed him a thin smile.

"Oh, just relax, for heaven's sake. I'm a law officer, sworn to protect you. I wouldn't let them get past your ears, not really."

It was one of Claudia's more imaginative ruses. She knew zip about carpenter ants, but so what, the kid didn't either. The ploy worked just swell.

"Now come on," she said. "We're both tired. The ants are hungry." She raised her voice, gouged him with a look, and pressed him tighter against the tree. "What's your damned name?"

"Robert," he said, all fight gone.

"Robert who?"

"Lindstrom."

Claudia grinned, gave him slack, and clamped a hand around his arm. She holstered the gun.

Buddy. Buddy Lindstrom.

"You're under arrest, Buddy," she said. "Maybe Shayla Kincaid will visit you in jail."

Her breath came almost naturally now, and she read him his rights. Then she lit a cigarette, offered one to Buddy, and walked him back toward Overton's house, scanning the ground for her handcuffs on the way. They were hooked neatly on the fence with a long thread from her jacket.

Plenty of charges to throw against this boy, yessir: resisting arrest, possession of drugs, attempted breaking and entering. Claudia pondered a list. When she was thinking clearly again, there might be more. Not all of them might stick, but that was okay. She'd learn what she needed before some public defender managed to get him sprung.

"Having a good day, Buddy?" she asked Lindstrom once.

He scowled and didn't answer. She didn't mind. They made it back to Overton's house just before it started to rain.

CHAPTER 18

THE DOG HAD ACTUALLY TAKEN THREE HITS. The medical examiner's report indicated one would've done it. But then, Claudia thought, the murderer obviously was not schooled in medical science. Everything about him was overkill.

Irene Avery had been less fortunate than the dog. The baseball bat was much more precise than whatever weapon the killer had used on Donna Overton. The M.E. easily distinguished fourteen crushing blows, but there may have been more. The woman's skull had caved in with two; three found her shoulders; nine met her face. A finger was broken. Her teeth had been jammed down her throat. And what could be determined by painstaking analysis was that she had died with her eyes open.

Claudia sat at her desk, toying with an unlit cigarette. She'd read the report several times when it was issued, and three times now, just within the last hour. She quickly scanned to the bottom. As with Overton, there had been no sexual assault. No foreign blood or fiber under the nails. No bite marks. Estimated time of death: Saturday, somewhere between two and three in the morning.

Presumption: Irene Avery had been nudged out of sleep—either by the killer or the dog—then efficiently executed.

"Criminy, Hershey, you'd think you'd have that thing memorized by now." Chief Suggs stood at Claudia's desk, his thumbs hooked in his belt.

"Not quite."

"Yeah, well you been starin' at the damn thing for an hour," he growled. "For all the time you're spendin' on it you coulda made your way through the 'begats' in the Bible and learned just as much."

For a brief spell, she had almost started to like the irascible chief of police. In her mind, he'd gone through a meltdown on her, too.

But Suggs wanted Markos bad. He wanted the murders cleaned up fast, and—what was it Mary Curtell had said about police in general—everything he needed was neatly laid out in black and white. Challenge from the detective didn't sit well with him, and he made little effort not to show it.

Reaching for an ankle, Claudia scratched distractedly at one of the cuts left by a thorn. She ached all over.

"The thing about the finger bothers me," she said at last. "It's inconsistent with everything else in the report."

"Oh, horseshit," said Suggs. "The poor woman got as far as openin' her eyes and raisin' her hand to defend herself, probably after the first swing of the bat. Her finger got busted."

"Then why isn't the rest of her hand bruised, too?" Claudia asked.

"Hershey, ain't you ever banged your finger against a door or a wall? Or had a baseball movin' at forty miles an hour tip your finger on a bad catch?" Suggs shook his head irritably. "Your finger breaks or fractures, but not your whole hand. In Avery's case, the bat glanced off her finger. That's all there is to it."

"Sure. And that's just the way it happened with Donna Overton, too, right?" Claudia stood deliberately. "I don't believe in coincidence. The X rays show the right index finger of each victim was broken almost identically."

Holding her hand out, she pulled backward on her own index finger, demonstrating the manner in which the mediums' fingers had been broken.

"So what?" said Suggs. "Look, we're talkin' about some big guy, someone who towered over both those women. He swung a bat at Avery, something else at Overton. In both cases they held up a hand and the finger pressed backward. It ain't coincidence at all, Hershey. It was instinct on their part."

He impatiently took a turn demonstrating the movement he presumed both victims had used in defending themselves. "Coincidence woulda been if both those women survived the kind of bashing this lunatic gave 'em. And talkin' about coincidence, there's no coincidence in all that dope you found in Overton's house and the fact that Markos is gone. The man—and we're talkin' about a man with a record of violence—the man had motive, and he had opportunity—"

"Then why didn't he take the drugs after he killed Overton?" Claudia demanded.

"Somethin' interfered, is all," said Suggs. "When we pick him up—and we will—we'll find out what that somethin' was. Meanwhile, he whacked Avery because she knew somethin' and then he sent that Buddy Lindstrom to pick up his stash when he figured we'd be busy chasin' our tails on the Avery murder."

"It's too neat."

"Look, Hershey. This ain't some kind of Agatha Christie whodunit. You told me yourself Buddy confessed that the drugs belonged to Markos and he was just acting on Markos's instructions by trying to get 'em back for him."

"He's lying," Claudia said swiftly. "He hasn't got the first clue where Markos went. All he did know is where he was stashing the drugs. He went to the house to rip him off. Now he's just trying to save himself, hoping we'll cut him a deal by acting like he can hand Markos to us. And if we listen to him, that's where we'll wind up chasing our tails."

"Buddy's not that smart."

"Neither is Markos."

The chief looked at Claudia for a long time. "You know, anyone else'd be happy as a pig in mud with the way this thing is turnin' around for us and thank the good Lord for it. Not only do we know who axed those women—"

"We don't know that for sure—"

"—but we got a line into the drug activity here as straight as a stripe down the middle of a road."

"It's two parts fairy tale and only one part the real world."

Suggs made a noise, threw up his hands, and clomped off.

Claudia closed her eyes and leaned back in the chair. This was the last place in the world she should be right now.

Carella and Moody were stomping the psychic block all over again, hoping to find witnesses missed during the first neighborhood canvas. Suggs was fencing with the press over the phone— badly, judging by the bullish voice Claudia heard when she slipped out of the station at four o'clock. And someone, probably Peters, was hunting down the duty judge in Flagg, trying for a signature on a search warrant for Markos's trailer.

Everyone was working except the lead investigator.

Unforgivable.

"Your neck feels like someone drove a spike through it," murmured Dennis. He stood behind her, his hands deftly working the muscles, sorting out kinks. "Pile on any more tension and you're going to need physical therapy."

"This *is* physical therapy," said Claudia, reluctantly opening her eyes. She really ought to leave now.

Across the room, a shaft of sunlight pierced a window and reflected off a metal tray holding art supplies. From there, it splintered into a thousand reckless points against the wall.

But the dining room where Dennis seated her with an iced tea and a sympathetic smile was paneled in dark wood and decorated in muted tones. A perfect shield against the world. Claudia felt herself responding. She closed her eyes again and didn't resist when Dennis's hands shifted purposely to her shoulders.

"You know, you ought to register those hands of yours, Mr. Heath," she said softly. "They're practically lethal."

Dennis said nothing. His fingertips floated to her collarbone, tracing circles.

Claudia sank further into the chair. She felt his breath on her and tried to think of something witty. Nothing came.

"You just need to unwind a little," said Dennis. His lips were at her ear; his fingers dipped lower, finding the soft spot at the bottom of her throat.

Willing him not to say another word, she shifted slightly, just enough to raise her lips to his. They kissed slowly, experimentally. She let his hands glide inside her blouse. One lingered at the silly bow affixed to the clasp on her bra. The other unlocked buttons, pushing the material of her blouse to the side.

Leave now.

But she didn't, and after an agonizing moment her bra fell free. Cool air rushed in, and when his fingers slid across her breasts, then lower, the heat from his hands took her breath away.

She thought she heard him whimper, then realized the sound was her own. She put a clamp on thought, took a ride on sensation.

He had four hands, six hands, a dozen. They moved expertly, drawing her from the chair to the floor, finding and undoing buckles and zippers, tugging at elastic, inviting the cold air everywhere.

And later, when she was putting herself back together, a little shyly, feeling rug burn, groping for her glasses, catching her breath, and raking a hand through her hair, she realized the tension was gone. They'd journeyed to another planet without leaving the room.

Dennis freshened their iced teas and sat across from Claudia. "Want something to eat?" he asked. "I can throw a sandwich together fast enough."

"What? A sandwich?" she showed Dennis a lopsided grin. "Doesn't tradition call for an omelette?"

"You watch too many movies," Dennis replied.

Claudia's smile flickered and died. The reference to movies reminded her of the séance video and, by extension, Donna Overton's brutal murder. "Look, I really have to get going," she said.

"Things aren't working out very well for you, are they?"

"They could be better. The case isn't going anywhere."

"I didn't mean just the case," said Dennis. He ran a finger along Claudia's hand. "The job, the town, Robin. You're going to bolt when everything's over, aren't you?"

"I don't know," she said honestly. "I'm a fish out of water here. I didn't count on that."

"It could be worse," said Dennis. He smiled. "You could be in Vermont."

"That'd be worse? How?"

"Not only would everyone know what you ate for breakfast before it was digested, but you'd be freezing your butt off on top of it."

"Something to consider."

"There's more." Dennis disappeared for a moment. When he returned, he slid an oversized painting in front of Claudia. "This is why you came here, isn't it?"

The picture was of Claudia and Robin settled companionably on lawn chairs in front of their Alice in Wonderland house. Laurel oaks towered beside them. Clouds like mountains rose up behind the house, stout against an azure sky. The painting suggested early morning, when everything still held possibility.

"It's beautiful, Dennis," said Claudia. She'd seen his cartoons, his sketches, some of his book and album covers. But the mastery of what she saw now took her breath away.

"Take it. It's for you. I'm selfish and I'm hoping you'll look at it now and then and still want what you see—and then be bullheaded enough to keep after it." Dennis pecked her on the cheek. "I hate the idea that you might just be a pleasant interlude in my life."

Was it possible to be seduced by a painting? Claudia sipped at her drink and scrounged for words. She thought of a response, discarded it, thought of another. Just as she began to frame an answer, her portable radio crackled from the table.

Claudia grabbed it and fiddled with the squelch button. As usual, the garble was too indistinct to interpret. The thing needed more than a new battery.

Dennis sighed and gestured toward a phone. Claudia set the painting down and called in. She listened silently when Peters's voice came on.

Eleanor Matheson was missing.

CHAPTER 19

A WOMAN LIKE ELEANOR MATHESON did not just walk away from her life. Oh, she might want to. She might even talk about it. But she wouldn't do it, couldn't do it. Breeding, propriety, fear—she could no more dodge them than her own shadow under a full moon.

Yet the Flagg County sheriff's investigators were lapping it up. Like puppies at the master's feet, they sat obediently before Richard Andrew Matheson while he spoke in hushed tones occasionally punctuated by a tremor in his voice. They sipped coffee from dainty cups and offered sympathy.

And Claudia had to hand it to the old goat. His performance was riveting, bolstered as it was with red, swollen eyes, uncombed hair, trembling hands. Had he begun to rent his clothes in grief, she would not have been surprised. She wondered how long he had rehearsed, or if he had at all.

She kept her mouth shut, though. Claudia hadn't made friends with the Flagg County Sheriff's Department. Its chief investigator, Monroe Spivey, could boot her off the estate anytime he wanted. Fact was, even though she believed the performance was staged for her, jurisdiction gave all authority to Flagg and none to Indian Run.

But it was all a load of crap. Matheson wanted them to believe that after he'd had an argument with Eleanor, she'd surreptitiously packed a bag and slipped away without a word to anyone. Just up and took off.

Worse, he told them, she'd left without her medication and, well, she simply wouldn't be able to cope for very long.

"It's my fault," Matheson said in a choked voice. He took a long pull on a cigarette, his face soulfully calculated when he turned tired eyes on Spivey. "I shouldn't have argued with her. I know how brittle she can be. But she'd stopped going to her shri— psychiatrist. Said she didn't need him anymore, didn't need her medication, either. Eleanor had gotten really defensive about how she conducted her life ever since the Indian Run police badgered her about that dead woman. And we—me, mostly—traded a lot of hot words."

Spivey shot Claudia a dark look, then turned to Matheson and encouraged him to continue.

"I didn't know she'd left until yesterday . . . it's a huge ranch and we have separate bedrooms . . . and then, well, something . . . pride, I guess . . . I figured she'd be right back." Matheson's eyes implored understanding. Spivey nodded again. "She took the Mercedes—the only car she'd drive—and . . . well . . . you've got to find her, boys. She's my life."

After a well-timed pause, his eyes flickered to Claudia. "What worries me especially is that this guy who killed the psychics, the one I read about in the paper—"

"Tom Markos," Spivey offered.

"Yeah, him," said Matheson. "He's still out there, and from what I hear he's capable of just about anything. What if Eleanor somehow runs into him? What then?"

Heads turned toward Claudia. She spoke for the first time, picking words with the care of a homemaker examining tomatoes for bruises. "Mr. Matheson, Tom Markos is a suspect, but we don't know for a fact that he's the killer, and—"

"That's not what your own chief told me, Miss," said Matheson, a hard edge creeping into his voice. "I talked to him myself. Chief Suggs told me there's a warrant out for his arrest."

Ah. So Matheson had specifically called Indian Run, put some pressure on Suggs. No surprise there.

"A warrant is not a murder indictment," Claudia said, "and at any event the likelihood of your wife encountering Tom Markos is as remote as a meteor hitting the earth. Markos is on the lam. Believe me, he's traveling in entirely different circles than your wife."

Matheson scoffed.

So that's how it played, thought Claudia. Despite his distaste for politics, Suggs had made a point of keeping the Matheson name out of any press accounts of the murders. It simply would not do to rile the man. But word must have trickled out that the rancher and his wife had been questioned, and Eleanor's visits to the medium were probably corridor gossip all the way to Tallahassee by now. It would only be a matter of time before the Matheson name would surface next in the press, and an enterprising reporter could give it a lovely spin.

But Matheson was no fool. Circumstance dictated that the best defense was a good offense. Turning up the heat on Markos would deflect any suspicion of Matheson's own involvement. Wife missing, killer on the run, give it a neat, tidy ending. And make Indian Run the heavy. The wife ran because she was demoralized, emotionally beaten up by the Indian Run cops.

Sure. If Matheson couldn't keep the taint from his name, then he would turn things to his advantage. It worked for Betty Ford; she wasn't a drunk, she was just overwhelmed by circumstance. In the end, she became an angel of mercy. People flocked to the clinic bearing her name. Drug addiction, alcoholism, dependency of any sort—they made for good public relations for those who knew how to work the media.

Matheson did.

Claudia suspected that when all was said and done, Eleanor Matheson would be "found" in a clinic somewhere, drugged to the hilt. Secretly and voluntarily—certainly under an assumed name—the story would be that she had checked herself in after a few tormented nights on her own—aware that her husband had been right, but too embarrassed to go to him. That's how Matheson might play it, and he had enough connections to make it work.

Or Eleanor would be found dead. If Matheson was skillful enough, she might not be found at all.

Whatever the scenario, his star would rise in a swell of public sympathy.

While Matheson nattered on, Claudia excused herself. No one urged her to stay. His eyes reflected triumph; he had made his point.

Quietly, she headed toward the front entrance where her car was parked, but then circled around back, letting herself in through the French doors off the patio. The king would hold court for at least another thirty minutes, she figured. Plenty of time to peek into Eleanor's bedroom.

The room was something out of a dollhouse. Silk curtains, canopied bed, roman bathtub, a vanity with marble counters and gold fixtures—even the deliberate scent of lilac hung in the air.

The detective poked around. Cosmetics appeared untouched. Drawers showed neat stacks of undergarments and lingerie. Inside the closet, a climate-controlled room that rivaled Claudia's entire bedroom in size, stood a six-piece matching set of Louis Vuitton luggage. Clothes hung precisely so, no untoward gaps between them.

Nothing suggested flight.

Of course, she reasoned, Eleanor might have taken a suitcase from elsewhere. In an anxious state, she might easily have overlooked some essentials. Indeed, it was possible she intended to purchase what she needed when she arrived at whatever destination she had in mind.

But this was a woman whose days drew shape from routine. She chaired community programs, organized events, planned major parties. Even her visits to Donna Overton had systematically fallen on the same days at the same hours. Little about Eleanor Matheson reflected the kind of spontaneity her husband expected the police to accept.

Trouble was, they *would* accept it. They would pursue the leads Matheson fed them. They would find his wife when he wanted her found, if he wanted her found—and they wouldn't start here. Claudia doubted they would even make the cursory check she was making now.

Hell, the man was an important figure in Flagg County. His influence could mean the difference between a "yes" vote or a "no" vote on a fatter budget for the sheriff's department. A carefully placed call could make or break careers.

No one messed with Richard Andrew Matheson, and certainly not when a scum bucket like Markos could take the fall.

After skirting the Matheson entourage, Claudia returned to her car and headed back to Indian Run. She arrived in time to hear the news: Peters had come back with a warrant, and with it, Suggs and Moody had tossed Markos's trailer. Without even working up a sweat they'd found a blue-jean shirt covered with what looked like crusted blood.

CHAPTER 20

THE REST OF THE WEEK DRAGGED. By Friday, Chief Mac Suggs was throwing new work on Claudia's desk. Peters, Carella, and Moody were returned to uniform and their regular shifts. Neither Tom Markos nor Eleanor Matheson had surfaced, and as far as Suggs was concerned, all that remained to conclude the murder investigations was paperwork and, of course, picking Markos up. The chief was confident that would happen soon.

"The bastard can't hide forever," he told Claudia in a celebratory mood, his tone a little smug. "He's hotter'n a jalapeño pepper."

That much was true. Markos's scowling face appeared daily in newspapers and on TV. The poor quality of the photograph the media used—a 1990 jail mug shot—exaggerated the sinister lines around the man's eyes, giving him a Charles Manson look. And though news stories carefully referred to Markos only as a "suspect wanted for questioning in connection with two murders," no one doubted that the big man was anything but a brutal killer who was to be feared. The stories made much of his arrest record; they documented his role in the distribution of drugs through Indian Run.

All that Suggs held back from the media was the stained shirt. Leuco malachite tests proved the stain was blood, and subsequent lab analysis matched it with Overton's. In court, the shirt would become key evidence.

Matheson scored headlines, too. In a news conference carefully timed to make the most of television's six o'clock deadlines, the grieving husband immediately offered a $25,000 reward for information leading to the whereabouts of his wife, plus a $10,000 reward for anyone who led arresting officers to Markos. He told reporters he had no reason to believe Markos had anything to do with his wife's disappearance, but because he offered rewards for turning up both, the link was irrevocably established—and his political position was solidified. Reporters gave it great press. Precisely because he denied a tie at the same time he offered a reward for Markos's head, they were certain that Matheson—and the police—were withholding something that definitely showed the burly fish-camp employee was responsible for Eleanor Matheson's disappearance. Denial, to the press, was just another word for confirmation.

Markos was a dead man. Matheson was a hero. Claudia was, well, overrated.

Suggs told her to leave things alone, and so she did.

"Isn't this great?" Dennis asked as he looped their second bass of the day on a stringer. "Couple more of these and the heck with turkey for Thanksgiving. We'll have stuffed fish instead."

Claudia murmured something appropriate.

It was Sunday. They were in the heel of Little Arrow Lake on Dennis's new bass boat, which he'd dubbed "The Hershey Bar." Boats, he told her, were supposed to have feminine names.

At four o'clock in the afternoon, a breeze was just starting to throw up a welcome chill. The fragrant scent of swamp lilies clung to the air. Now and then, a cormorant skittered by. Great herons took flight, their graceful necks like aerial steering columns.

As she watched Dennis cast out again, Claudia thought it plenty sufficient to sit in quiet contemplation and allow the marshy environment to dispense its magic. But Dennis was here to fish, and she struggled to get into the spirit of it, admittedly less awed by what the lake could produce from its depths than by what it boasted from its banks. She looked distractedly at her own line, but it wasn't moving. It hadn't moved in the last hour.

Downright bored finally, Claudia gazed a half-mile north across the lake. She and Dennis had scouted there earlier, and she marveled now that from where she sat, nothing showed but dense forest that stretched the length of the lake. Distance rendered invisible the tangled water hyacinths that crept irrepressibly toward the bank. Nothing showed of the bank's irregular hedges—massive thickets of horned beakrush and sword grass, cattails and saw grass, some towering to ten feet. The bank was at its most lush; in spring, a maintenance crew would be dispatched to harvest the foliage. Just enough would be cropped to allow anglers closer casting into choice fishing ground. The measure riled the alligators, but it pleased the paying customers and, of course, that was the whole point.

Right now, though, the foliage was thickly matted and tough. And even up close, if you weren't looking you'd never notice that just beyond a particular wedge of nasty waterweed was a small recess that allowed access to the bank and a crude clearing among the trees some ten feet in.

Claudia knew it was there only because Buddy Lindstrom had told her about it. And the deal was, if Dennis wanted her to fish with him, he had to bring her there first.

Like a tourist scouting shells along a beach, Claudia had sorted through the clearing, Markos's place of business. The ground was trampled by footprints and littered with discarded cigarette butts and beer cans. Two glassine bags, empty but for powdery residue, were wedged into the fork of a red maple like coins jamming a vending machine. She slid what she found into paper evidence bags for the lab while Dennis watched and kept an uneasy eye out for alligators.

"Good place for commerce," he commented at one point. "Your boy's pretty clever. It's not visible from the lake, and unless you're willing to get your feet wet you'd never get out of your boat."

"Uh-huh," Claudia said. She looked at her own sneakers, black with mud. "From what Buddy Lindstrom said, this is where most trading went on." She pointed into the woods, past maples and oaks and a cluster of impossibly tall cabbage palms. "About a quarter mile through these woods puts you right on a secondary road that skirts the town. Whoever distributed to Markos would come in off the road, hide a vehicle in the woods, and meet him here."

"And Markos, I take it, was more than willing to get his feet wet?" Dennis asked. He watched her slide a cigarette butt into an envelope. "He'd just motor on out here like he owned the place and make a pickup?"

Claudia nodded. "Hell, yes. There's good money in drugs. Markos would pull his boat out of sight and cut deals over beers. Then he'd load the stuff in his boat, motor back to the fish camp, and at a convenient moment put the drugs in his van. Later, they were stashed behind Donna Overton's medicine chest."

"Nice racket," said Dennis.

"Probably small-time by Miami standards, but sizable enough for a place like Indian Run." Claudia watched Dennis slap something away from his neck. She hid a grin. "Buddy had no trouble giving up Markos in exchange for a plea bargain that'll put him back on the streets in a year or two."

Dennis and Claudia spent forty minutes chasing off bugs and foraging for drug paraphernalia in the small clearing. She was tempted to try and pick up the trail Markos's distributor used to and from the highway. But no. Let Suggs assign someone who gravitated toward the outdoors. The gnats were after blood.

"You having a good time?"

Startled back to the present, she looked up and smiled. "The lake's really peaceful," she said truthfully.

"No pun intended, but I figured you'd get hooked," Dennis said.

Claudia rolled her eyes and told him not to be too hasty in his assessment. As profound as the lake was in its beauty, fishing in it likewise invited occasional anxiety.

She judged Dennis's vessel reasonably sized as boats went, but it moved unpredictably. The water itself reached depths of fifteen feet in places, and it harbored sinister marine life. Snakes slithered at the lake's edges. Logs metamorphosed into alligators. Kamikaze flies the size of pecans and with the raspy volume of lawn mowers swooped cantankerously. Small wonder that Robin refused to come along.

When Dennis offered Claudia a chance at the tiller, she politely declined. She rummaged for a cigarette and lit up while he slowly maneuvered the boat to a new spot. A thin wisp of smoke curled skyward, then vanished. She studied the thin tube between her fingers. In another week, maybe two, she planned to give them up again. Things could kill you.

Of course, death could come at you from any direction. Look at the Reverend Donna Overton. In the end, cigarettes were the least of her problems. Hell, the woman had barely gotten past the first cigarette in a fresh pack when she made the mistake of opening her door, and there death stood.

"Let's try our luck here," Dennis said. He cast out. "The guy at the camp says the bass go deep this time of year."

"What? Oh, sure. Sounds good to me." Claudia recklessly let out line, her thoughts still on the dead medium.

How very ordinary that night must have seemed. The woman had come home, dropped her purse, kicked off her shoes, and made for the kitchen—something like that. Paused to get a glass of water from the tap, then pulled out a cigarette. Dropped the pack on the counter. Maybe wondered if anything was on TV worth watching at that hour. Or maybe she would just smoke her cigarette, and turn in for the night. Maybe—

She moved so abruptly the boat rocked. She looked at the cigarette in her hand.

Damn!

"Dennis, we've got to go back, right now," Claudia said. She doused the cigarette in the water and dropped the stub into an old coffee can Dennis used for litter. "There's something I have to do."

"Whoa, whoa." Dennis shaded his eyes with his hand, peering questioningly at her. "I don't get it. What's the rush?"

"I need to get to the 7-Eleven."

"Now? Right now?" Dennis's face registered exasperation. "What do you need that can't wait?"

"It's not what I need that can't wait. It's what Donna Overton needed that couldn't wait." Claudia started to reel up her line. She stopped long enough to glare at Dennis until he began taking his in, too.

"Okay, okay," he said, surrendering. "We're back to turkey for Thanksgiving."

Claudia laughed shortly. "Actually," she said, "I'm not done fishing. I'm just going to fish in another place."

CHAPTER 21

CLAUDIA JABBED THE FAST-FORWARD BUTTON on the VCR and fidgeted while the videotape ran to the end. She punched STOP, then hit REWIND and backed the tape up. Too much. Then too little. On the fourth effort the tape played precisely where she wanted it. Lucille Schuster's coquettish face swam into focus. She was handing cash to the medium and saying her good-byes.

Lots of background chatter: a woman chiding someone for slopping a drink on her; two men debating the administrative savvy of the junior high principal; a voice whining that they were running out of ice; someone crabbing about a kid who egged his car.

And then, yes! There—the break she'd been looking for—there it was. Overton was sorting through her purse, digging out car keys, but then still rooting around.

Claudia hunkered lower in her chair. She rested her elbows on her knees and her chin on her hands and watched. The medium, mild annoyance crossing her face like a shadow, looked up at her hostess. "Damn. I don't suppose you smoke?" she asked.

And then, Schuster, a little haughtily: "Sorry, never picked up the habit."

Lighting her own cigarette, Claudia leaned back in the chair. Other than Sally, the dispatcher, and an occasional patrol officer who wandered in, she had the police station to herself. And damn good thing, she thought. Suggs would have a coronary if he knew Claudia was dickering around with the tape.

In an irritable moment the evening before, she'd made the unpardonable error of curtly suggesting to a radio reporter that he should think—just for once, think—not only about the repercussions of calling her at home (and how had he gotten her private number?), but about the possibility that there just might be other suspects besides Markos. Were all reporters equally brain-dead? Did they always move in packs, bloodhounds bent on only one scent? Caught off guard as she was and annoyed as hell, it all just slipped out. That she didn't elaborate seemed not to matter. The reporter seized on her comment about suspects. He edited her observations about the press, then aired the remark about Markos as a live exclusive during every newsbreak.

Plugged as tightly into the community as a wine cork, Suggs learned of the broadcast within minutes of its first airing. Before calling Claudia, he waited just long enough to hear the report first-hand. Then he got her on the phone and for twenty minutes treated her to invective dependent on every barnyard profanity he could summon without losing breath. Afterward, he personally stomped to the radio station to set the record straight. In a honey-spun voice he told the reporter that Detective Lieutenant Claudia Hershey was "in error," her judgment "understandably" clouded by exhaustion. Did the reporter know the police had been putting in eighteen-hour days? He rambled at length, repeatedly denying that anyone but Markos need apply for top billing in both of the mediums' deaths.

Feeling blessed, the reporter launched the second exclusive before the chief roared out of the parking lot. As for Suggs, he was not yet spent. He called Claudia back, gave her hell for another half hour, and told her to keep her damned fool mouth shut and her damned fool hands off the case. It was closed. Period.

Except it wasn't. She put the end of the video through its drill one more time, but there was no doubt. The Reverend Donna Overton, bona fide medium and nicotine addict, had run out of cigarettes. Smokers didn't idly shrug that off. Which meant that if Overton wanted a cigarette badly enough—and the detective assumed she did—then the medium had to stop somewhere on her way home to buy a pack. In Indian Run, the only store open at that hour was the 7-Eleven, just about midway between Schuster's house and the medium's.

With effort, Claudia pushed aside her mounting excitement. It was a shot in the dark, nothing more. Markos's shirt, stained with Overton's blood, certainly counted for a lot. She couldn't explain it. Still, she noticed her fingers trembled slightly as she riffled through Overton's case file, looking for the crime-scene report. But yes, there it was. Among the potential evidence inventoried was one unlit cigarette, found on the kitchen floor. The pack Claudia believed it came from was on the kitchen counter, and it showed two cigarettes missing.

Donna Overton had driven to the 7-Eleven and purchased a pack of cigarettes on her way home. Like any smoker, she lit up immediately and finished that first one off in the car. The next cigarette, the one found on the kitchen floor, would have been her second, had she not been brutally interrupted.

Of course, it was possible that the medium had gone straight home and opened a pack kept there. But Claudia thought not. She didn't recall seeing any other packs in the woman's house.

No, what had happened was the medium ran out of cigarettes,

stopped at the 7-Eleven to buy some, and was followed home by her murderer. There might be a witness, someone who wouldn't have given the medium a thought. Someone who might even have seen or spoken with the killer.

It was almost six by the time the detective got to the 7-Eleven. A group of teenagers on skateboards outside the store scowled at her when she passed, whether making her for a cop or merely showing scorn for her adult status, Claudia didn't know or care. She ignored them and went straight to the counter. A clerk pointed out the manager's office.

The manager, a skinny man with rosebud cheeks and a prematurely receding hairline, straightened when she flashed her shield. Claudia told him only that she was working on a case in which his customers on Halloween night might be relevant, and asked about video the store's surveillance camera might have captured.

The manager visibly winced. "Oh, boy," he said. "Normally, I could help you. We'd have the whole cast of characters on tape. Problem is, we . . . well, we had a lot of decorations hanging up. Orange balloons, cardboard skeletons . . . that sort of thing. The camera lens, it was blocked by some black crepe paper that came loose and fell down." He cleared his throat and examined one of his thumbnails. "We didn't get bupkis."

"You're kidding, right?"

"I wish." He watched anxiously while Claudia jotted something on her notepad. "You don't have to include that in your report, do you?"

"What about the clerks?" she asked. "Who was on? I'll need to talk to them."

The manager thought for a minute. "That would have been Mark Yastrepsky and Eddie Winn. They're roommates. We call them Mutt and Jeff." The manager described the pair. "I always put them on the same shift."

"When do they work next?" she asked.

"Well, actually, they don't," the manager told her. "They quit last week. We have fairly high turnover." He tried to smile. "I'm not doing very well, am I?"

"You have a phone number for them in your files?"

"Just a second." The manager turned to a file, then recited a number.

Claudia scribbled the number on her notepad, thanked the manager, and went to the phone booth outside. The teenagers still lurked near the door, just a few feet from the booth. She glared at them until they skulked off. One of them mumbled something about "stilts." The rest of them laughed.

When the kids were out of earshot, Claudia slipped a quarter into the machine and dialed the number the manager had given her. She pulled her jacket a little closer around her; a wind was kicking up. The number rang once, and the moment she heard a connection she began to speak. In the next moment, she realized she was talking to a prerecorded voice. The number had been disconnected.

Damn, damn, damn. It was going to have to wait. She slammed the phone down. As she headed to her car she noticed that one of the teenagers was already back at the booth, checking to see if the coin had bounced back out.

In retrospect, the most incredible aspect of Claudia's marriage to Brian was that it took nine long years to finally disintegrate. He blamed it on the police revolver she strapped to her hip nearly four years after they took their vows. She blamed it on the women he strapped to his hip at about the same time. The divorce papers merely described their dissolution as the result of irreconcilable differences, and in reality the stiff legal document was probably more to the point. They shared far more differences than they did common ground. In fact, of common ground they claimed only music. Early on—very early on—it seemed enough.

Brian's skill with a piano was effortless. He was as much at home with a complex Bach overture as he was with New Orleans jazz. His fingers didn't merely caress a keyboard; they made love to it.

Claudia met him in an inky blue club where Brian had a three-month gig. The club, a step-down tavern in the Cleveland flats, encouraged customers to debut their talents every Wednesday night. On a girlfriend's dare and bolstered by two drinks, she toted her oboe there one Wednesday night and went solo. Closing her eyes to stave off terror, and silently vowing to kill her girlfriend, she drew the instrument to her lips and began. Beneath a sultry light that spun highlights through her hair, she softly executed a haunting melody made all the more ethereal by the oboe's somber tones. To Brian, on a break and watching from the bar, she was an exotic. And to Claudia, meeting him immediately afterward, he was an electric charge.

Four months later, they were married in a simple ceremony. Robin arrived less than two years later, and the badge, two years after that. By then, Claudia had long come to recognize that what she originally admired in Brian as refreshingly spontaneous and cavalier was just window dressing for recklessness and irresponsibility. He couldn't and wouldn't hold a job. He pooh-poohed monogamy. He never put the toilet seat down.

To Brian's disappointment, she was not the mysterious siren to whom he had been drawn. That gypsy hair? Under the bathroom's fluorescent lighting it was merely ordinary. Her quiet nature was cloying. She cared too much about a steady income.

They argued over money often. And eventually, having discovered that her English degree was sufficient for little more than secretarial positions, Claudia learned a weapon in order to earn a decent paycheck. Brian countered with a new playmate, the first of many. Even then, she stubbornly clung to the marriage long past the time when it made even marginal sense. There was Robin, of course. Beyond that, however, giving up was not in Claudia's nature. As for Brian, he didn't much care one way or the other.

They parted when Robin was seven. Now and then, when Brian thought about it, he sent his daughter a card. He called half a dozen times a year. On three occasions he arranged visits, never for more than one week.

Claudia regretted only that she didn't divorce him sooner. Living with him disoriented her in the way that unexpectedly rearranged furniture did. And it was that sensation that momentarily seized her that evening as she returned from the 7-Eleven.

When she opened the door to her house, her mind full tilt on the murder investigation, she came upon a picture of domesticity so complete that she fleetingly believed she must have somehow entered a neighbor's home. Dinner flagged its intent with an intoxicating scent of freshly cut vegetables and spice. Music—her kind—filtered quietly from a radio. Store-bought carnations, set among baby's breath, sat artfully arranged in a vase on the dining room table. The house itself had been beaten into submission with a vacuum and polish.

One hand on the door knob, the other clutching keys and briefcase, Claudia filtered the transformation. Her mouth fell into an oval.

Giggling, Robin peeked around the corner of the kitchen. "Close your mouth, Mom. You look like you just swallowed a can of hair spray."

"Is someone coming over?" Claudia asked.

Marty immediately came to mind. Somehow or another, the woman had become a part of their lives. Not a big part, but a part—a phone call here, a brief visit there, a story or joke in between. Claudia uncomfortably vacillated between liking and resenting the younger woman.

"Unless *you* invited someone, it's just the two of us," Robin answered. "Although," she continued, sternly poking her wrist watch, "five more minutes and it would've been just me. You would've been eating hot dogs."

"Sorry about that, kiddo."

"Never mind." Robin adopted a mincing voice and a perfectly erect profile. "The menu du jour, madame, features salad with a light vinegarette dressing, chicken almandine in a lovely cream sauce, cheese soufflé, steamed broccoli, French bread, and strawberry cheesecake for dessert."

"Well, wow." Genuinely impressed, Claudia shook her head and moved toward the kitchen. She sniffed the air. "Mmm, to what do I owe this pleasure? Are we celebrating something?"

"Hah! I knew you'd be suspicious!"

"Well . . . ."

"But as a matter of fact, there *is* something to celebrate," said Robin. She disappeared into the living room. A moment later, she handed Claudia a paper. "Check it out."

It was an algebra test with a B clearly marked in red on top. The calculations meant nothing to Claudia, but she scanned the sheet as if they did.

"That's fantastic!" Claudia told Robin. She pulled the kid into a brief hug. "I knew you had something between those ears," she said. "But how come you waited until Sunday night to show me?"

The girl made a face, though her eyes reflected pleasure. "I was going to show you Friday, but you worked late. Then I started to think maybe it would be neat to surprise you like this"—Robin gestured toward the pots on the stove—"just because, you know."

Claudia smiled. "Yeah. I know."

"And by the way, you're out of Windex and paper towels now. The windows took a whole roll."

In between stirring pots and getting food on the table, Robin prattled on about her day. It had taken her forever, scouring the place—and did Claudia notice she'd done the laundry, too? Dinner was a breeze—really, Mom, you ought to learn how to do more than broil—and hey, the cheesecake came out of her own little stash of money. Haw, haw. Don't say I never bought you anything.

They ate leisurely, exchanging stories of the day. It wasn't until the dishes were done and Claudia flicked on the nine o'clock movie that Robin made her move.

"So, Mom," she began when the first commercial came on, "that B that I got—pretty impressive, huh?"

"Mm-hmm. A definite step in the right direction."

Claudia checked her daughter's hopeful expression and sighed. She should have recognized that the turnaround in Robin was too abrupt to ring true. There were no free lunches.

"All right, kiddo," she said. "Give it up. What's on your mind?"

"Nothing."

"Nothing, huh?"

Then: "Okay, there is one thing," Robin blurted. "There's this fund-raiser for the band coming up next Saturday. They're holding a fishing contest out at the lake, and positively everyone's going to be there. It's like this major gig."

"Robin, you're not in the band, and you hate fishing," said Claudia, measuring her words, waiting for the rest.

"I know, but it's a really big deal, Mom." She listed all her friends who would be going. She mentioned a few boys. "And it's going to be supervised. The principal'll be there. The band director. Couple of teachers. It's going to be totally righteous. I have to go!"

This was tough and Claudia took her time answering. Easiest, of course, would simply be to say yes. A week or two of tranquility would surely follow. But this wasn't "Little House on the Prairie."

"No."

"Why?" Robin wailed. She punched a pillow.

"Because you're still grounded," Claudia reminded her wearily.

"Yeah, but it's, like, three weeks come tomorrow."

"And you were grounded for six."

"You're ruining my life! Why can't you just cut me some slack? Marty would."

Low blow. With her Mary Poppins disposition, Marty Eckelstrom had become for Robin a mentor, the older sister, the benevolent aunt—ready with sympathy, fast with answers, a prestidigitator with words.

"Look, kid," Claudia said after a moment, "Marty's not Mother Teresa. She's also not responsible for you. I am. And never mind that anyway. We've been over this before. You did this to yourself."

"Please!"

"Do I stutter? I said no, and that's final."

The movie came back on. Sylvester Stallone flexed muscles as he reached for a machine gun. Why didn't they ever run anything new?

"I might as well be dead," Robin muttered. "I haven't gone anywhere. I'm busting my butt on homework. I'm seeing that stupid geek teacher twice a week for tutoring—"

"Give it a rest, Robin. I mean it."

"It's not like I'm ever even going to need algebra."

Claudia clipped her daughter with a look, and they watched the rest of the movie in strained silence. Muscles bulging like diseased fruit, Stallone wiped out a village. Claudia thought of Dennis and considered calling him later. She surreptitiously glanced at the stubborn set to Robin's jaw and contemplated caving in. But no. She had to tough it out. Robin had to tough it out. Inconsistency hadn't done anything but merit her daughter's contempt.

While fireballs blazed around him, Stallone boarded a chopper and hightailed it out of the jungle. Claudia watched without seeing. How the hell did other parents do this?

When the eleven o'clock news came on, Robin went to bed. She muttered a frosty good night. There were no Disney hugs.

Claudia watched the news up until the sports. There wasn't a word about Markos. Thank God for small favors.

Then, flicking off the television and rising, she made coffee, pulled files from her briefcase, and turned her attention to Donna Overton's smoking habits.

CHAPTER 22

THE CALL CAME AT TEN-THIRTY. Claudia had just finished typing the narrative on a vandalism report, one of the nickel-dime cases Suggs had dropped on her desk to show her who was boss. She snagged the phone irritably and barked her name.

When there was no response except the hissing of the line, she said it again. "Hershey."

And then: "It wasn't me who did it. I told you that."

Markos?

Claudia swung from the typewriter to her desk. She hunched over the phone, cupping the receiver with her free hand. "Where are you?" she whispered.

She was answered with a scornful laugh.

"All right, all right, never mind," said Claudia. She thought rapidly, Markos's big face looming in her mind. "Uniforms are all over the state like white on rice, Markos. You're in deep."

"No shit, cop. I read the papers."

"Then what do you want?"

His answer was so long in coming that for a moment Claudia thought he'd hung up. "I didn't kill Donna, and I didn't kill that other broad." A pause. "I know who did—and I got proof."

She mindlessly doodled clef notes on her desk pad and said, "I'm listening."

"Uh-uh. Call off the posse first."

"Get serious, Markos." Claudia's pen danced over the pad. "Even if I wanted to, the machinery's in motion. And they got you dead to rights. They can place you at the scene."

"Bullshit. They don't have anything on me, and you know it."

"No, I don't know it."

"You do," he insisted. "If you didn't, you'd-a said 'we' got you dead to rights. But you said 'they.'"

Ignoring his supposition, Claudia said, "Are you telling me you weren't at Overton's house the night she was killed?"

"I was there, all right. But I wasn't there first. I was there too late."

Claudia's skin prickled. "Markos, come on. Give yourself up. You can tell your story then—"

"Damn it, Hershey! It's not a story!" An edge of desperation underscored his tone. "And if I walk into the middle of the street with my hands up, some shit-kickin' cop with his eyes on that reward money is gonna turn the street into Dodge City. Nobody's gonna wait for me to tell my side."

"So what do you want me to do?" Claudia colored in a quarter note on the staff she'd drawn. "You looking for a special invitation?"

"Meet me. Alone. No weapons. I'll tell you—"

"Are you nuts?"

"—what I know. You get things going in the right direction. Get it in the paper that you have another suspect. When I see that, then I'll come in. I know I got drug charges against me, but the state won't fry me for that."

"Markos, you're full of crap," said Claudia. She glanced around to make sure no one was listening. "I don't know what kind of scam you think you're running, but if you really have a name, you could give it to me right now. We don't need this cloak-and-dagger stuff. You can—"

"Yeah? While I make it easy on you, giving you time to run a trace on the line?" Markos's voice boomed. "You're probably working on it now. But I'm watching the time. We deal alone, or I don't deal."

Claudia scoffed. Another television favorite. In two minutes she'd have the call traced. In another five, someone would be slipping bracelets around the big man's wrists. Right.

But she knew he would never believe that. "All right, look. You're afraid of the phone? Fine. Then stick this so-called name and this so-called proof in an envelope and mail it to me."

"Screw you! This is all I got. I'd be nuts to let it out of my hands."

"All right. Send me a copy. Or fax it."

"No! A copy wouldn't mean a damned thing. No, what I need is to be sure you're getting it, not some cracker who's gonna toss it aside and then trace the postmark. No way. I want to deliver it so's I can see you got it, so's I can see your face."

"Why should I believe you would trust me, Markos?"

"I *don't* trust you. But I trust the rest of 'em less. So I deal with you—just you where I can see what's coming at me—or I don't deal."

Claudia capped her pen, buying time. "I have another question. It's even better. Why should *I* trust *you*?"

"Because I heard you on the radio, Hershey. I heard you say there might be other suspects. And next thing I know, I hear that cracker Suggs on the radio sayin' you're full of shit, making you look like a rookie."

She took a breath. "So what?"

"So I know cops, Hershey. And it has to burn your tail to know you're the lone ranger on the case, the only one who isn't buying into the web the rest of 'em are spinning."

"Not good enough."

"Well, it's all I got. Meet me, or I stay low just like I have been, and the guy who did Donna and that other woman, he maybe does another."

Claudia could hear Markos lighting a cigarette.

"That'd burn your tail even more, wouldn't it, Hershey?" he said softly.

Sheer lunacy on her part. Desperation on his.

"All right. When and where?"

The detective scrawled directions and a time. She tapped her pen rapidly against the desk pad. "Markos, don't underestimate me," she said quietly. "This is no boat ride we're taking together. You set me up and I can guarantee you won't see daylight again."

"And if *you* set *me* up, cop, we'll die together," the man said. He hung up abruptly.

The meet wouldn't go down until three in the morning. Claudia cleared a few more reports, her attention so distracted she had to back up on several and make corrections.

Suggs prowled past her desk a few times, glowering at her but otherwise leaving her alone. Their conversations had been sparse and perfunctory since the radio fiasco. Carella, Peters, Moody . . . they held her at arm's length, taking their cue from the chief. Claudia understood. She was on her own, a fish swimming against the tide.

At noon, she called Victor Flynn. The algebra teacher was polite. Yes, Robin was doing better. Yes, she was showing up for all the tutoring sessions. It was apparent she was studying, and her concentration was stronger.

"Is it safe to assume she's going to pull her grade up to at least a C?" Claudia asked. She reread what she'd just typed about a shoplifting incident at Philby's, then grabbed the bottle of correction fluid.

"Well, it's looking good," he said, his tone noncommittal. "No guarantees, but there definitely is progress."

She pictured Flynn pulling on his sideburns. "Is Robin doing well enough that she doesn't need to continue with any after-class tutoring?"

"Actually, no. I think it would be to her advantage to stay with those for another week or two," he said.

"Even with the progress she's making?"

"It's probably the best time," said Flynn. We're approaching some tricky material. I'd just like to make sure she gets a good handle on it before we, uh, part company."

The guy was a pompous jerk. Claudia understood exactly why Robin hated being around him more than necessary. Still, he was the expert. And another week or two wouldn't kill her daughter.

She started to thank the teacher, but he interrupted to ask whether the police were confident they would be able to arrest Markos shortly.

"I can't tell you how nervous it makes all the students, this man being on the loose," he told her.

"Well, I shouldn't think it would be that much longer before we find him," said Claudia.

"You're sure, then, that Markos is the murderer? I understood from someone who had overheard a radio broadcast that you, uh, had reservations about that."

Claudia massaged her forehead. What a mistake that had been, opening her mouth. She cursed her own impatience and assured Flynn that the case was nearing completion. She had, she said, indeed been mistaken.

"Well, the sooner that man's put away, the better," he said.

"Right," said Claudia. She eased Flynn off the phone, then immediately dialed Elaine Kincaid's number. She'd been meaning to ask about Shayla for days.

"I took your advice, Detective, and Shayla's in a residential treatment program in Tampa," the girl's mother said. "The doctors tell me she's doing much better. I'll be seeing her this weekend."

"I'm glad to hear that," said Claudia. At least that was one thing she hadn't fouled up. "The boy who was selling drugs to her will probably get treatment, too. He was really just a small part of it."

"Yes, well, I'm not so sure I feel as charitable. Although, I hope you get that character who was bringing the drugs into Indian Run in the first place," said Mrs. Kincaid. "Murder, drugs, he sounds like one sick man."

"Markos."

"Yes."

Everyone wanted a piece of Markos.

"I don't think we're too far away from him now, Mrs. Kincaid," Claudia said by rote. "It's only a matter of time."

Hard work and skill were never enough to carry any case. Politics determined priorities. The legal system dictated decisions. Manpower influenced direction. And luck played a role; some cops would say the biggest.

Claudia wasn't sure about that, but she recognized luck when it came to her. And when she pulled up in front of Mark Yastrepsky's apartment and found him and the other clerk, Eddie Winn, packing a U-Haul, she knew luck had touched her twice: tracking their address through the bureaucracy of the power company; getting to them before they took off.

She recognized the pair from the description the manager had given her. They were both young, Yastrepsky tall and sinewy, Winn short and thick. *Mutt and Jeff*, Claudia remembered the manager had told her.

Yastrepsky was loading a much-used cardboard box in the truck when the detective introduced herself with her badge. He wore a blue and white bandanna around his forehead. Sweat stained the material.

After peering at the shield and laminated identification card, Yastrepsky showed uneasy surprise. "Oh, man, a detective? Just for a couple of parking tickets? Man, I thought that was ancient history by now."

"I told you we should've just paid the things," Winn said dispiritedly. His eyes were round and wide, level with Claudia's chest. "We're not trying to get away with anything. Just moving back up north."

"Yeah," offered Yastrepsky. "Wages stink big-time down here."

"I'm not here about tickets." She pocketed her ID. "I'm here to see what you remember about Halloween night at the 7-Eleven."

Mutt and Jeff looked at each other, relief and confusion evident on their faces. Neither asked why she wanted to know.

"Not a whole lot to remember," said Yastrepsky. "It was busier than usual, and some of the customers came in wearing costumes." He shrugged. "Sold a lot of six-packs and lottery tickets—"

"And Cokes and ice and chips and cigarettes," finished Winn. He plucked at a hangnail. "I think everyone was partying but us."

Claudia ran them through the drill. She showed them a picture of Overton. She showed them the mug of Markos, and an old news photo of Matheson without naming either of them.

The pictures of Markos and Matheson drew blanks. In fact, what they knew about the murders themselves would fill a thimble; neither read past the sports sections of the papers. But after a lot of prodding, Winn said he thought that yeah, the medium might have been the same lady who stopped in for cigarettes. See, he remembered only because she wanted a whole carton, and they were out. So okay, she was going to settle for a pack, but then she wanted the boxed kind and they were out of that, too. The woman fussed a little but settled for one soft pack.

Naw, he didn't remember exactly what time, only that it was before midnight.

"Was she by herself?" Claudia asked, already making a mental note to find out whether Overton generally carried boxed packs of cigarettes. It was exactly the small sort of detail that could establish her presence in the store.

Winn shook his head. "I don't know. I think so, but there were other people in the store. I just remember she was holding up the line, carrying on about how we didn't stock what she wanted."

"That's it?"

"Yeah, that's— Wait a minute!" Winn looked excited. "I remember one other thing about this lady, yeah. She paid with a fifty-dollar bill." Winn slapped his forehead. "I don't know how come that didn't register right away, but at the time it really irritated me because I was running low on change." Winn nudged Yastrepsky. "Remember me saying something about that?"

Yastrepsky nodded, but she didn't put much credence in the gesture. Friends automatically tended to agree with each other on what seemed to them like inconsequential matters. But it was another thing to check. The video from the séance wasn't clear enough to show the denomination of the bills Lucille Schuster had handed Overton when the medium was leaving. But Claudia recalled that Overton's wallet was just a few dollars shy of one hundred. Yes, she very likely had broken a fifty for that last pack of cigarettes.

She had Overton at the 7-Eleven and it would hold up in court. She needed to put the killer there, too.

The detective looked at Yastrepsky and Winn. They weren't rocket scientists, but they were her best bet.

"Fellas, I need you to think harder." Claudia gave them her best no-nonsense look. "I want to know about every customer you remember that night, mostly those who came in between about ten-thirty and eleven, and anyone else you might've spotted hanging around outside."

"Oh, man," said Yastrepsky. "You know how many people pop in and out? This is, like, impossible."

"Then make it possible," said Claudia. "Think now and think hard, or you can come with me and think at the station while you're paying your tickets and whatever late fees go with them."

Winn winced.

"On the other hand, if you think well enough, I can probably overlook the tickets," Claudia continued. "I don't think anyone will follow you up north to make good on them."

Yastrepsky sighed elaborately. He jerked the bandanna off his head and ran a hand through his hair. Winn stared off vacantly. She could see the wheels turning.

"Look," she said, "think about customers the same way you did to remember Donna Overton. You said some of them were in costumes."

Slowly, with Claudia guiding each step, the roommates regurgitated faces. They'd seen Little Bo Peep. A gorilla—no, two gorillas. One dude made-up to look like Fred Flintstone. A woman trying to look like Madonna, only she didn't come close—a "heifer," Yastrepsky said, giggling. One guy with buffalo breath in an all-black costume. Another dressed as a Keystone Kop. Still another in a tuxedo and just a black mask.

The detective fired questions at them: Did any of the customers—think hard now, she said—did any of them come in around the same time as the medium? Did any of them stare at her? What all did these people buy? Did any of them just come in and not buy anything?

"Man, my brain's worn out," Yastrepsky complained. "Mind if I grab a beer while we talk?"

Claudia shrugged impatiently, then waited while he dug one out of a Styrofoam ice chest in the front of the truck.

"The guys in gorilla suits—I think they bought beer," said Yastrepsky, looking at his own.

Winn nodded. "Yeah. I think that's right."

Suppressing a sigh, not knowing how much was bullshit just to shut her up, she nodded for them to continue.

"Let's see . . . Madonna, I think she bought one of those little travel boxes of aspirin," said Yastrepsky.

"Bayer," added Winn. He looked up at Claudia, pleased. "I remember because she made some stupid joke about wishing it was a real drug."

"Hey, man, this is kind of like a game," said Yastrepsky. He took a swallow of beer. "It's like, um, free association."

"Yeah, well, free associate some more," said Claudia.

"Okay, okay, we're just warming up now," said Yastrepsky. He narrowed his eyes.

Claudia hoped it was for more than effect.

"All right. Here's another one, man. The guy in the all-black costume? The one with bad breath? He bought a bag of ice. Then he came back a little later and bought a second one."

"What else, what else?" Claudia asked irritably. She fished a cigarette from her pocket and lit up.

"Well," said Winn slowly, "the guy in the tuxedo, he picked up a package of corn chips—or some kind of chips—but then at the last minute he just put them down and walked out. That was kind of weird."

"Naw, people do that all the time," said Yastrepsky. "They get impatient in line, figure they can do without."

Yastrepsky and Winn argued the point until Claudia cut them off. The exercise was getting her nowhere. They remembered some of the customers in costume, and few who weren't, which stood to reason. But they couldn't be sure about who they saw when, and she finally let it go.

Maybe something would be important later. Meanwhile, luck had shown a benevolent streak. At least she had Donna Overton at the store. For what that was worth.

CHAPTER 23

BY THE TIME THE LIGHTS WENT OFF in the house, the man had been crouching in the shrubs for almost forty minutes. But he waited another twenty minutes, making sure. When he stood, cramps jackknifed through his calves. It was insignificant pain, though. What tormented him most was the voice screaming at him.

Her power was diminishing, but it wasn't gone. Not yet.

As silently as a lizard, the man weaved cautiously through the shrubs. They lined the six-foot privacy fence, affording protection intended for the homeowner. The big man liked that. Probability was working in his favor. He didn't feel nervous. Just purposeful. In a way, he had become something of a public servant. They should be thanking him, not hunting him down like some wild animal.

When he arrived at the back door, the odds doubled. With effort, he contained his delight. The lock was old and simple. He dismantled it with a screwdriver in less than two minutes and slipped from the shadows inside.

For a moment he hesitated, getting his bearings and waiting for his eyes to adjust to the dark. The voice had stopped, but it was just a trick, of course. Something to throw him off. He waited, head tilted, listening. Light snoring filtered from the bedroom. A clock gently drummed a steady beat. From the kitchen, he heard the refrigerator cycle on.

Slowly, each footstep as deliberate as a cat's, the man moved toward the bedroom. There were, he knew, two of them: a husband and wife. He would have to be swift.

When he rounded the corner of the bedroom door, partly in a crouch, the man paused long enough to caress the knotted tree branch he carried. Over two nights' time, he had sanded and polished the bottom of it to make the grip sure, and it felt good in his hands, even through the thin gloves. The weight was comfortable; the swing, excellent.

Their names were Harold and Betty Lancashire, he a psychic and she a medium. They cuddled like spoons, wrapped as one, a comforter pulled to the tops of their shoulders.

From the doorway, the man watched through dispassionate eyes as they slept. He took no joy in his mission, but neither did he feel remorse. The two were merely vessels, evil vessels for the voice—she more than he, but he would have to go, too.

In four steady paces, the man reached the bed. A floorboard creaked and Harold Lancashire stirred slightly. But his eyes never opened to see the thick branch when it rocketed toward his brain. And in the time it took for Betty Lancashire to pull away from dreams and open her mouth in sleep-drugged confusion, the branch was already whistling toward her face to silence her forever.

The man grunted heavily with each blow he delivered. Muscles bunched at his shoulders, tightening his forearms. He stood with his feet apart, the shirt pulling a little looser from his slacks every time he drew his arms up to raise the branch. Blood answered the strikes. In seconds, it tinted the perspiration on his face.

But he didn't stop. He raised the branch, brought it down repeatedly in precision blows until he could no longer recognize their faces. Two minutes passed. He waited, gulping air, watching the comforter spasmodically jerk where the woman's foot played out an erratic and final dance.

When he caught his breath, he leaned toward the bed. Wearily, he pulled the comforter down and reached for the woman's hand. The medium. He sucked in a final lungful of air, grabbed Betty Lancashire's right index finger, and snapped it backward. The woman was elderly and the finger broke as easily as if he had stepped on a twig.

After he pulled the comforter back up, the man looked down on the pair, satisfied. He listened: nothing from the voice.

CHAPTER 24

DRESSED LIKE A PROWLER, Claudia stood silently at the side of her daughter's bed and watched her sleep. One leg poked outside the covers, bent from the knee over the side of the bed. Headphones from a portable radio were still clamped to her head. The mother smiled and gently removed the headset. Robin never moved.

After closing the door, she went back to the dining room. Quarter to two in the morning. She pushed herself through a grueling round of exercise and reviewed her plan. Nothing could be left to chance. Then she scribbled a casual note. If her daughter woke, she would read that Claudia had been called in to work.

At five to three, the detective pulled her car to the edge of the Feather Ridge Golf Course where the fourteenth hole stood a hundred feet from a densely wooded area. Markos had chosen well. Nothing stirred, and from the fourteenth hole—a narrow dogleg that cut sharply right of the fairway—isolation was assured. He wanted her out in the open, in the middle of the green, shielded by nothing more than a prayer. Twice earlier, Claudia had reconnoitered the area, once at dusk and once in the dark. Knowing the layout shored her confidence. Still, her best guess at what he might do remained but a guess; she had to be sure what she would do.

Guided only by the dim illumination of a half moon, she stepped away from her car, pausing briefly to get her bearings. If Markos had driven, she saw nothing of his vehicle. But she knew he was here somewhere. He would have made a point of arriving long before she, watching to ensure that she had come alone.

Cautiously, Claudia began her perambulation toward the fourteenth hole, a tiny plug swallowed by dark and marked only by memory. When she got there, she turned around and scanned the woods, identifiable now only as a splotch slightly darker than the open area around it. She waited, not moving.

Markos's first surprise was coming up behind her. The detective hadn't heard his steps across the soft grass, and she stiffened when she felt the revolver against the back of her neck.

"Looks like you don't know your way around a golf course any more than you know your way around a lake," he said with a trace of amusement in his voice.

"Put your gun away, Markos." Claudia labored to inject authority in her tone. "Weapons weren't part of the deal."

"Well, now, I guess you weren't listening too well," he said. "I told *you* not to bring anything. I didn't say I wouldn't." He chuckled from the throat. "Now turn around."

When she did, the big man ordered her to hold her arms out. Reluctantly, she complied.

Markos clucked disapprovingly at the gun clipped to her waist. "Looks to me like you weren't listening at all, were you?"

Claudia shrugged.

"Of course, I figured as much," he said. "I figured you'd be carrying, but it's still a disappointment, Hershey. Now hand it over real slow."

With her left arm still outstretched, she carefully withdrew the .38 from its trouser holster. She held it out. Markos took the weapon, examined it briefly, then tucked it in his waistband.

"So okay, Markos. Can we get down to business now?" Claudia started to lower her arms.

"Uh-uh. Back up. That's better." He casually waved his gun. "We're not done yet." A faint smile showed through his beard. "Take your jacket off, and then your pants."

Claudia's breath caught in her throat. Markos's second surprise.

An owl hooted low and mournfully. When it stopped, the only sound she heard was her own uneven breathing. "You're out of your mind," she said slowly.

The man's smile broadened. He was enjoying himself. "That's not very polite for a lady," he said. "But then, you're really not a lady. You're a cop. A pig with tits." Markos's eyes narrowed. He brought the gun level with her chest. "Strip, Hershey."

Claudia's heart banged erratically. She measured the distance between them. No good. If she charged him, she would be dead before she made contact. And stalling would change nothing.

Hesitantly, she shucked the jacket. She kicked off her shoes. When she stepped out of her slacks, stumbling once, the material swished audibly against her skin. Throughout, her eyes held his face. She tossed the slacks on top of the jacket.

The ankle holster with its silver-plated .22 showed clearly.

"Not much more than a peashooter, but I'll take it anyway," he said. There was no surprise in his voice.

Claudia handed it over, shivering. "Satisfied, you bastard?"

"Now the shirt," said Markos. "Let's go the distance."

"Come on, Markos. It's damned cold out here. There's nothing else on me."

"Just do it."

When she stood free of her clothes, he made her rotate once. His eyes traveled leisurely up and down her body. Then he nodded approvingly.

"Very, very nice," he said in a husky voice.

But indecision threaded his tone. Claudia heard it, understanding suddenly that although his original intent was merely to disarm her—perhaps humiliate her, demonstrate her vulnerability—there stood but a fragile moment before he might bow to more.

She couldn't let him take it.

Swiftly, she reached over and picked up her shirt. She snapped it casually, as if she were merely shaking off wrinkles at a launderette.

"All right, Markos," she said briskly, sliding the shirt over her arms. "You've got my weapons. You've had your fun, but the show's over. Let's get down to business. I'm freezing my butt off."

Without waiting for a reply, she snagged her pants from the slick grass. The man grunted something, but he didn't stop her, and she finished dressing quickly.

Claudia ran a hand through her hair. She glared at him. "You either talk to me now, and fast, or I'm leaving."

"Slow down," he said. He gestured with the gun. "I'm still making the rules."

"Markos, what do you want from me?" she said, not even bothering to keep the exasperation from her voice. "If you called me out here to talk, talk. If you called me out here to shoot me, then shoot me. Otherwise, screw you, I'm out of here, and believe me, you won't find another cop in this state who's even mildly interested in what you have to say."

A cloud scuttled past the half moon, momentarily drawing a blanket over what little light touched down. When it passed and Claudia could see again, Markos was pulling a cigarette from his jacket pocket. He shook one loose, then held the pack toward her.

She took one, waited for him to light both. The gun remained in his hand, but he lowered it. They both took a step back, watching each other.

Smoke rose around Markos's face. He shifted his weight to one hip. "That guy who put out the reward money on me . . . ."

"Matheson?"

"Yeah, him. He's the one who killed Donna." He took a pull on his cigarette. "He's the son of a bitch you should be after."

Claudia felt her heart buck, but she looked at Markos with practiced skepticism on her face. "This is it? This is the best you can do?" she asked. "Matheson's the bad guy and you're really just a victim."

Agitated, he fumbled with his pocket again. He thrust a sheet of paper toward her. It was badly rumpled from many creases.

Squinting, the detective said, "What am I looking at, Markos? It's too damned dark to read anything."

From another pocket, he produced a penlight. He handed it to Claudia. "That's a page from the back of Donna's scheduling book. Matheson was paying her to keep her mouth shut about his wife's visits. Donna told me the wife said Matheson hated her seeing a medium. Said he was worried it would ruin his career if the public found out."

She ran the penlight quickly over the page.

"He also hated that she blabbed everything under the sun," Markos continued. He blew a plume of smoke. "Man had a couple of women on the side. And he had a couple of interesting business deals on the side."

It was all there, in neatly penned notations. Full names. Dates. Amounts.

"I figure that some expert somewhere can verify that the handwriting is Donna's," said Markos. "And someone can probably verify that the page came out of the scheduling book, which I'm sure you cops now have."

Claudia nodded to herself more than to Markos. "So Donna was blackmailing him?" she asked.

"No," he said impatiently. "She'd never do something like that. Too prissy."

"What, then?"

"Look, Matheson approached Donna when he found out his wife was seeing her. He'd already told the wife to stop, but she didn't. She just changed the days she was going. But when Matheson figured that out, his next move was to pay Donna to keep her mouth shut about everything. See, he offered her the money."

"Quite a boost to her income," Claudia said. "But so what? It's not exactly illegal."

"Not at first, but it got to be that way."

"Like how?"

"Like when I found out about it." Markos shrugged. "See, Donna, she never liked the arrangement. Oh, she loved the money all right, but it made her real nervous. Me, I felt real comfortable with it. Fact is, I thought it should be more."

Big surprise, thought Claudia. "Go on," she said.

"I put the squeeze on the son of a bitch, and he upped the payments. Hell, he had the juice."

She was beginning to understand.

Markos flicked his cigarette away. It glowed briefly on the dewy grass. "I didn't tell Donna right away, but the first time Matheson doubled the amount it all came out."

"So what you did, Markos, was turn things into an extortion scheme."

"You're pretty bright for a cop." He smiled thinly. "That's exactly what I did. Matheson's filthy rich. He could afford it."

"What went wrong?"

"Donna." Shaking his head, Markos said, "I should've known. Me and her, we was oil and water. A bad mix. It was really a simple shakedown, no big deal, but it bothered her more and more. We fought about it. Finally, she booted me out of her life. Said good-bye."

"You're really an enterprising soul," Claudia said dryly. She crushed her cigarette. "Did Donna know about your drug dealing, or the supply behind the medicine chest?"

Markos looked up. "No to both. Aw, she could've if she'd ever given it much thought, what with the way I'd come and go. But I don't think she wanted to know much about me—you know, what you don't know can't hurt you."

"Hardly true in Donna's case," she muttered.

"Anyway, it was the drugs that made me go back," he continued. "I gave it a while—figured the hell with the Matheson thing and the hell with Donna—but the drugs, uh-uh. No way was I gonna let more'n twenty G's in good dope sit in her house."

"Oh, but you're a cold bastard," said Claudia.

"Go to hell!" Markos leveled the gun at the detective briefly, but it was just for show. "It wasn't that way at all. Truth is, I liked her. Maybe loved her, best I could."

"You had a funny way of showing it."

Ignoring her, he said, "I tried to talk to Donna a few times, but she wasn't having none of it. Then I figured I'd just slip in quiet-like one night, cozy up to her, make nice, maybe she'd come around."

"And even if you couldn't salvage the relationship, you could get your drugs."

"Right. And I could get my drugs." Markos sighed. His voice softened. "The night I went back—Halloween—I let myself in through the front door. Still had the key. I was a little surprised the lights were still on because Donna usually went to bed by eleven at the latest, and this was, I don't know, maybe one, two in the morning."

Katydids began shrieking in unison. Claudia waited, studying Markos's expression. His eyes blindly wandered the flat grass.

"I found her on the kitchen floor, and I . . . I didn't recognize her. I went over to her, bent down, tried to lift her some. She was gone, though."

It explained Overton's blood on his shirt. If his explanation were true. "So what you did was run," said Claudia.

Markos looked up. "Hell, yeah, I ran. I knew I'd be first on the cops' hit parade. But it was Matheson who killed her—or had someone kill her. Had to be. And the other broad, too. She was Donna's best friend. Donna probably told her everything."

"Interesting theory," she said finally, "but so what? Matheson may be slime, and he may have had good reasons to protect his political career, but that doesn't make him a murderer. No jury on earth will buy it."

"They will if someone investigates him as thoroughly as I'm being investigated," Markos said darkly. He pointed at the paper in Claudia's hands. "Doesn't that tell you anything?"

"All right," she conceded. "It's a start. And I'll look into it."

He exhaled slowly. "At first I thought I could handle this. Murder's not exactly uncommon in this state. There'd be some new hits and the push for me would taper off, at least enough for me to breathe."

"You figured wrong."

"Yeah. And I can't keep running. I also don't want to be shot down like a dog."

Claudia said nothing. She folded the paper twice and stuck it in her pocket. Then she moved to hand Markos the penlight. A quarter-inch shy of his hand, she let it slip from her fingers. It fell to the grass with a barely audible thud.

They bent simultaneously to retrieve the instrument, and in that second Claudia made her move. She delivered an awkward shin kick to the inside of Markos's leg, then deftly landed a hammer fist to the top and middle of his forearm.

He bellowed. His gun flew behind him and skittered across the wet lawn. When he whirled to fumble for it, she dove for the fourteenth hole. The snub-nosed .38 she'd planted there earlier was as she'd left it. She plucked the revolver out, rolled once, and from a flat-belly position took aim.

"Freeze, Markos! I got you sighted, and even as dark as it is, at four feet I won't miss." Claudia pulled the hammer back, letting him hear the unmistakable click. "Put your hands to the moon. We're playing by *my* rules now."

Breathing hard, the man turned slowly, his hands raised. "You bitch," he said.

"You're being melodramatic," she responded evenly. She exhaled and rose carefully, her arms outstretched and steady. "You should be grateful, Markos. Someone else would shoot you down like a rabid dog. I'm going to let you live."

For a moment, Claudia flirted with the idea of making him strip.

She would not forgive him for the private performance he'd forced her into. But naw. Except for the disrobing, their meeting went more or less as planned. He'd found the guns she'd intended him to find, and not the one she didn't. Believing her defenseless, he'd relaxed just enough for her to create an opportunity.

She tried to tell herself it hadn't been as close as it was.

"Let's go, ace. And don't be stupid and try anything," Claudia warned. She collected the weapons. "I'm tired. I'm cold. And I'm cranky. It would take very, very little for me to pull the trigger, and we both know it."

With the gun trained on Markos's back, she walked him back to her car. Along the way, she gave him the Miranda spiel.

Then: Two counts of murder one. Possession and distribution of drugs. Extortion. False imprisonment of a police officer. There would probably be others, but it was a good start.

"You silly, freaking bitch," Markos said sourly as Claudia forced him across the hood of the car. "I didn't kill anyone!"

She produced a set of handcuffs and a set of leg cuffs. In moments, he was secured. She turned him around and held the gun at nose level.

"Your status as a murderer is for jurors to decide," she said mildly. "My job is to take you into custody before someone beats the breath out of you and deprives them of that opportunity."

Let him sweat it.

Prodding him with the gun, Claudia forced Markos into the trunk. He cursed violently.

Smiling, she slammed the lid, then rapped the top with her keys. "Don't worry, Mr. Markos," she called out cheerfully. "The car's department issue. It's a piece of shit, complete with air holes courtesy of lots of rust. So relax. Just close your eyes and enjoy the ride. I'm an excellent driver."

With her trophy in the trunk, Claudia drove back to the station, humming to classical music on an all-night station.

CHAPTER 25

PULLING RANK WAS AN OPTION Claudia had exercised sparingly, and casually at best, since her arrival in Indian Run.

First, need rarely dictated it. Her role was foremost that of a detective. The lieutenant title she'd brought from Cleveland served solely as glitz to shore up the small department's faltering status with the town council. She understood.

Second, Sergeant Ron Peters was a capable, if somewhat unimaginative, organizer whose methodical ways kept patrolmen in all the right places at all the right times. Indeed, scheduling was the most taxing part of his supervisory duties. A lieutenant was overkill, and Claudia accepted that.

Third, there was Chief Mac Suggs. He liked his image as the paternal father, ruler of the roost, chief honcho, law enforcement deity. And no, there would be no graven images before him—especially no female graven images. Claudia had a little more trouble with that one.

Finally, because most officers were good-old-boys born and bred in Indian Run or in "them parts thereabout," with few exceptions they viewed her as they would some exotic species who had somehow slipped past customs and might harbor unknown viruses. At best, she could expect indifference. At worst, sullen resentment. Claudia made do.

After all, if it ain't broke, don't fix it. In that context, being a lieutenant was superfluous and remained that way until fifteen minutes past her arrival at the police station with Tom Markos.

It was four-fifteen in the morning when Claudia pulled up. The station should have been deserted, a token salute to safety. But lights blazed from the windows. Patrol cars lined the street out front. Voices rode the cool night air.

One eye on the station entrance, one eye on Markos, she eased her prisoner out of the trunk. He glared hatefully, but the steam had gone out of him and he said nothing. Claudia hustled him inside, depositing him on the scarred bench beside the front desk.

An old cracker named Stan Caruthers held down the desk as night duty officer. Caruthers, with a wisp of oily gray hair combed over his bald pate, was something of a mascot. Long past retirement age, he nevertheless refused to give up police work, even though at night it amounted to little beyond an occasional call about a barking dog. That was fine by Officer Stan, as he was affectionately known. After all, the best old movies were shown in the predawn hours, and since most were not in color, the small black-and-white set on the desk suited him just fine. But the TV was off right now, and he did a double take when he saw Claudia with Markos in tow.

"I don't believe what my eyes are relayin' to my brain!" he drawled, peering over the top of half-moon glasses. "You got Markos already! Wait'll the chief—"

Claudia waved an impatient hand. "What's going on here?"

"Say what?" The officer's milky eyes registered confusion.

"I said, what's going on here?"

Caruthers shook his head slowly. "You're foolin' with me, right? You got this-here fella in bracelets and you don't know?"

"Obviously not," said Claudia irritably. She could hear the chief's voice booming in the back somewhere. "You want to fill me in, Stan? Please?"

"Well, hell's bells, honey! You've just become the best part of it!"

"Come on, Stan. Quickly, quickly! What's up?"

"Well, all right, then." Caruthers adopted his best storytelling pose. "Not more'n twenty minutes ago two more bodies turned up, blood so fresh on 'em you could paint with it," he said. "A husband and wife, dead in bed. He was one of them-there psychics. She was a . . . whatchacallit . . .a medium." Caruthers shot Markos a dark look. "Now ain't that just some kind of coincidence, huh?"

What little flesh showed between Markos's beard and eyebrows turned white as enamel. His lips moved, but nothing came out. His eyes sought Claudia's.

"Shit!" said Claudia. She slapped the desk counter with her hand. "Who found the bodies?"

"A grandson, some young pup who was spendin' the night." Caruthers gave Claudia a doleful look. "Poor kid, the noise woke him up. Must've been terrified. Hard to say how long it was before he even peeked out. Claims he didn't see nuthin'."

"How old's the boy?"

"Five, I hear-tell. His parents are on their way to collect him."

"Who's on the scene right now?"

"Moody, and Carella's on the way."

Claudia nodded. They could hold things until she got there. "Crime techs out?"

"They been called."

"Okay. Give me the short version fast, Stan."

Delighted, the old officer filled her in, disappointed when she interrupted him or hurried him along. It was a moment he would relive for a long time. He didn't want to be deprived.

"All right. Look, get Markos processed and into lockup, and start pushing the paperwork," Claudia told him. "I'll—"

"Son of a bitch! This is a total crock! You can't railroad me for—"

She whirled on the big man. "Shut up, Markos."

Turning back to Stan, she said, "I'll take care of the reports later. There's going to be a bunch." She reeled off a list of felony charges and put Markos's revolver on the desk. "Tag this and get it in the evidence locker. I've got to go find the chief." As she was leaving, she heard Officer Stan telling Markos that yessir, boy, he was in a heap of trouble.

Claudia pushed past three patrolmen and into Suggs's office. The chief was shouting into the phone, red-faced and sweating. He slammed the receiver down the moment his eyes fell on his detective.

"Where in hell have you been, Hershey?" he roared. "Markos is makin' fools of us and dog meat out of the people we're supposed to be protectin', but you're not at home. You're not—"

"I've been—"

"—answerin' your portable. Your vehicle ain't showin' on any street. We got ourselves a double homicide and—"

"I just—"

"—the one homicide dick I got is out carousin' like a bitch in heat!"

She let him go on, watched him pop Tums, listened to him catalog sins and omissions and invoke God's name in every conceivable way. Waste of time, he called her. High heels lookin' for brains. A disgrace to the fine callin' of law enforcement.

A cluster of officers gathered just outside the office. This was good theater, fodder for weeks of stories. And still she let him go on, until he was spent, physiology demanding that he pause for air.

Then she quietly closed the door, her posture betraying nothing to the cops just outside. But when she turned back to Suggs there was heat in her eyes.

"You're a blind man, Suggs, a clown in costume," Claudia said hotly, wielding words like a blunt instrument. "You want so badly to protect your image and believe that Indian Run is sacrosanct that you're willing to trade justice for expediency."

"Just a damned minute, Hershey. I—"

"No! *You* wait a minute, Suggs, because I'm not finished." Claudia crossed to the chief's desk. Her voice rose slightly. "I've got your Tom Markos right outside this door. I picked him up tonight and—"

"That lowlife's right here?"

"Shut up and listen to me!" she hissed. "He'll do hard time for pushing drugs. And you can throw the rest of the murders at him and maybe even make a circumstantial case for at least Overton's death. But in the end, when it goes to a jury, he won't do time for murder because he didn't have anything to do with them—not hers, not these latest two, and not Avery's."

"That's rubbish, Hershey, and I've had just about enough of it." Suggs grappled for a Tums. "Your stubborn streak's rubbed out any common sense you might've had."

"No, sir!" Claudia violently shook her head. "The time of death on this Lancashire couple is going to show he's innocent—I don't need a medical examiner's report to know it—and if you book Markos now, you're going to be eating your badge in front of the whole town while more people die."

She told him about the meeting at the fourteenth hole, the sequence of events, the timing. She told him about Matheson, quickly showed him the paper, explained its significance, that it implicated him at least as strongly as Markos, but like Markos, not strongly enough. Suggs looked at Claudia a little less certainly.

"What you have is some sick animal out there, Chief." She inhaled. "He's a sociopath, and that makes him a loose cannon. Donna Overton was his first victim, and probably for a specific reason. Somehow, she set him off. The others—Avery and Betty Lancashire, anyway—they're dead just because they talk to spirits. That means something to your killer, something a whole lot more involved than what we can even guess at."

The chief grunted. "I don't know," he said lamely. He rubbed his eyes. "It don't make sense. It—"

"It does make sense," Claudia insisted. "It makes sense to him, and he will kill again."

Suggs looked away. He stared at the wall, at the mounted fish. "You're talking about a serial killer, aren't you, Hershey? The worst kind. Someone who doesn't play by the rules."

"Yes, maybe." Claudia thought about it. "But he's not a serial killer in any conventional sense, at least I don't think so. Doesn't fit the profile."

"Meaning what?" The chief turned back to her.

"Meaning—I don't know—ninety percent of the known serial killers murder because of some sexual drive, some perversity that compels them to kill again and again. We already know our killer's not in this for sexual thrills."

"Then we're in way over our heads."

"Not necessarily." Claudia paused to light a cigarette, most of the venom out. "There's a certain logic to what this guy is doing. Overton's death, I think, was spontaneous, but not random. She did something or said something that triggered him, and probably at some point when they'd met."

"But we've been over the client list, friends, associates. We've gone full circle on that."

"Yeah, we have, but we're still missing something, something that's right under our noses." Smoke drifted to the ceiling, where countless cigarettes had already colored the acoustical panels a dull yellow. "Look. Every indication is that Overton let him in, and only a few minutes after she got home. He might not have planned to kill her, for that matter. But rage, whatever was building, exploded. He bashed her hard and fast, intentionally broke a finger, and got out. Then he knocked over the jack-o'-lantern and probably left a footprint in it—"

"Which we'd have if Ridley hadn't mucked up the crime scene," Suggs muttered.

"Yeah. Anyway, he didn't stop to make it look like a robbery. He didn't knock himself out covering his trail. In Avery's, he did. But he also left his signature with that finger. Whatever it means to him, he has to do it. And this couple tonight, I bet we'll find the same thing."

Suggs pinched his nose between a finger and thumb, thinking. "Then I guess there's only one question, Hershey." The chief looked up. "Can you find this guy? Stop him?"

"Maybe. Yes, I think so. But not your way."

"Meaning?"

Claudia hitched an eyebrow. "Meaning I need full authority out there"—Claudia gestured behind her—"full authority over every man, every move. And with your complete backing. I can't be second-guessed. I *won't* be second-guessed."

"That's a lot," Suggs said stonily.

"We've both made mistakes with this, Chief." She reflexively removed her glasses, gave them a quick rub on her shirt. "Me, I came here to get myself and my daughter away from the underbelly of police work—I wanted to take us away from all of that. So I've been half stepping. I've let my instincts and experience be diluted because resisting, having to prove myself, pisses me off. And you, you've encouraged that because I'm not the package you thought you bought."

"Hershey, I don't know if I'll ever really take to you," he began slowly. "You got a way about you that, aw hell, just rubs me wrong."

"Granted, my bedside manner leaves something to be desired."

A weary half-smile found its way to Suggs's face. "Yeah. Something like that."

"So?"

"So, looks like—"

The door flew open, and the old night duty officer pushed in, breathing heavily. "We got a problem with that feller that's been brung in, that—"

"Markos?" Claudia said sharply.

Caruthers nodded, panting. "Yeah, some of the boys, they—"

Before he finished, she was out the door. Commotion sounded from the all-purpose room.

Markos was on the floor, on his knees. Bobby Ridley, the officer who had taken the original call on Donna Overton, gripped him from behind. Standing over Markos was Lester Fry, a fleshy patrol officer whose father had been on the force before him. Fry had a reputation for using his fists on the streets; he was using them now.

Mesmerized, a half dozen patrolmen stood in a semi-circle around them.

"Fry!" yelled Claudia. "Get your hands off of him!"

Fry paused with one arm raised. He smiled insolently. "What's the matter, Detective? Haven't you ever seen a man take a tumble down the stairs before?" His fist chopped Markos's kidney with a thwack.

"Let him go!" Claudia made her way toward the fray. She shoved a patrolman out of her way. "I said, let him go!"

Thwack! Thwack!

"Move, damn it," she muttered, pushing her way forward. When she got to Fry she grabbed a handful of shirt and yanked back, grunting with the effort. He stumbled, cursing. But before he could push her off, Claudia slammed him against a wall, hard. She pulled him off, then threw him against it again.

Fry roared, and tried to break her hold. But she sought the pressure point under his nose with a finger, and jabbed up. Tears sprang to Fry's eyes; his hands closed around his nose.

Claudia grabbed his collar and put her face in close. "You're history, Fry." She whirled, aimed a finger at Ridley. "You too. Both of you."

"Wait a minute!" said Ridley, looking wildly around for support. He pointed at Markos, who lay curled on the floor, blood seeping from his mouth and nose. "This guy made me into a fool! He's—"

"You made yourself into a fool, Bobby," said Claudia.

"But—"

"But nothing. Turn in your badge and your gun." She turned back to Fry. "Yours, too."

"You bitch," said Fry. He touched his nose gingerly. "You have no right."

"I have every right, Fry." Claudia gave him room, stepped back. She took them all in. The chief stood silently at the door, watching. "You crossed the line here, and we both know it. Wearing a badge doesn't give you license to do what you just did, and I won't have it."

Eyes riveted to Suggs.

He sighed and said gruffly, "You heard the lieutenant, and she speaks for me. 'Bout time y'all figured that out. You, Ridley—and you, Fry—you're out of here."

Claudia and Suggs locked eyes. Then she rattled off instructions, pivoted, and left, snagging Sergeant Peters on her way out of the room.

"I'm going out to the Lancashire house," she told him. "While I'm gone, get someone to rouse Matheson and bring him in here. I'll be sending Moody back here. I want him to sweat Matheson and find out where Eleanor is."

Peters's eyes widened. "We don't have jurisdiction."

Claudia nodded. "Don't worry about it. He's still part of a murder investigation. Meantime, I'll take the heat."

"You know he won't come without a lawyer."

"Fine by me."

"Oh, boy."

"And Ron, get someone else to round up Lucille Schuster. I don't care if she has to sit in this station for the next two days. She's going to remember more than she's told me, before she leaves."

Claudia spent a few minutes with Suggs, then grabbed her purse to go. As she strode toward the station-house door, every eye was on her. No one said a word.

CHAPTER 26

THE INDEX FINGER WAS BROKEN, snapped as casually as a pencil. Claudia gently replaced the woman's hand, then signaled the crime-scene technician to move in close for a photograph of the finger.

"His, too?" The technician gestured at Harold Lancashire's still form.

She shook her head. Not necessary. He was a psychic, not a medium; his finger had been left untouched. The killer sought those who spoke to spirits. Anyone else in his way was incidental. And the finger—it held particular significance for the killer. It fueled him further, somehow. It told his story.

But what?

What?

It was Tuesday, six-fifteen in the morning. Claudia had been up around the clock. She needed food, coffee. She had to touch base with her daughter, something more than the telephone calls that tied them together lately. She yearned for a shower.

With a final look at Betty Lancashire, Claudia stepped outside. Garish red and blue lights pulsed significantly from patrol cars. Mitch Moody spotted her, came over.

"I heard about the excitement at the station. How are you holding up?" he asked.

"I've been better." She cleared her throat. Too many cigarettes. "Anything from the canvass?"

Moody shook his head. "Not so far. We banged on every door, but nobody saw anything. Nobody heard anything. Our best bet is still the boy, but his parents aren't letting us within a foot of him."

Claudia nodded. "Where are they?"

Moody gestured toward a parked van. "The boy's sleeping, and the parents are waiting for you, but they're real, real itchy. They want to get him home."

"Understandable." She pulled at a cramp in her shoulder muscle. "I'll go talk to them in a minute."

"By the way," he said, "you connect with Carella yet?"

"No."

"Yeah, well, he's been dogging that lawn boy—"

"Billy Pyle?"

Moody nodded. "The kid's got a thing with peeking in windows, all right, but from everything Carella could find out, he wouldn't as much as pull the wings off a fly. Dumb as a lamb, but gentle as one too."

"Emory's sure?"

"As much as he can be." He shrugged. "Still making a couple of checks on his own, but he told me this morning he doesn't think they'll go anywhere. You know"—Moody scratched an ear, looked down—"a couple of us, uh, got a little uncomfortable about how best to play our hands, what with the way Chief Suggs was blustering about Markos and all—"

"Look, it's okay, Mitch."

"No, no, I need to say this." Moody sought Claudia's eyes. "We should've stayed with you all the way. Carella at least followed up, but—"

"Forget it, Mitch. Really."

It was always there with cops, the guilt, the backward look, the idea that if only they'd done this instead of that, if only they'd made one last call, one last follow-up, pointless death would simply stop.

"I've been around the same blocks you have, Mitch," she said gently. "I just went around them first. That's all. Let's just let it go, all right?"

After a brief pause, Moody said, "Okay. Um, what next? You want me to head back to the station? I don't think there's anything else I can do out here. Crime techs'll be here another hour or so."

"Where's the M.E.?" asked Claudia. "He should've come and gone by now."

"Car trouble."

"Great."

She thought for a minute. "Tell you what, Mitch. Go on back. Peters radioed in that Matheson got there about ten minutes ago. Kicked and screamed the whole way, and he's furious. And his lawyer's on the way."

"Ouch."

"Uh-huh, but we can turn that to our advantage." Claudia gave Moody a sharp look. "Don't cave in. Push him, and push him hard. I talked to Suggs and he'll be in there with you, ready to lay some old-fashioned fire and brimstone on Matheson. Let Matheson know he's all alone. Two things need to come out of your interview: an admission that he was feeding Overton with hush money and a location where we can find his wife."

Moody shook his head. "He'll never go for it."

"Yes he will," said Claudia. She smiled thinly. "He'll give up

Eleanor for an opportunity to distance himself from Overton and Markos."

"You're convinced he's got Eleanor stashed somewhere?"

"Not a doubt in my mind," she answered firmly. "And what you need to do is show him that we're prepared to believe him where Overton is concerned, and keep it quiet—if he plays ball on Eleanor."

"But actually, Eleanor's nothing we even have to worry about. It's Flagg's case."

"We need her," she said.

"I don't get it."

"Politics, Mitch. One-upmanship. We're about to look like jack-asses because Sug—" Claudia bit her tongue. "—because we've been pushing Markos as the killer. Now we're taking it back, and we're about to alarm everyone with the prospect of a crazy out there. It's not going to go down well."

"Basically, you're talking damage control."

"More like survival. The press is going to be all over us," said Claudia. "We've got to cut all ties to Markos and Matheson fast, and the two are so bound together that this is the only way we can. If we don't eat our mistakes now, we'll be eating bigger ones later. Some-one—maybe even the governor—will send down a task force to take over. We'll never get a chance to pursue the leads we need to."

"What leads?" asked Moody, exasperation showing. "We don't have any leads."

"Yeah," said Claudia briskly. "We do."

The boy wore pajamas printed with floppy-eared puppies. A speck of blood half the size of a dime stained one leg cuff. The parents hadn't noticed. Right now, they were grateful believing he hadn't seen his dead grandparents. He had, though. He may have seen the killer.

Christine and John Dillard watched protectively as Claudia gently closed her hands around the boy's. His name was John Joseph Dillard Jr., but everyone called him J. J. to avoid confusion with his father. He had soft eyes moist with tears and round with fear.

All of them were crammed in the back of the Dillards' van. The parents refused to bring the boy anywhere near the house. The van served as a cocoon.

Claudia hated herself for having to do this, but there was no choice. She smiled at J. J., asked him about puppies, about games, about his favorite cartoons, anything to warm him up, to compel trust in a night where it had been shattered. Her eyes never left his face. Her hands stayed on his, a tiny polygraph for truth.

Then, finally: "J. J., honey, you know how it is when you watch a really scary show, and it's hard to go to sleep because you think the bad guys are hiding somewhere? That maybe they're in your closet?"

"Monsters!" said J. J.

Claudia gave his hands an approving squeeze. "Right! Monsters." She thought rapidly. "Did you ever see a monster yourself, J. J.?"

The boy nodded solemnly.

"You did?"

He nodded again.

"All by yourself?"

"Mm-hmm."

"Wow, that must have been scary! And you must have been awfully brave to look."

J. J.'s mother was holding him on her lap. The boy tucked his face into her arm. She stiffened visibly. "I think that's enough, Detective," she said in a low voice.

Claudia released one hand long enough to hold a finger to her lips. She shook her head, gave Christine Dillard a cautious look.

"J. J.," she said, rubbing her hand over the child's, "you saw a monster tonight, didn't you?"

There was no response.

"What did the monster look like?" Claudia persisted. "Big?"

Almost imperceptibly, J. J. shook his head affirmatively.

"Look at me, honey," she coaxed. "Please?"

Reluctantly, J. J. turned his face back.

"The monster was big. As big as me?"

J. J.'s eyes drifted up and down Claudia. He nodded.

"What else did the monster look like, J. J.?"

"Black," the boy answered.

Black. A black man? Or merely dressed in black? The detective probed gently, consciously framing everything in terms of a monster.

"Black everywhere," J. J. said finally, "only not his face. And he had . . . he had shiny eyes and big black circles around his eyes."

Puzzled, Claudia said, "Like a raccoon?"

The boy turned to his mother. "What's a r'coon?"

"It's a fuzzy animal, baby. You remember. It has big black rings around its eyes."

"Like a r'coon!" he announced triumphantly to Claudia. "A monster r'coon!"

She rewarded him with a smile. Good. Make it a game. Distance it from reality. That would come later, in nightmares, at odd moments. One day, in adult grief.

"Did the monster have antennas, J. J.? Did he carry anything with him?"

Feeling his small hand tense in her own, Claudia wished she could take it back. Too late. J. J. furrowed his brow. He began to cry, and he pulled away again.

"No more," John Dillard said sharply. "Please leave now."

Claudia patted the boy's hand. "You're a good boy, J. J."

She looked at the parents tiredly and thanked them. Dawn was breaking when she got out of the van. She stretched, rotated her shoulders.

Dear God. The boy had seen it all.

Because he had, Claudia knew where to look.

CHAPTER 27

CLAUDIA SLEPT WITHOUT MOVING for three hours. She didn't think she'd drift off, but she did. When she woke, ravenous, Robin had already left for school. They'd missed each other coming and going.

After a shower, a hit-and-miss round of exercises, and a long overdue, bone-numbing, two-mile jog, she went back to the station. Suggs had gone home, but Mitch Moody was still there, weary but jubilant.

"I'll be damned if you weren't right, Claudia," he said. "Matheson stormed and threatened, but he opened up easier than canned tuna."

Claudia exhaled relief. "So where is our misguided Eleanor Matheson?"

"Hold on, just a sec." Moody went to his desk and shuffled through notes. "Some place in Orlando called Pyramid. It's a pricey psychiatric center. Has a spa, workout room, tennis courts, and shrinks who don't bat an eye the whole time they're charging you $200 an hour. She's there under an assumed name."

Claudia whistled. "And?"

"And—you'll love this—Matheson freaked when he saw the notes Overton kept of the money changing hands." Moody blew a kiss in the direction of Markos's cell. "The lawyer kept advising him not to say anything, but Matheson told him to shut up.

"Anyhow, turns out that for the first two payments—the ones for a thousand bucks—Overton and Matheson met in a parking lot at a Publix store in Flagg. He'd give her an envelope. But when the price went up he had one of his flunkies make the drop to her home personally. And even though Markos upped the ante, Matheson swears he thought Overton was just as much involved.

"He said he was desperate, trying to figure out what in the hell to do to turn things around when she was killed. And then when we came to visit, he went over the bend and concocted this business about Eleanor doing a Houdini act. He's begging us not to let the media know."

Claudia laughed. "Good job, Mitch." They exchanged high fives.

"I can't claim credit for the whole thing," said Mitch. He shook his head admiringly. "You should've seen Suggs. He rode Matheson like a cowboy on a rodeo bull."

The image elicited a chuckle. But Claudia's expression turned serious again almost immediately. "What about Lucille Schuster? Right now I need her more than Matheson."

"She flat-out refused to come. Told Benny—"

"Puppy face? That new guy on patrol?"

"Uh, yeah," said Mitch uncomfortably.

"Damn it, Mitch. Someone with a little experience should've been hitting her." She sighed. "Never mind. That was up to Peters. What'd she say?"

"She told Benny she'd talked to us enough. As far as she was concerned, she'd done her civic duty—that's how Benny says she put it—and she wouldn't even hear of riding in with him."

"That was it?"

"Told Benny it was her bottom line."

"That's what she said, huh?"

"That was it."

Claudia glanced at her watch. Ten-thirty. "I bet I can make her change her mind."

Lucille Schuster was leaning against her desk, serenely quoting Dickens, when Claudia stormed into her classroom unannounced. Thirty-two heads swiveled toward the door. Any break in routine was welcomed. Schuster's face turned white.

When the detective reached the woman, she turned her back to the class. The kids couldn't see her face. They couldn't hear her words. To judge intent, they didn't have to.

"Mrs. Schuster," Claudia said so quietly the teacher had to lean in to hear, "I'm investigating four homicides that occurred in less than a month. It makes me very edgy. Do you follow me so far?"

Lucille Schuster nodded mutely.

"Good, because when I'm edgy to begin with, I tend to take it personally when people ignore my invitations. Still with me?"

The woman blinked furiously and nodded.

"Excellent."

"I—"

"Don't interrupt."

The teacher whispered an apology.

"You ignored my invitation to review a tape with me this morning, a reasonable request which the young but fully certified Officer Benjamin Kramer was good enough to convey on my behalf. So now I'm here in person to issue the invitation all over again. Personally. I'll be exceedingly disappointed if you say no."

The clock in the room was of the old-fashioned variety, a big round job with a tick designed to throw sheer terror into students during exams.

Claudia heard it and allowed herself a thin smile. "Tick-tock, tick-tock, Mrs. Schuster," she said. "Are you going to join me over coffee back at the station now, or would you prefer to think it over in a cell?"

The teacher tensed. "I, um, I . . . what about them?" She gestured plaintively toward her class.

Claudia turned and took a lingering look at the students, smiling. "Well, now," she said quietly, her eyes still on the kids, "we're both government employees, aren't we?"

"I . . . yes, I guess."

There would be hell to pay for this later, but Claudia's ugly mood was gaining on her. Turning full face to the students, she swept her arms magnanimously and said, "Class dismissed."

The first time Claudia watched the video, she'd been mildly amused by the Halloween costumes, the absurdity of the party. Grown men and women playing dress-up, showing off as geisha girls, clowns, Zorro, Abe Lincoln . . . .

Right now, the third time into the video in as many hours, She wasn't amused at all. And Schuster—the most she'd learned from the woman was that Overton had been paid with two $50 bills. It further established that the medium had stopped at the 7-Eleven, using one of the fifties to buy a pack of cigarettes.

Schuster sat stiffly, her forehead furrowed as she watched the tape journey the length of the party. Now and then she offered commentary, but nothing she hadn't already said, and nothing of consequence.

Claudia fantasized slapping the woman silly. A cardinal tenet of all homicide investigations was that everyone had something to hide. And everyone lied: suspects, witnesses, family members. Lucille Schuster was doing both now, and the detective knew it.

Draining her coffee cup, Claudia hit the VCR's PAUSE button and stood to stretch. As angry as she was at the teacher, she was more so at herself. What was she missing? Overton had left the party before eleven Halloween night. According to the medical examiner, it was impossible that she had been killed after midnight, twelve-thirty at the latest. The party continued on; not a single guest left before one.

"Excuse me, Lieutenant?" Lucille Schuster stood abruptly. She toyed with a pendant.

They were the only two in the all-purpose room. Suggs, Carella, Peters, Moody—they'd watched halfheartedly the first time through, then one by one slipped out.

"Are you finished with me yet?" Schuster asked petulantly. Her confidence was growing. Color was restored to her face. "I've answered all your questions. And not counting the first time I came down to watch the video with you, this is the third time we've been through it. There's absolutely nothing else I can tell you, and I have classes to teach this afternoon."

"I'd be finished with you if I thought you were trying," Claudia said curtly. "But I don't, so I'm going to keep asking you questions and we're going to watch this video another dozen times if we have to."

Lucille Schuster sighed elaborately. "Then may I please use the ladies' room?"

Claudia waved disgustedly. The party was the key. Had to be. And Schuster was holding something back. Maybe just a little. Maybe quite a lot.

While the teacher was gone, Claudia sought Moody. "Mitch, wasn't it you who checked into Schuster's husband's alibi the night of Overton's murder?"

Midway through pouring fresh coffee for himself, Moody paused. "Yeah. He sells pharmaceuticals and was at a seminar in Dallas. He didn't get in until the next morning. He was there. I got half a dozen people corroborating his presence."

Claudia nodded thoughtfully, watching Moody doctor his coffee with a sweetener. "Okay, but what about his flights? Did he come in nonstop? Change planes? Does everything check out?"

Moody shifted uncomfortably. "Well, I . . . ."

"Trace them, Mitch. His presence doesn't mean a damn thing if his travel itinerary doesn't check out."

Damn it! Another hole she could drive an eighteen-wheeler through, and it was her fault. The potholes were everywhere; she should have anticipated most.

"I'll get right on it," Moody mumbled. He hurried off.

Claudia filled her own coffee cup and returned to the all-purpose room. She settled irritably into her chair and jabbed the FAST-FORWARD button on the VCR. Okay. She knew she was obsessing at this point. But she was obsessing because she knew she was missing something.

Shit. What?

And then, at precisely the point when the tape began to roll once more, Claudia saw it. She'd been watching the trees and missing the forest. Suggs had been right about that much.

There, almost at the point where the Reverend Donna Overton was saying her good-byes—a script Claudia had committed to memory word for word—the background chatter that she'd glossed over began to stand out. Someone off camera, a man, judging by the voice, was grousing about ice. They were running out.

She pushed the FAST-FORWARD button. The tape ran almost to the end before she stopped it, then backed it up marginally.

The party was winding down, and the drunker he'd become, the more hideous Tom Orben's camera aim had been. The man was practically careening off walls, and the images he shot bounced like gravel off a dump truck. But one shot showed clearly. It was a nothing shot, one of a hundred random details: a hand with tongs plucking an ice cube from a filled plastic bucket.

Claudia shot out of her seat. When she flung the door to the ladies' room open, Lucille Schuster was applying fresh lipstick. The two women exchanged the briefest of glances in the mirror before Claudia slammed the door behind her. She closed on the woman swiftly.

"You sanctimonious, lying bitch!" she snapped. "Someone went for ice shortly after Donna Overton left your party. Now I want to know who went!"

Schuster warbled. She put a hand to her throat and said, "No, there's got to be a mistake. I . . . are you sure? I mean . . . I don't remember. There were so many things going on. I'm not sure . . . ."

Claudia turned lethal eyes on Schuster and banged the metal towel holder on the wall an inch to the right of the woman's face. The clatter ricocheted like gunfire. Schuster gasped and tried to put a hand up to shield her face. Claudia batted it away. Schuster's lipstick skittered into the sink.

"You'd better start telling me what I want to know," Claudia said. "You played your good-hostess role to the hilt. You stayed sober—you were the only one to stay sober. So don't tell me you don't know who went for ice."

Schuster looked wildly around. "You don't understand," she blurted. Tears fell freely. "They'll fire me if this party gets out! I wish I'd never had it! And this person who went, if you knew him at all, you'd know he never could've . . . ."

Riding anger, Claudia pressed in close enough to count the pores on Schuster's face. The teacher wore Obsession perfume. "Five seconds," she said, her voice steady and low. "That's all you have to start talking. Five seconds. One. Two . . . don't even imagine I'll let you out of here before I get what I want. Three. Four . . . ."

Pinioned so closely, Schuster had nowhere to look but Claudia's face. The detective's unwavering eyes dispensed fury made all the more impressive through her lenses.

Lucille Schuster flinched on the count of three. On the count of four she whimpered pathetically. But there was nowhere to go and nothing to do but tell, and so she did on the count of five.

Claudia fished the lipstick from the sink. She handed it to Lucille Schuster without another word, gave her a long look, and left her crying against the bathroom wall.

CHAPTER 28

"ZORRO'S OUR MAN? Zorro? The guy with the black cape and the sword?" Carella's chair scraped against the linoleum as he sat. "I'll be damned," he said wonderingly. "I never would've thunk it."

Claudia tilted her head in acknowledgement, waiting for everyone to get settled. Although Lucille Schuster had slunk off hours earlier, she'd held Victor Flynn's name to herself until she had time to make a few cursory checks. To be sure.

Now, it was five o'clock. Mitch Moody had arrived with two six-packs of Coke and a pizza. His dark hair was slicked back, still wet from a hurried shower.

"Okay, Hershey, it's your show," Suggs said. He wrestled with the flaps on the pizza box and pulled out a steaming piece. "You've told us who the star is. Now read us the script. And tell me why this teacher gets the Academy Award, because if we're wrong again, I'm gonna be hung by my balls."

As patiently as possible, Claudia laid it out. When Donna Overton left the Halloween party, Victor Flynn good-naturedly offered to make an ice run. He arrived at the 7-Eleven within moments of the medium. She bought cigarettes. He purchased an eight-pound bag of ice.

Then he followed her home, perhaps lingering outside in his car for a few minutes, thinking, maybe even struggling to resist. But he couldn't. Overton had set him off at the party, said something that unleashed a murderous rage suppressed long ago. The urge built to a pressure point until killing her was the only way to release it.

"Would've been simpler to just off himself," Suggs muttered. He poked a string of cheese into his mouth. "The son of a bitch is gonna wish he had when we haul him in."

"So then what?" asked Moody. "She just let him in?"

"I think that's exactly what happened," said Claudia. "She would have recognized him as a guest from the party. She would've been confused to see him there, but probably not alarmed. Maybe she thought she'd forgotten something and that he was bringing it by."

"Sounds like a lot of conjecture," said Suggs.

"It is," said Claudia, "and so's the rest, but I think we have a shot at it."

"Yeah, well, I'm all ears."

"They wound up in the kitchen," she continued, seeing it play out in her mind. "Either he came at her right away and chased her there, or for some reason she led him there, maybe being the good hostess, being polite, offering him something to drink."

The scent of pepperoni fouled the air, contributing to the spiraling headache Claudia had been unsuccessful in banishing with aspirin.

"We know he killed her there," she said softly. "It probably didn't take very long. It—"

"I don't suppose you know what he iced her with," Suggs interrupted.

Claudia smiled wryly at the chief's unintentional pun. "She was killed with the bag of ice he'd just bought at the 7-Eleven. Bludgeoned to death by eight pounds of ice intended for drinks at the party. It would've been like swinging a concrete block at her."

Hot cheese plopped to the table beside the chief's elbow. "You're yankin' my chain," he said. "You gotta be."

"No." Claudia fired up a cigarette, then pulled papers from the Overton file. "This is the inventory report from the crime lab, some of the stuff they bagged at the scene. One of the items listed is a heavy staple. It was found on Overton's kitchen counter. This afternoon, I compared it to the staples used on the necks of the ice bags at the 7-Eleven. We'll need it authenticated by the lab, but there's no doubt in my mind that we're going to find a match."

"The staple broke off the bag while he was whacking her?" Peters asked.

"Mm-hmm." Claudia shuffled through the file, produced another report. "The report said that some of the blood on the floor had been diluted with water. We figured it came from a glass we'd found on the floor, the assumption being that she'd gotten a drink from the tap and during the beating it spilled onto the floor."

"So you're sayin' that between the time Flynn killed her and we went in, the ice had melted, diluting the blood," said Suggs.

"That's how I see it," said Claudia. "The lab dusted the glass for prints—Overton's were on it—but they didn't run an analysis of residue in the glass itself. We'll get them to do that now. But I bet they'll find traces of Diet Coke. It was Overton's drink of choice."

She guided them through the rest. After Overton was dead, Flynn returned to the party, stopping at the 7-Eleven for another bag of ice. Most of the guests had been drinking like fish; they had no perception of how long he had been gone. They didn't notice how withdrawn he appeared afterward. They didn't notice that the Zorro hat and jacket were gone. They didn't notice that he wasn't wearing his glasses—thick, black-framed spectacles.

Claudia opened a labeled evidence bag. She shook it gingerly. A small screw fell out.

"Take a look at this," she said, carefully holding up the screw between the forefinger and thumb of her right hand. "The crime techs swept it out in a piece of dust trapped between the counter and the refrigerator in Overton's kitchen."

Suggs edged in closer to the table to squint at the tiny piece.

"Now watch," said Claudia. She took her glasses off with her left hand, holding the eyewear beside the screw. "Look at the stem on the frame of my glasses," she said. "See how it's hinged to the eyepiece with a screw?"

When she was satisfied all of them had a good look, she put her glasses back on. "The screw we found in Overton's kitchen wouldn't fit my glasses, but it's a close match. And I bet it's a perfect match for the glasses Flynn wore to the party."

Carella whistled.

"In the first part of the video, Flynn wears glasses. He has them on through the time that Overton leaves." Claudia put the screw back in the evidence bag. "Later in the video, long after Overton is gone and Flynn's returned with ice, he's not wearing glasses at all."

"Knocked off, bumped off, something, when he was beating Overton to death," said Peters.

Claudia nodded. Then she told them how she'd met Flynn two days after the murder, called in because he was concerned with Robin's faltering grade.

"That much was true," said Claudia. "The kid's grade had just about dropped off the edge of the earth. But that's not why Flynn called me. He called me to fish, to see if he could learn anything about what we'd found. It's a small town and Robin's one of his students. For that matter, probably every kid who marches through eighth-grade algebra is.

"Anyway, my name was in all the TV, radio, and newspaper reports as lead investigator in the murder. He didn't have to be a brain surgeon to arrange to meet me without calling suspicion to himself."

"So the guy's a nutcase, but he ain't stupid," Suggs grumbled.

"No, he's not stupid." Claudia shook her head, calling up Flynn's face. "Weird, though. He has a lot of nervous habits," she said, "and one of the things he kept doing was fooling with his glasses, like they were too tight. And they were, because they were new, a replacement pair."

She watched the information register in the faces around her.

"The so-called 'r'coon' eyes that little J. J. Dillard saw in the 'monster' at his grandparents' house, those would've been Flynn's new glasses," she said. "Just like the old ones—thick-framed, black, heavy."

"We're gonna have to check with retail optometry shops all over Flagg County, maybe beyond," Suggs said. "There's a couple places you can get new glasses made up in an hour."

"Let's hope our whacko didn't drive to Kansas to get them," said Carella. He swallowed noisily and took a swig of Coke. "And let's hope someone can ID our man."

With a sardonic chuckle, Claudia said, "Even if he used an assumed name, anyone who fitted Flynn for glasses will remember him. His breath is enough to level Milwaukee."

"Maybe," said Carella, "but luck's been in his favor all the way."

"Not anymore," she said. "It's turning our way now. Overton was spur-of-the-moment. Not random, but almost instinctive. We should've been able to plow through the holes he left us, but we didn't see them because we were looking for something else."

"Something that made sense," Peters said.

"Standard motives—money, sex, drugs, like that," said Moody.

"Like that," Claudia repeated wearily. She thought again about everything they'd missed—she'd missed. Had it still been Cleveland, would she have approached the case differently? Looked harder at the video from the beginning? Even remotely considered the teacher?

Victor Flynn: the Caspar Milquetoast of mathematics.

Victor Flynn: the avenger, personified as Zorro.

Victor Flynn: the quirky customer at the 7-Eleven, with buffalo breath.

Victor Flynn: a murdering bastard with four deaths to his credit.

Appetites sated, the quintet of cops around the pizza box stared unseeingly at the debris. Claudia felt queasy now, nausea competing with the headache. She couldn't remember a time she'd felt so thoroughly exhausted.

"So, Hershey," said Suggs at length. "What's your read on this guy? Why the mediums? Why the fingers?"

Sighing, she said, "I'm not sure. When you watch the part on the video where Overton does her thing, you'll see that Flynn reacts visibly when she points at him. But so did a lot of the guests. The only difference is that he doesn't seem to come out of it later."

The chief leaned back in his chair and patted his belly. "Looks to me like we have enough to go round this guy up right now."

"No, not yet." Claudia shuffled through notes she'd prepared earlier. "What we have right now is circumstantial. Good stuff, but it all needs verification." She nodded toward Peters. "Grab a pen, Sarge. Here's what needs doing."

Over the next half-hour, she laid it out. The staple and precision screw had to be run down. They needed to learn whether Flynn had recently purchased new glasses. The Zorro costume may have been a rental: From where? Was it returned? In what condition? Blood stains?

Stills of Flynn from the video had to be obtained. Possibly, close-ups on his face would show the glasses he originally wore were old. And his face, they would need an ID from Mark Yastrepsky and Eddie Winn. The pair had driven to Indiana; had to be tracked down for a signed statement.

The video also showed a variety of places where Flynn had stood in Lucille Schuster's house. Crime-scene techs needed to look for traces of pumpkin on the carpeting, traces he might have tracked in from the smashed jack-o'-lantern at Overton's.

"Whew," said Carella. "Schuster may not cooperate. And it's a long shot."

"Very," Claudia acknowledged. "But it could help us put him at the scene of the murder and we have to take it. As for Schuster, she'll cooperate."

Suggs barked a laugh. "She looked a little rattled when she left here earlier today. Give her a talkin' to, did you?"

"We talked," she said noncommittally. "Look, there's more. Obviously, Flynn needs to be put under around-the-clock surveillance." Claudia nodded toward Peters. "Get your best people out there in plain clothes and unmarked cars—their own if necessary." She raised an eyebrow. "No new puppies this time, Ron."

Peters grunted acknowledgment.

"We also need a history on Flynn, and fast," said Claudia. "He doesn't whack people because an algebra problem keeps him up at night. There's something in his background that provokes his rage. I'll take care of that myself."

"Lieutenant," said Carella, "all of this is going to take a lot of time."

"It can't take a lot of time," she said quickly. "We need to move, and move quickly—two, three days, tops. Call in favors, push, whatever you have to do. And for heaven's sake, this has to be kept quiet. If there's a leak, he'll run—or worse. He's probably already fidgety because of the announcement that we've eliminated Markos as a suspect."

"He's no lightweight, is he?" Peters asked softly.

"No, and that's another thing," said Claudia. She looked sharply at each man in turn, holding Suggs's eyes the longest. "That man teaches my daughter, and he tutors her after school. For that matter, he's in contact with a lot of kids. He'd better not be able to take a leak without our knowledge. And I want a discreet drive-by at my house at regular intervals every night until we pick him up."

"Hershey," Suggs said softly, "I understand how you feel, but this boy's not after kids, he's—"

"I don't care who he's targeting!" said Claudia. "If anyone underestimates Flynn, and my kid—anyone's kid, anybody period—gets hurt, I promise you there will be hell to pay." A vision of Robin laughing, joking, flickered through her mind. "Don't anybody fight me on this point. I mean it."

He nodded slowly. "Okay, Hershey, okay. We'll watch him. And if the man so much as blinks wrong, we'll be on him like a duck on a june bug."

They split up tasks, then watched the video one more time.

"That tape is like a road map if you know how to read it," said Moody afterward. They were breaking up, getting ready to pump the phones, hit the streets, maybe work in a little sleep. "Flynn's signature is all over it."

"Let's just hope we don't find his John Hancock anywhere else," Suggs said.

CHAPTER 29

HERSHEY KNEW. The man could tell it by the way Lucille Schuster looked at him, or rather, refused to look at him. None of the usual hallway chatter, the casual touch on his wrist. The woman didn't even pause, just swept right past him, head low, eyes averted. Not even "Hello, Victor."

And he should have guessed as much. Through the window of his classroom, he had seen her escorted down the hall by Hershey, a skyscraper on legs. Lucille's posture signaled uneasiness, but he'd turned it aside. The cops were after Markos, after all. And the detective, she was back to vandalisms, petty burglaries, routine matters. It wasn't commonplace for a police officer to appear in the school, but neither was it cause for alarm.

No, best to stay cool; and so for hours he'd waited, teaching by rote, looking for the familiarity in greeting with Lucille's return. When it didn't come, he knew. And even if he ignored the signals, he couldn't ignore what he heard on the radio when he got home: Markos was in custody but no longer a suspect in the murders. Victor Flynn paced, fighting panic. He snapped off the radio, clamped his hands over his ears.

Hershey. He didn't know how. But he knew it was she who had turned all eyes to him. The others were merely followers.

They would come for him soon. A day, maybe two or three. But they would come, and with the enormity of that knowledge, Victor began to whimper. Tears stained the bottoms of his lenses, blurring his vision. His body shook. He got on his hands and knees and pounded the floor and wailed.

It was all over, and when they had him they would want him to die. It wasn't fair.

For a long time, Victor sobbed. Dark fell, inviting shadow, but still he lay until exhaustion alone dried his tears. He didn't rise, though; there was no reason. Instead, he measured time with each breath that he felt on his arm, curled under his head. Let them come, then.

But then he heard the voice, the voice he had stopped so many times, so finally.

What? Wait a minute. What was she saying?

Victor pushed himself to a knee. He peered into the shadows, listening. She was asking him something, her voice scornful: Didn't he know that he could never be rid of her? That it wasn't meant to be?

Fool! They were part of each other, and no matter what he did, no matter how often he tried, she would always be there with him; and now, not because he deserved it, but because he had no one else, she would be there for him, too.

Get up, she told him firmly. *Stand like a man.*

"Mother?" Victor said plaintively. He rose, trembling. "They're going to come for me. That woman, she knows, she—"

The voice spat contempt. The detective could be stopped; it would not take much. *Take stock of your situation*, the voice ordered. *Think of who you are. How far you've come. The woman is nothing beside you. Beside me.*

Victor nodded. Yes. He was beginning to see. It had been a mistake, trying to make his mother go away. He was nothing without her. All she had ever done was help him. Like she was helping him now.

In a voice barely above a whisper, Victor asked for instructions. And as she had always done, she told him what to do. She told him how to do it.

There was a way.

CHAPTER 30

IT WAS NEARLY MIDNIGHT when Claudia's plane touched down. With a windchill factor of twenty, the temperature stood at a bone-numbing twelve degrees. An earlier snow, now turned to dirty crust, hampered movement; and by the time she collected her overnight bag, signed for the rental car, and checked into her room at the Holiday Inn, it was after one o'clock in the morning.

While she rummaged for her toothbrush, Claudia toyed with the idea of calling Robin. It was the Thanksgiving holiday and she felt entitled to a little sympathy. Sustaining resentment took work, and in off-guard moments Robin seemed unable to keep it up.

She turned on the bathroom tap. Florida faucets never truly released cold water, but what gushed from the Minnesota tap made her teeth ache. Working briskly around her back teeth, Claudia thought she could coax Robin into a giggle with little more than a slapstick snow story. Embellish it a little, but keep it short.

She spit into the sink and set the toothbrush beside her deodorant. She wiped her mouth on a hand towel and turned off the bathroom light. Yup. Robin would thrill at the image of her mother slip-sliding from car to door. But the resolve that pointed her toward the phone wavered the moment she lifted the receiver. She sighed and set it back down. No, better not. It would be after two in Florida. Robin needed her sleep, and for that matter, so did Marty, who had agreed to spend the night.

Although Claudia carefully avoided the word *baby-sitter*, Robin vigorously protested the notion of anyone staying with her—until Claudia said that Marty wanted to, thought it would be fun. Ah. It was Marty. That made it different.

The truth be told, the mother had few options. No way was she about to let her daughter stay alone overnight, even without the menace of Victor Flynn. No way. The kid was thirteen, just in that stage where she experimented with makeup but still watched a cartoon or two if she thought no one was looking. And unfortunately, Marty was the only woman with whom Claudia had become even marginally friendly; and she wasn't about to unload the kid on anyone she worked with. And Dennis—well, propriety said no.

Shivering, she kicked off her shoes. The damned hotel rooms

either roasted you in the summer or froze you in the winter, no matter where you were. And this was the downside of November in Minnesota, a no-nonsense state where cold sadistically lingered into spring.

After setting her travel alarm, Claudia lay beneath the blanket and tried to argue herself to sleep. It was Thursday—well, Friday, by now. If her meeting at nine went well, she was prepared to take Flynn by Monday, maybe sooner. Moody was still tracking Flynn's glasses, but over the last two days the rest of the pieces had come together and she was confident that would as well.

So screw you, Flynn. An airtight case was on its way to the state attorney. The press would shut up. The psychics and mediums would stop calling. *You will kill no more.*

As she twitched toward sleep, it struck Claudia that it was altogether fitting that Flynn's roots would be in one of the nation's most relentlessly cold states and that he would mark his first murder with a bag of ice.

Victor Ronald Flynn, now thirty-four, was born and raised in a rural, lake community due north of Duluth. Winds howling off Lake Superior commonly dropped temperatures to freezing nearly two hundred days of every year. The region rarely sustained ninety-degree ranges more than two or three days annually.

While Claudia pumped the gas pedal to spark life in the car, the thought spun fresh shivers along her spine. Cleveland certainly scored high in cold, but she had been away from it just long enough for her blood to thin. She wondered whether Flynn's had.

Working backward from his current status as a teacher at the junior high, she had spent two frustrating days collecting data on Flynn, an exhausting process that showed him as something of an enigma. For despite his insipid expression and wooden demeanor in the classroom, he was not as soft as his stature suggested. When they took him, they would have to exercise more caution than anticipated.

Claudia's spotty information showed that before teaching, he worked an assortment of jobs as a laborer. There were stints at a cannery, a dairy farm, then later at Lake Superior's loading docks. Before he drifted into teaching—another curiosity—he had been employed as a wilderness guide in a remote Wisconsin wildlife park. The job didn't last long; Flynn's stiff personality made the paying customers uncomfortable.

But then there was a gap. As if he didn't exist at all, the trail stopped abruptly for a four-year period between Victor Flynn's departure from cold country to less-taxing climates in the southeast. And of his childhood, Claudia knew almost nothing, though it was the very little she had learned that brought her now to Minnesota.

The engine wheezed once, twice, then turned over. Claudia sighed and angled out of the parking spot. Fresh snow was beginning to fall. She hoped her meeting would not take long; with luck, she might be able to get an early flight back. It would be at least sixty degrees in Indian Run.

Even with the snow, she made good time by staying on primary roads as much as possible. It was five to nine when she pulled up in front of the retired psychologist's home, an impressive cabin nestled in a copse of trees.

Franklin D. Washington met Claudia at the door. They sized each other up briefly while exchanging introductions, and then Washington ushered her to the den.

The former counselor, a portly seventy-one-year-old black man whose wiry hair had gone to white, gestured to an overstuffed chair. He prodded a newly started fire in a brick-laid fireplace. It hissed and spat, radiating warmth in a circuit that embraced Claudia's chair.

During the requisite small talk, Washington laced his hands across an ample belly. He wore soft corduroy slacks and a green-and-white flannel shirt. Were it not for his dark eyes, steady and bright with intelligence, he might have been mistaken for a retired butcher, or perhaps farmer. But stripped of twenty pounds and buttoned into a suit, she imagined him an impressive figure to the countless youths who had found themselves before his desk over the course of a thirty-five-year career associated with the courts. She wondered how well they responded to him.

"Well, Detective," Washington began, "you've come a long distance to see me, and not because you're interested in comparing notes on the weather patterns here and in Florida." He smiled indulgently. "Although you were rather cryptic by phone, you're obviously here to learn what you can about Victor Flynn."

Claudia found herself addressing Washington as "sir" while she explained what gave Flynn status as the primary suspect in four slayings. She told him what meager information she had acquired on him through Social Security records and telephone calls to former employers, colleagues, and acquaintances; and she showed him photographs of Flynn made from the video.

Throughout, Washington said nothing. His face remained impassive when he looked at the pictures.

"What's interesting is that he has no criminal record," said Claudia. "In fact, we haven't been able to turn up as much as a parking ticket on him. The only evidence that there may have been trouble in his past is here, in Minnesota."

"I see. And because you've learned that the courts referred him to me for counseling, you want to know what that trouble was," said Washington matter-of-factly.

"Yes, sir, I do."

"The problem, of course, is that anything Victor Flynn may have told me is privileged information."

She nodded.

"Nevertheless, you would like me to tiptoe around professional ethics and tell you what law prohibits me from revealing."

"I wouldn't be here if I didn't believe there might be vital information that would help me," said Claudia. She tried to choose words as carefully as Washington did. "There are gaps in Victor Flynn's background. It's my belief that you know something about them."

"Well, Lieutenant, what have you already learned about your man?" asked Washington. He clipped the end off a cigar and lit up.

"Victor Flynn came to Florida a little over a year ago and began teaching in Indian Run," said Claudia. "Prior to that he taught in rural communities in Louisiana, Mississippi, Alabama, and Georgia—always in places where he had identified a teacher shortage, places where background checks were cursory at best. He never stayed long."

"Does that make him less of a teacher?" Washington asked softly.

"No, sir. By all accounts, he did his job adequately."

"So?"

"So he never graduated from any college or university, at least not that we can find record of," Claudia said. "We're still chasing public school records and running down a list of private schools, and—"

"On that I can save you some time, Lieutenant," said Washington. "Victor Flynn never even graduated from high school. He never attended high school at all—or any school here. Until his mother's death when he was sixteen, Victor was taught by her at home. I would imagine that anything he learned after that was self-taught."

At Claudia's expression, Washington shrugged. "That isn't privileged information. You would find that out for yourself given enough time."

"Sir, time is exactly what I don't have." She recognized impatience in her tone and spoke more slowly to curb it. "I have no authority here, and even if I did, public offices are closed until Monday. I can't wait that long."

Obviously, Washington knew a good deal about Flynn. His stubborn refusal to yield information would have been admirable under other circumstances, but not now.

"I need your help," Claudia continued. "I don't need to look at transcripts or records. I just need to know the gist of them—why he was referred to you."

Washington puffed silently. His eyes never strayed from Claudia's face. At length, he carefully placed his cigar in an ashtray, got up, and disappeared into another room. When he returned, he handed her a small, yellowing newspaper clip.

"Read that, Lieutenant," he said. "Perhaps it will suggest questions to you that I would feel comfortable answering."

The faded clip was an obituary for Frieda Ostermann Flynn, dead at the age of forty-two. Claudia glanced up once, then read on. Frieda was identified as a seamstress. Survivors showed only Victor, sixteen then. There was no mention of a husband, and Frieda had been buried at county expense. Cause of death was not provided.

"Presumably, Ostermann was Frieda's maiden name," said Claudia.

Washington waved a hand. "One might draw that conclusion," he said.

"Reading between the lines, it could also be inferred that Flynn—Frieda's husband, Victor's father—was not a major part of her life. He might even have been a fly-by-night acquaintance, good only in name."

"Reasonable speculation given that no husband—late or otherwise—is listed as a survivor," said Washington.

Claudia glanced at the brief account again. "Also, presumably, Frieda Ostermann Flynn barely subsisted on her income as a seamstress," she said. "No government body readily parts with money, for burial or otherwise. Victor and his mother struggled to make ends meet."

After pausing to relight his cigar, Washington inclined his head.

"Forty-two is young to die," said Claudia, "but the obituary doesn't show any cause of death. Except at the family's request or under circumstances that might be regarded as embarrassing, newspapers generally print that information."

"I'm not well-acquainted with newspaper procedures concerning obituaries—and I hope I'm not for a good long while—but yes," said Washington, "that stands to reason."

She sighed. "Mr. Washington . . . sir . . . please. I know you're uncomfortable with this discussion, but if you know how Victor Flynn's mother died, don't make me guess. Tell me. I can try and research records to find out, but I absolutely don't have time. I won't press you for details on your sessions with Flynn because it would bring me nowhere. But his mother's death—it's relevant, isn't it?"

Rising, Washington moved to the fireplace. He bent to stoke the fire. Without turning, he said, "It took nearly two weeks to establish her identity at all. To begin with, she had been dead for at least a week when her body was discovered."

Claudia's heart skipped a beat.

"Back then, of course," Washington continued, "forensic science was far inferior to that which is available today."

"Mr. Washington, please . . . how did she die?"

Moving slowly, as if plagued by arthritis, Washington returned to his chair. "She was found by a schoolboy in a wooded area adjoining her property, less than two hundred yards from her house." The psychologist's eyes locked onto Claudia's. "Her face was virtually gone. The rest of her was remarkably intact, not accounting for what the natural elements had done to her."

"He killed her, didn't he?" she asked softly.

Washington said nothing at first. Then: "There was an investigation, of course. Naturally, it wasn't as exhaustive as it might have been had the victim been wealthy or powerful. Ultimately, no one was ever charged." Shadows from the fire danced across Washington's face. "The courts, meanwhile, followed the book and referred the boy to me for counseling. It was assumed that the traumatic nature of his mother's death might be troublesome for him to deal with. We're talking about a sixteen-year-old boy with no other family."

Excited, Claudia said, "How did he strike you? Was Flynn remorseful? Traumatized? And in discussion with him, did he ever confide—"

Washington held a cautionary hand up. He shook his head, not unkindly. "You're stepping over that line, I'm afraid."

"I'm sorry."

"You know, if you were to explore the newspaper library, you would find another interesting obituary, that of a woman named Oresta Mueller." A small smile played at Washington's lips. "Oresta was Frieda's only friend—and perhaps she was really more of a professional acquaintance. They spent a lot of time together, but what's interesting is that as frequently as they saw each other, even to Frieda the woman was known only as Reverend Oresta Mueller, sometimes simply 'Madam' Oresta."

"A medium," Claudia said.

"She communed with spirits, yes," said Washington, "and I

gather hers was not a gentle nature."

"Meaning?"

"Meaning, Lieutenant Hershey, that those who sought the Reverend Mueller's spiritual services could expect fire-and-brimstone advice, straight from whatever 'spirit guide' supposedly spoke through her. Frieda sought Madam Oresta's spiritual counseling, and she relied heavily on it."

"And in turn used it to nurture and raise her son the way any other parent might use Doctor Spock," said Claudia. She looked up thoughtfully. "Under the medium's influence, Frieda's way would have been . . . what? Exacting? Maybe even harsh? The stuff of nightmares?"

"One might speculate as much," said Washington. He examined his cigar. "For this area, the good Reverend Mueller did financially well until her death six months after Frieda's."

"Her death, was it like Frieda's?"

Choosing his words carefully, Washington said, "She was mugged, yes."

"Mugged." Claudia shook her head. "Where was Victor?"

Washington shrugged. "The boy had vanished. He'd been placed in a shelter immediately after his mother's death, but a month later he simply disappeared."

"Was there—"

"Really, Lieutenant, I've gone far beyond what I intended in trying to help you," said Washington. "As much as I respect the difficult time frame under which you're operating, if public offices weren't closed because of Thanksgiving I would not even have agreed to meet you."

"I understand. And believe me, I appreciate your help, but please, just one last question," Claudia persisted. She studied Washington's face. "It's important."

"And I already have the answer," Washington responded. "Yes, in both cases, autopsies showed an index finger had been broken."

CHAPTER 31

WITH THE TELEPHONE RECEIVER cradled between her chin and shoulder, Claudia squinted at the numbers on her calling card, then punched the appropriate digits on the dialing plate. She cupped a hand over her right ear to hear better. The terminal was jammed, and no one was going anywhere; the airport was socked in by snow.

Marty answered on the third ring, the surprise evident in her voice when Claudia identified herself.

"I expected to see you rolling up any time now," the younger woman said. "Where are you, anyway? It sounds like you're calling from the bottom of a well."

"I might as well be," said Claudia, vexed. "I'm still in Duluth, waiting to board a plane that I'm now told won't be leaving until sometime tomorrow morning. Snow is descending like the wrath of God."

"It's bad here, too," said Marty. "A miserable sixty-eight degrees, a threat of rain—"

Claudia chuckled wryly. "You been taking lessons from that kid of mine?"

"I might make her my next research project."

They laughed again.

"Listen, Marty, I hate to ask, but would it—"

"Don't worry about a thing, Claudia," Marty interrupted. "I'll stay the night. My briefcase travels well, and it's all I really need. Besides—and don't dare tell my aunt I said this—it's refreshing to be away from all her . . . energy. She can be a little daunting at times."

"You sure?" asked Claudia. "Because between the delay and plane changes, I probably won't be in until . . . mmm . . . tomorrow evening, maybe even early night."

"I'm sure."

"Okay, and thanks. Can you put Robin on for a sec?"

"I can put her on, but not in a sec. She's in the shower."

The kid showered at night. She showered in the morning. The only thing she did more often was change clothes.

Disappointed, Claudia asked Marty to tell Robin her mother missed her and would see her the next night.

"So what about you? Are you heading back to your hotel for some sleep?" Marty asked.

"Nah, I don't think so. I've already turned in my car. And anyway, maybe God and the airport director will change their minds and open the runways sooner than we're being told. I'm just going to find myself a good paperback and hunker down on a chair."

After hanging up, Claudia called Peters at the station, relaying the same information about the delay, asking for a case update. No, Flynn's activities hadn't deviated. Yes, they'd hounded the FBI. The agency's profile would be dispatched no later than Tuesday. And yes, Carella thought he had a match on the glasses. Sergeant Peters got eight minutes.

In the next call, Dennis got twenty. He missed her so much he was combing his carpet for her hairs. He bet he could weave them into ribbon. Did he really have to learn how to cook an omelet? They had to go fishing again; next time he would bring insect spray. Claudia hung up agreeing to meet for dinner Sunday. What was with her? For the first time in years she found herself actively missing a man. He had a paunch. When he shaved, he missed patches at the corner of his chin. She suspected he sometimes wore the same socks two days in a row. And his idea of a good time was fishing. Loneliness swept in.

Claudia wandered dispiritedly toward the gift shop. She flipped mindlessly through the Studio cards, identified with the Ziggy cards, then bought a book, a pack of cigarettes, and a small stuffed teddy bear she hoped Robin wouldn't be too old to enjoy. When she found the coffee shop, she settled into a chair, opened the book, and began to read. It looked to be a long, long night.

Claudia gazed through the thick window of the 747, which magically had lifted off at ten-thirty in the morning. The novel was long finished and now, stiff, cranky, and tired, she filtered information in an effort to trap sensible explanations. Of the many perplexities in Victor Flynn's character, one that Claudia found most confounding was his penchant for mathematics—for that matter, for teaching altogether.

From everything she knew, he was not at ease in social situations. The video showed a man who struggled with banter, whose sentences evaporated into shrugs. Likewise, much of his life had been spent in work more attuned to things physical, not cerebral. Yet somewhere along the line, he had learned—indeed, possibly taught himself—enough about math to secure employment in schools. And socially skilled or not, he had managed to portray himself convincingly enough that no one ever checked his qualifications.

Where was the common denominator in a man who could sling fifty-pound sacks as a laborer at a seaside port, teach the intricacies of algebra to adolescent children, and murder women without hesitation—even his own mother?

Knowing Victor Flynn—peering into the dark recesses of his soul—wasn't her job. As a homicide investigator, it wasn't necessary that she grapple with what motivated him. Shrinks and lawyers could do that. She had only to prove that he had killed, and then take him to jail. She could do that now.

Still, was it control? There was a certain logic in that, she thought. Mathematics were precise; the numbers could be controlled so that they always came out the same way, the only way they could. And the jobs that had required physical strength—those, too, demanded a control that in its most absolute sense belonged to the man wielding the muscle.

Claudia tried to imagine Victor Flynn's upbringing. She had driven by the house in which he was raised by Frieda Ostermann Flynn. Small and unpretentious, it was one of many widely spaced houses in a quiet neighborhood whose ethnic makeup was largely of German extraction.

What kind of routine defined Flynn's days as a youth? Did one monotonously drag into the next? With only his mother for company, how did he bridge loneliness? Were Frieda's ministrations sufficient? She fed him, clothed him, tutored him. Was it enough?

For that matter, Claudia mused, was it even her?

Frieda didn't work alone. What nurturing she provided was governed by the Reverend Oresta Mueller's tyrannical spirits. They guided Mueller; Mueller guided Frieda; Frieda funneled their dark wisdom and unrelenting discipline into young Victor. How long did it take before he confused them all? How long before he rebelled? And what sort of fury must he have stored?

Most connecting flights were on schedule. Claudia perfunctorily smiled a thank-you at a flight attendant bearing cold drinks and pretzels. She tore the package open and plucked a few out, chewing methodically. The captain's voice scratched over the intercom. In another thirty minutes, the plane would touch down.

When Victor Flynn killed his mother and then Mueller—the spirits, really—he made sure they would never look at him again, never speak to him again, and never point a finger at him again.

And maybe they hadn't, until Donna Overton raised a finger at the séance. Maybe . . . .

Claudia closed her eyes. Trying to unlock Flynn was like trying to unlock a combination safe with a toothpick. The exercise would make her nuts.

Crickets and cicadas trilled with the enthusiasm of a gospel choir. A frog bugled in throaty response. Two blocks over, a dog barked faintly. Claudia idly tuned in, warming to the reception. It was seven-fifteen and home had never looked so inviting.

Too much sitting had provoked spasms in her back. Her eyes burned. Smart would have been returning to the Holiday Inn the night before. But never mind. They would pick Flynn up before the night was over. Afterward, a twelve-hour stretch in bed. Some time with Robin. Then Dennis.

Humming lightly, Claudia unlocked the front door and went in. Marty was parked on the couch in front of the TV. She rose and greeted Claudia warmly. The silver streak in her hair flared with each step.

"You're a sight for sore eyes," said Claudia, meaning it. She unceremoniously dumped her overnight case and stretched. "I can't *believe* how tired I am."

"Want some coffee?" asked Marty.

"Twist my arm," said Claudia, pantomiming. She looked around curiously. "Robin in her room?"

Midway to the kitchen, Marty paused and said, "No, she's not home yet." She glanced at her watch. "Should be any time now."

"Wait a minute. What am I missing?" said Claudia. "Where'd she go?"

"Wow, you must be bushed," said Marty. "It's Saturday. That fishing tournament? The fund-raiser? It's today, remember?"

Claudia's eyes darkened. "I remember Robin asking me about it, all right. I also distinctly remember telling her no. She's grounded."

"Uh-oh," Marty said uncomfortably. She sighed. "Look, Claudia, I'm sorry. I didn't know. Robin, she never said a word about that."

"Yeah, I bet she didn't." Claudia pressed a fist into the small of her back. "I don't want to put you on the spot, Marty, but what exactly did Robin tell you?"

"Well, she asked me if I'd drop her off and pick her up, that it looked like you wouldn't be able to make it back in time to do it yourself."

Claudia swore softly.

"She didn't actually say she had permission," Marty said swiftly, trying to placate. "It was just sort of implied."

With a wan smile, Claudia said, "Don't try to protect her. She knew exactly what she was doing, Marty, and I bet the subject came up almost the moment you told her that my plane wouldn't be getting in until tonight."

Marty nodded feebly.

Claudia took her jacket off and hung it on the back of a chair. "The only thing that surprises me is Robin's timing. You'd think she would intend to be back before me. What time was this thing supposed to end, anyway?" She irritably peered through a window. "It's been dark for at least an hour."

Marty checked her watch again. "Actually, she called about a half hour ago. Said she was going to stick around and help clean up. I guess there were booths and refreshments, things like that. Anyway, she said I didn't have to bother going out for her. Someone was going to give her a lift home."

First the report card. Now this.

"I'm gonna kill her," Claudia said matter-of-factly. "Plain and simple, I'm just gonna kill her."

"Oh-oh, I'm sorry. I—"

"Did she say who was going to drop her off?" Claudia asked, sinking into an armchair.

"Yeah, it was one of the chaperons, a teacher, the one she doesn't like." Marty pursed her lips thoughtfully. "The name will come to me in a minute."

Claudia felt her chest constrict. She straightened. "Marty? The name—it's not possible that . . . you're not thinking of Victor Flynn, are you?"

Marty snapped her fingers. "Yes! That's the one, the algebra teacher who—"

Claudia shrieked and vaulted from the chair. "My God, no!" Her face twisted, fell to white. She grasped Marty's wrist. "What else, Marty? Quickly, quickly. What else did Robin say, and how did she say it? How did she sound?"

Stunned, Marty worked her mouth soundlessly.

"Please, Marty? What did Robin say?" Claudia frantically pumped the younger woman's wrist. "I have to know now!"

"Well, I . . . I . . . it didn't seem. . . ."

Claudia squeezed her eyes shut. She released her grip, fought for breath.

Calm down, calm down. Give her room. Let her think.

"Marty, nothing you've ever tried to remember is more important than what you're trying to remember now," Claudia said hoarsely. She tried to blot the perspiration from her hands. "Please help me."

"Claudia, I . . . it was just a brief conversation." Marty blinked spasmodically, confused. "It was over in five minutes. Less than that."

Slow down. Don't rattle her again.

"It could be important, Marty. Even five minutes. It could be . . . please try to remember. Think. Think!"

Tears fell freely down Marty's face. "She said . . . she said that Flynn was going to drive her home when everything was packed up.

That he'd volunteered to finish up and that she'd offered to help him."

No. Please, God, no. NO!

Claudia inhaled sharply, brought both hands to her lips. "How did she sound, Marty?"

"I . . . she sounded a little funny."

"Funny how, Marty? Worried? Distant? Was her voice quivering?"

"I don't know, Claudia, I don't know!" Marty bit her lip.

"All right, all right." This couldn't be happening. This could *not* be happening. "Take your time," Claudia said. "Close your eyes. Try to remember picking up the phone, hearing Robin's voice."

"Okay. All right. She . . . ." Marty briefly closed her eyes. "She sounded stiff, somehow. Formal. I . . . I didn't think much of it. She would've been tired and . . . ."

"Quickly, Marty. What else did she say? What else?"

"She said—what was it—yes, she said that Flynn—only she called him 'Mister' Flynn—that he had some important advice about fishing. She repeated that it was important."

"What, Marty? What did he tell her to say?"

"I'm not sure this is exactly right, the exact words, but," Marty let out a sob, "his advice was that the biggest and the best fish were caught only when you fished alone."

Her world spun out of control in a heartbeat.

Flynn. Robin.

Claudia whirled from Marty and into the den without another word. She was gone for thirty seconds. When she returned, it was with a flashlight and her revolver. She secured the holster at her waist and slid the gun into it.

Victor Flynn had escaped surveillance. It didn't matter how. He was on his own, and he had Robin.

"Listen to me carefully, Marty," Claudia said. Her voice still trembled but her hands were almost steady. "I'm going out to the lake. If you don't hear from me in forty minutes, call the police and tell them to get out there. Do not call them sooner."

"Claudia, what's going—"

"Just do it, Marty!" said Claudia. "This man wants me out there. If I don't go, he might kill Robin. And if I show up there with reinforcements he'll kill her without hesitating. If there's any way to stop him I have to fish alone."

She didn't say the unspeakable, that Robin might already be dead.

Claudia flung the front door open and sprinted into the night.

CHAPTER 32

VICTOR FELT GIDDY. It was Providence . . . divine intervention . . .
something.

After all, he didn't know that the girl would attend, not with
any certainty. Oh, sure. She was popular, one of those giggly ones
who clustered in hallways and crowed at boys. They moved like
packs of wolves, these girls, always together, always sniffing out the
action.

So yes. It did stand to reason she would attend an event the students all deemed so important.

And yet, anything could have happened. He had taken quite a
risk to leave his house without detection just to embrace a possibility. Fortunately, Mother had been right. Of course. She was
always right. She was his strength, his life. He would serve her well,
make her proud at last.

Victor grinned, one hand on the tiller, the other one with a knife
at the girl's throat. He could feel the pulse in her neck beating like
hummingbird wings.

"Thank you, Mother," Victor said softly into the night. He nodded, hearing her reply. "Yes. She'll come, too."

Fog thick as paste shrouded the trees, camouflaging the lake
beyond. Powered by humidity, the rising mist dampened the air
and cast a stillness that trapped noise like an empty room. What
moved was not visible; sound shrieked.

Claudia's heart ran like a jackrabbit. She felt its feet thump
inside her flesh, swore she could hear it. And she was cold. Where
fear seized her skin, gooseflesh stood out.

This was not Markos on a golf course where only the dark created
uncertainty. Here, dark brought companions in its shadow: foliage
as tight as rolled wire and sharp as razor blades; uneven terrain pit-
ted with shell made slick by the damp air; insects with radar scopes
calibrated for blood; countless creatures that slithered restlessly.

And the lake—a vast pool deceptively still.

Flynn knew this world. Claudia could not even see it.

Counting off breaths, she talked herself down. With a will
granted life because her daughter's was at stake, she reached into

the backseat of her car and groped for the jacket thoughtlessly discarded there weeks earlier. It smelled mildly of mildew. The cuffs curled inward. But the jacket was black and Claudia needed its protection. And it dispensed warmth; she needed its heat.

Armed thusly with a gun, flashlight, and jacket, she quietly latched the car door and set off. She mouthed words soundlessly: "I'm coming, baby. I'm coming."

After guiding the boat past a clump of water hyacinth, Victor Flynn maneuvered toward a wedge of giant bulrush and sword grass, foliage somewhat flattened by previous visitors to the small clearing. With the announcement of Markos's drug activity, an enterprising newspaper photographer had thought to memorialize the setting for an accompanying story. Others had followed suit, and Victor had encountered no difficulty in identifying the location while pretending to participate in the day's fund-raiser.

Now that made him smile. He had actually caught two panfish. Mother appreciated the irony.

Surefooted and confident, Victor stepped out of the vessel. He flashed the knife at the girl. She clambered out unsteadily, whimpering. Victor made no effort to hide his disgust. Silly vapor-headed ninny. She still didn't fully recognize a rational number from a real number. She showed absolutely no appreciation for the simple beauty of a Venn diagram. One time he'd actually overheard her giggling to a friend that algebra was the mental equivalent of a hemorrhoid.

Outrageous!

But the girl was not giggling now. Tears streaked her face as he looped cord around her waist and arms, binding her to a tree. She shuddered uncontrollably, wide, hollow eyes turned in appeal toward him.

Victor watched dispassionately. She was of no real concern. He didn't care if she lived or died. For him, she represented little more than—

Abruptly, he crooked his neck and listened. Now and then he nodded. He smiled broadly, then threw his head back and laughed aloud. What a fine idea! Of course! While they waited for her mother—and yes, yes of course, she would be coming—he would give the girl a quiz. The teacher pondered the possibilities. The quiz would be challenging, but not unreasonable. If she passed, he would consider allowing her to live. If she failed, then she would die.

Despairing, Claudia guided her flashlight over the rentals, trying to remember what Markos had done, trying to remember what Dennis had wanted to teach her and that she refused to learn. The motors were intimidating, bloated boxes of metal made all the more sinister beneath the gleam of the light. If she took one—if she took one and could even get it started—Flynn would hear her coming. In his arrogance, he probably expected it.

She settled on a canoe, an old aluminum-framed vessel. To wrest advantage from him, she would have to forfeit speed for silence and hope for the advantage of surprise.

The canoe was seventeen feet long, and light. Claudia awkwardly lowered herself into it, gasping when it dipped beneath her weight. Twice before, while in college, she had paddled a canoe with friends. She wasn't competing. She wasn't interested in the nuance of how it rode the water, or what paddling method best suited its sleek design. Most of whatever technique she had learned eluded her now.

Cautiously, she knelt in front of the center thwart, her hips uncomfortably perched on its hard edge. When the canoe stopped rocking, she carefully picked up the paddle and dipped it into the lake water. She pulled the oar back and shifted it to the other side, struggling to find a pattern. At first, the boat wobbled erratically and threatened to go in circles. But then, as she experimented, it slowly straightened out. Her breath caught sharply when she realized she had put twenty feet between the canoe and land. What had Dennis said about depth here? Where exactly did it drop off?

With each left-handed stroke of the paddle, the revolver rubbed mercilessly against Claudia's skin. Within minutes of leaving land, her knees felt as if they were grounded on marbles. She shut the pain from her mind, thinking instead about what Flynn was doing. And how Robin was responding.

Once, she thought she heard a laugh. It made her flesh crawl.

Claudia pulled harder on the paddle, silently counting cadence. She wished she had talked to Robin sooner. She wished she had belted her. Wished she had anything. Because if Robin mouthed off, Flynn would kill her.

Oh, God, Robin, keep your mouth shut. Please, God, don't let her talk back. Don't let her make him mad. Don't let her underestimate him.

Something splashed in the water close by. Claudia bit her lower lip, resisting the urge to cry out. She stayed close to the banks, rounding the lake and using the shapeless forms against its edges as a guide. Could he see her? Was he watching her approach? She calculated moves, planning and discarding strategy, trying to anticipate the best opening. Her senses were on full alert. Sound suggested distance; scent carried proximity.

He was there in the clearing. She knew it. She knew he would choose a place they could both find. It was part of his game—his mother's game. Claudia narrowed her eyes, raking memory for the layout. He would expect her to glide into the opening where passage was most manageable. That would not do. No. She would come in on him thirty or forty feet from the left instead, make a loop into the woods, and take him from behind.

The girl wasn't even trying.

Well, of course, Victor knew she was frightened, and so he had started simply, even giving her a few basic definitions that she should have memorized at the beginning of the school year. But she sat there mutely, sniffling, just staring wide-eyed, her tears still coming and snot beginning to drip from her nose.

Disgusting, absolutely disgusting.

"Listen to me," he hissed. He pinched her arm. "Listen! I'm going to give you another chance. This is an easy one. List the set of prime numbers less than twenty."

A second passed, two, three.

"Well?" Flynn demanded. "What's the answer?"

Robin's shoulders quaked. Her lips trembled. "I . . . that would be two, three, four, five, six—"

"No!" Victor slapped her once, lightly. "You're not paying attention! Go back to the beginning and think! Think, think, think!"

When Robin began to sob openly, Victor clamped a hand over her mouth. He said contemptuously, "The answer is two, three, five, seven, eleven, thirteen, seventeen, and nineteen."

The stupid little fool. She would never amount to anything. He had gifted her with his expertise for months—even private sessions—and look at her! Pathetic.

"Pay attention, Robin." Victor slowly took his hand from her mouth. "Answer this one: If x plus five equals twelve, what value is x? A fourth-grader could figure it out."

Robin swallowed. She blinked back tears. "It's . . . it's x equals seven."

"Well! You got one right! Very good, Robin. Very, very good." Flynn clapped facetiously. "Let's try another easy one." His eyes narrowed, and he spoke rapidly. "True or false, Robin: If every element of A is an element of B, then B is a subset of A."

The teacher shifted to his knees. "Come on, come on. I'm waiting, Robin. True or false?"

Nothing.

"Answer me!"

"I, um—"

"True or false!"

"True!" she blurted. "No. Yes. I don't know."

"False!" said Victor, livid. He cuffed her again. "It's false, false, false! This is what happens when you don't listen! You just refused to pay attention in class, didn't you?"

"I tried, I—"

"Liar!"

Slap!

Robin twisted sideways, trying to shift away from him.

Flynn laughed maniacally. "Are you paying attention now? Hmm? You are, aren't you? Hmm? Hmm? What's the matter, Robin? Cat got your tongue?"

Slap!

"Let's take a little break, shall we? And then we'll try a few more."

Claudia heard the first slaps the moment she stepped out of the canoe and into the water. Her heart lurched. She struggled to keep her footing and dug her fingernails into the palms of her hands to keep from calling out.

The son of a bitch! That sick, sick son of a bitch!

The water was deceptively deep, even among the reeds. They caught at her feet like tentacles. She swallowed hard, feeling the water almost at her waist. Had to block emotion. Had to push aside fear. Can't let him hear you coming.

Horned beakrush snagged her jacket. She pushed the coarse blades aside and waded toward the bank. With nearly every step she had to pause and untangle weeds. Icy water numbed her legs. Her eyes flitted wildly, watching for alligators. Snakes. Every shadow was alive.

Pausing two feet from the bank, she cocked her head and listened, trying to distill sounds. A voice, she could make out a voice now. Low and deep. Flynn's. And then it was gone. Cattails rustled gently with a breeze. Then, nothing more.

They were close, though; Claudia felt it.

Slowly reaching beneath her jacket, she pulled at the .38, tugging it out. She smelled the leather from its holster; smelled, too, her own perspiration, the scent of fear. Her arms ached from pulling on the paddle, and her hands shook. But she dared not turn on the flashlight.

Insects danced at her face as she moved cautiously onto the bank. She batted at them once, then ignored them. They were part of it, this marshy jungle. She wished for the stealth of a cat. Tried to think like one, imagining their padded feet as she set her own down, following instinct as she thought they might. And slowly, on a crouch, she made progress into the trees, moving resolutely forward, then beginning to circle in.

Come on, Victor, where are you, you lunatic. Make some noise. Step on a branch. Talk to me, you son of a bitch.

As if in answer, Victor moved abruptly, his form suddenly looming in the inky shadow. Robin simultaneously let loose a piercing scream that would travel through Claudia's nights in an eternity of nightmares:

"Mommmyyyyy!"

Claudia bellowed and thrashed blindly through the trees. She fumbled with the flashlight, and on the run fired once into the air. Panicked birds rose instinctively, their wings beating thunder. The flashlight's beam arched crazily, touching on Robin long enough for Claudia to see the look of terror starched on her face.

Anguished, Claudia stumbled into the clearing and straight toward her daughter. The blow caught her at midsection less than a dozen paces away and she went down hard. The flashlight flew left. Its beam spiraled, then vanished in a thicket of weed. The gun thumped against earth.

Pain spasmed through her lungs and into her spine. She gasped and rolled. She gulped at the air, fearful of blacking out. Tears stung her eyes.

The second blow glanced off a shoulder while she struggled to one knee. Claudia fell to her side and looked around wildly. Four feet to the left she spotted the weak glow of the flashlight. Its beam toiled facedown in the weeds, feeding the clearing with less than the power of a night-light. In the next instant it flickered briefly, momentarily cut off by shadow. She scissored to her back and kicked out savagely. Her foot struck something solid; she heard Flynn grunt.

Biting her lip, Claudia lurched to her feet. She couldn't make him out, but Flynn's feral breath assailed her and she swung blindly, clipping material—his shirt, she guessed. Clawing the air, she made a grab for it, snagged something, and pulled fiercely.

For an infinitesimal moment, they clutched each other like drunken lovers. Then, with an upward twist, he yanked back and pulled free. The bat, the stick—whatever it was—made its round once more. He caught her hard just below the left knee, and Claudia spun, yelping. The force of the blow threw her against a tree; she wrapped an arm around it, hiding, catching her breath. Something stung her eye and clouded her vision. She blinked furiously until it cleared.

From less than twenty paces, Robin sobbed raggedly. Claudia

yearned to close the distance, to somehow reassure her. The despair in her daughter's voice kindled her own. But she dared not move, not without thinking. Another mistake would be fatal.

Suddenly, Flynn shouted Claudia's name. His voice was high and mincing, taunting. He was enjoying himself. He urged her to come out. In the next moment his voice shifted. Now he was talking softly, no longer to her. The words were indistinguishable. Once, she thought she heard him laugh lightly.

Claudia shuddered. She had no light. No weapon. Wasn't sure she could trust her left leg. Her glasses had been knocked away.

Taking measured breaths, she evaluated her options. There was but one. Because she could not rely on physical strength, she would have to lure him out—and soon—before he turned his attention back to Robin.

She had to make him come after his mother. One more time. One final time.

Groping along the trees and using them as a shield, she painfully inched back toward the water. The candle glow from the flashlight gave her perspective. She trained her eyes on it. The leg was bad; she limped, cringing with each step. With effort, she tuned Robin's cries out, putting all of her energy into Victor Flynn.

Become the cat. Smell him. Hear him.

A few feet from the bank, Claudia stopped. She groped for words, then called his name softly. Heard an answering rustle.

"Victor," she said, "you're doing it all wrong again. You're clumsy. Nothing but a fool. You haven't learned a thing, Victor."

Silence. Even Robin's cries had stopped.

Almost on all fours, Claudia crept toward the reeds. She culled words from Overton's voice on the video. "You've proved it again, Victor." she scoffed. "I've been wasting my time with you. You're nothing. Nothing! You'll always be nothing."

Another rustle, but still no reply.

Claudia inhaled silently. Her heart beat rapidly. Something moved across one hand; she recoiled, almost cried out. Her voice sounded ridiculous to her. Fraudulent. He was probably laughing, creeping toward her. Or Robin.

Once more. Give it one more shot.

Claudia tested new words. "The truth is, Victor, without me you're less than the air you breathe," she bullied. "You don't have the strength of a puppy's tail. And I'm tired of you, Victor. I'm bored, and disgusted." She laughed derisively. "You don't deserve me. You never deserved me. And I won't help you anymore."

"Mother?" The voice was sudden, plaintive and confused. "Don't say that. Why are you talking like that? I'm a good boy. I've done everything you've said."

There! To the left, just twelve feet away. She could see him now, orienting himself to her voice.

Come on, you son of a bitch. Come on . . . .

"You're not being fair, Mother," Victor said. "Don't do this to me, please. Mother?"

The more contemptuously Claudia talked, the more childlike Victor responded. She hardly knew what she was saying. She understood not a word that Victor uttered in return. But he was coming, following the voice.

Snakelike, she crawled closer to the water's edge, concealed by the tall grasses. He was closer to her than he was to Robin now. Something thorny tore at her hands. She heard him stumbling toward her, faster. She could measure his breaths by her own.

Six paces! She could see him!

Five paces! Three!

NOW!

Claudia exploded from the reeds, faced Victor Flynn, and pointed a quivering finger at him.

Flynn stopped dead.

Come on, you son of a bitch! Come on, come on!

A second stretched into two, three, four. And then he roared and charged, stumbling in rage through the bulrush.

Just in time, Claudia saw the knife. She dropped low, fear gripping her throat. The knife swooped. It sliced her left hand. She looked up, saw him raise the knife again. She grunted and thrust a fist at his groin. Flynn howled and bent; Claudia swung again, missed. She scampered backward crab-like and pushed to her feet. Pain stabbed at her leg. She winced, clutched at it, and slipped on decaying vegetation. Water sluiced over her shoulders, splashed on her face. Something jabbed her side.

Flynn hooted, a vile sound that hammered spikes of terror into Claudia. He straightened and launched himself forward.

In that instant, she remembered. She fumbled for her jacket pocket. Her fingers felt for the fishing lure, still imbedded in the piece of Styrofoam from the day she purchased it. She yanked it out, pinched its hooks free from the chunk of Styrofoam.

The knife glinted dully when Flynn raised it and threw himself at her. Claudia desperately drew her own hand up, the lure cupped in her palm, one hook stuck against a finger. She kicked out simultaneously, hobbling him at the ankle. He toppled toward her and she thrust the lure upward. It caught against something soft. She pushed in and twisted.

He let go and bucked, writhing and screeching. He raised his head from the water and clawed at his eye.

Claudia rolled sideways to her knees. She glanced at Flynn, grimaced, then pushed to her feet. Water cascaded from her jacket, weighing her down. She wobbled unsteadily, automatically scanning for the knife.

He wouldn't be down long. He was hurt, but he would get up. He, too, would search for the knife. Claudia splashed at the reeds, trying to find the instrument by feel. Her hand radiated pain clear through her fingers. She jammed her hand under her arm for a moment, hoping to staunch the blood. Then she looked some more.

Nothing. Nowhere.

Claudia thought that Flynn must be on top of it, or else it was too hidden by reeds to be detected. But if he found the knife first, he would kill her. He would find the strength to kill her, and then kill Robin.

Resolutely, she turned back toward him. He lay more quietly now, groaning. Somehow, she would have to move him, now, and quickly. Sloshing through the water, she took two steps closer. It was difficult to focus without glasses, and at first she thought her eyes were playing tricks on her. But no. Something had moved. Not Flynn; there, just beyond him.

Claudia squinted for a closer look. She saw the water part three feet away. Something luminescent flared, then vanished.

In the second it took to understand what she was seeing, the alligator's jaws clamped down on Flynn's shoulder. He twisted and screamed. Claudia stumbled backward. A few moments later he started to gag, his screams muffled by the water.

Paralyzed with shock, she could do nothing but watch in horror. The beast's great tail thrashed the water into foam. Mist swirled in primordial response. Something else, then: Robin's voice, faint, raw, and frightened. Claudia shook herself and frantically navigated toward the bank, using the reeds as levers. By the time she found solid footing, the lake was still again except for the beating of her heart.

Numb, Claudia reached Robin at the same time she heard the distant wail of police vehicles. Could it have been only forty minutes?

She dropped on her knees beside the girl, murmured reassurance, held her briefly, fumbled at the cord. Robin shivered convulsively, could not stop crying. The moment the binds were off, she pushed her body into her mother's embrace.

Claudia marveled at how small she seemed, how fragile.

"Shh, there, baby, there. It's all right now." Claudia held her tightly, drinking in the smell of her daughter's hair. "It's all over."

She tipped Robin's face to her own. "It's okay now. We're going to go home in a minute."

"You lost your glasses," Robin said thickly, still snuffling. "You can't see without them."

Claudia laughed mirthlessly. "Yeah. I lost my glasses." She cradled Robin against her, rubbing her good hand up and down her daughter's bare arm, trying to warm her.

Across the lake, the reds and blues flashed. A second later, a spotlight threw out unnatural daylight. The chief's husky voice barked through an amplified horn.

"Hershey! Hershey, you out there?"

She stood, croaked an answer, cleared her throat, and tried again. She called out a location, waited for the response.

"All right, Hershey. We're coming. Just sit tight."

The cavalry was on its way.

Leaning against the tree, her child nestled against her, Claudia sat tight and waited.

CHAPTER 33

THE FIRST DAY, she was too heavily sedated to do more than sleep. The second day, she was well enough to sit up and appreciate the pain. Two cracked ribs, eleven stitches to close the gash in her hand, skin swollen from insect bites, bruises the color of eggplant—a garden of injuries a long way from harvest.

Suggs's was the first voice she heard. Claudia cracked an eye. He stood at the foot of the hospital bed, taking survey.

"'Bout damn time you opened your eyes, Hershey," he growled. "Got a truckload of cases piling up on your desk. Nothing fancy. Just a bunch of minor whodunits."

"I can't wait," she muttered through swollen lips. She groaned and shifted.

"You know you passed out on the boat?" He picked at a fresh roll of mint Tums, held it out.

Claudia shook her head. She wanted a gallon of mouthwash.

She asked Suggs about Flynn.

The chief's jaw tightened. "Well, Hershey, he's not gonna hurt anyone ever again. He's put the spirits to rest, his own and his mother's."

She nodded and looked past the chief. She squinted and spotted Marty and Robin. Dennis stood beside them, a half-moon grin stretching his lips. She winked at him, then smiled feebly and gestured for Robin to come over.

"Hi, kid," she said, taking her daughter's hand.

"Hi."

"You all right?"

"Fine," said Robin. "Just a bunch of bug bites. I have lotion on them."

"Marty watching out for you?"

She nodded, eyes downcast.

"Hey, what's this? What's the matter, baby?"

A tear formed. Robin shrugged, tried to wipe it away with a shoulder.

"Come on. Your eyes are leaking." Claudia squeezed Robin's hand. "Everything's all right. Really, it is."

"No it's not," Robin blurted. "It's all my fault. Look at you. I almost got you killed. Nothing would've happened if—"

"Hey, hey," said Claudia. "We don't know what would've happened no matter what, huh? There's no point in looking back, kiddo. We're here. We're alive. Now come on. Show me some teeth."

Robin sniffled, offered a small smile.

"Ah, that's better," said Claudia.

A moment passed, then another.

"I . . . so you're not mad at me?" Robin picked at her polish with a fingernail. Fluorescent green this time. "I mean, at least not much?"

Claudia hooted. "Hell, yeah, I'm mad at you! And yes, much! But not because Victor Flynn took a poke or two at me." She tapped a finger against Robin's hand and asked softly, "You know why, don't you?"

"I know," she said simply. "I know and I'm sorry." She sought her mother's eyes. "So I guess I'm probably, like, grounded for life now, huh?"

Oh yeah, that. Claudia groaned inwardly and propped herself on an elbow. "This is important to know? Right now?"

Robin made a face. "Well, you know . . . ."

"All right," said Claudia, trying to focus. She toyed with Robin's hand. "The truth is, I haven't really given it a whole lot of thought yet," she said. "But I do know that grounding you didn't seem to work that well. So I don't know. It might be that I'm going to have to find something more imaginative, or maybe just more direct."

"Like what?" Robin persisted.

Claudia pursed her lips in thought. She beckoned her daughter closer and whispered something in her ear.

Robin blanched, slipped her hand out of Claudia's, and backed a step away.

"Oh, come on," the mother teased. "What are you worrying about? I won't even be out of bed for a week. I won't be up to speed for another couple days after that."

She watched her daughter retreat and smiled to herself. Well, better that the kid be chased by nightmares of her mother than nightmares of Victor Flynn. Claudia sighed and closed her eyes.

They'd do just fine, the two of them. Just fine.